# COYOTE'S PEOPLE

# COYOTE'S PEOPLE

# ANDREW MCBRIDE

**THORNDIKE PRESS**
A part of Gale, a Cengage Company

LIBRARY OF CONGRESS CIP DATA ON FILE.
CATALOGUING IN PUBLICATION FOR THIS BOOK
IS AVAILABLE FROM THE LIBRARY OF CONGRESS

ISBN-13: 978-1-4328-6728-7 (hardcover alk. paper)

Published in 2021 by arrangement with Andrew McBride

Printed in Mexico
Print Number: 01          Print Year: 2021

In memory of Jon Dooley

# ACKNOWLEDGMENTS

Thanks to David Hewitt and Richard Hearn for their friendship and support over a lot of years, and to Johnny D. Boggs for some recent good advice.

*Coyote's People* is a work of fiction. However, it is based (loosely) on real events that occurred in Arizona in the 1870s. Some of the characters are based (very loosely) on real people, although I've changed the names. A few instances of speech by these characters and some extracts from newspapers, letters, and reports are taken, or paraphrased, from history.

# PART ONE

PART ONE

# CHAPTER ONE

Around him men stood with rifles raised. They stared into the darkness at the Apaches that might be there, waiting to attack.

Choctaw swallowed a rock-sized lump of fear in his throat. His arms trembled slightly, and his hands ached, holding his Spencer carbine up to his shoulder. He looked along the barrel past the front sight. Beyond was the gray gloom of the Gila River Canyon.

A few minutes ago, all had been peaceful. The freight outfit was camped just south of the river, wagons coiled into a defensive circle. The crew, thirteen bullwhackers, had finished their evening meal. Pipes were being smoked and dusk was deepening when the stock became nervous, and the teamsters also.

They had reason to be, here in southern Arizona Territory. They were deep in Apacheria, where the White Mountain and the

Chiricahua Apache country overlapped. Six Murphy wagons full of goods, the guns, ammunition, and gear of the outfit, the coffee, bacon, and tobacco in the mess wagon, would tempt any sizable war party. Apaches weren't said to be keen on beef, but they would want the mules inside the corral.

The men found cover, behind wagons and elsewhere, and stood to arms, watching the skyline. Above, a full moon hung like a dollar of blue ice cut out of the night, turning the ground before them into a checkerboard of black and silver. One of the teamsters called, "Who's out there?"

Choctaw couldn't see who the speaker was, but he recognized the voice of the wagon master, John Shadler.

There was a small sound, like a faint musical note, and a blackness showed against the gray and came nearer and stepped into moonlight and became a man walking towards them.

Shadler called, "Hold it."

The approaching man halted.

The wagon boss asked, "Who are you?"

The newcomer said, "Prospectors." His English was accented, maybe Mexican. This fit with what Choctaw could see of him in the uncertain light: the shape and wide brim of his hat, and what he was wearing, maybe

12

a serape. Although he was bigger than most Mexicans Choctaw had seen.

Shadler's voice came again. "How many of you out there?"

"Four."

"Okay. Come ahead."

The stranger strode forward and Choctaw saw he was indeed wearing a battered sombrero and serape. And big-roweled spurs making that slight music. This man carried a Henry rifle. Something flashed on his right cheek. A thin scar, like a blue weal, across the bone. There was a rustle of movement, a rattle of hooves, and three more men filed from the darkness, leading four horses and a pack mule.

Around him, Choctaw heard teamsters sigh out their relief. Weapons were lowered.

The four men halted in a group just short of the wagons. They all appeared to be Mexicans. Shadler walked over to them, his rifle hanging in his right hand. He told them, "We can't do much talking. And we've got to keep our voices down. We got a lot of oxen here, and they get spooky at night. Stampede real easy."

The scar-faced man seemed to be the Mexicans' spokesman. He said, "I understand."

"Where you headed?"

"Tucson. Mexico. We been prospecting upriver a ways. Up the Gila Canyon. No luck, so we decide to go back to Mexico."

"Prospecting, huh? Where's your pack animals? How come you only got one mule?"

"We sold 'em to get horses. Better for to go quick through Indian country."

"See any Apaches?"

The big Mexican shook his head.

"Any signal smoke?"

"No."

"All right. Throw your horses in the corral. You can camp over there," Shadler indicated. "And I'd appreciate it if you keep the noise and talk to a minimum. Like I said —"

Scar-face smiled faintly. "I know. The oxen."

Choctaw was one of the two youngest members of this outfit, alongside a boy named Finn. Both were seventeen. Their main job was looking after the mules. But this evening they were given an additional task, night herding.

So, whilst the other teamsters slept, Choctaw and Finn patrolled the calf yard and corrals and made sure no thieves made off with the livestock. Then it was daybreak and

14

the outfit rose from their blankets and began their daily routine. They skipped breakfast and got moving, whilst the night herders and night guards slept in the wagons. Round about ten, after covering maybe eight miles, the freighters halted. The stock needed a few hours' rest if they were going to haul through the afternoon.

The teamsters started on their morning meal. Finn and Choctaw had learned the hard way that if they slept in and missed breakfast, they wouldn't eat again until dusk. So both were awake as the cookfires were lit.

Choctaw sat under the lead wagon. He hadn't been in Arizona long but had already realized shade was precious out here. You grabbed it whenever you could.

A lesson Finn didn't seem to have learned. He straddled the tongue of the same wagon, shaping a cigarette. Which showed he was crazy, in Choctaw's opinion. It was only midmorning, it was February, and yet the sun was already fierce. And Finn, being so fair-skinned, was peeling badly. He was a lanky, straw-haired boy with a pleasant face you'd have trouble remembering.

Choctaw was luckier, as he was more dark-complexioned. His skin had tanned almost as brown as an Indian's in sun and wind. But his features had nothing Indian about them. As far as he knew, he didn't have a drop of Indian blood in his veins. But being born at Fort Towson, in the Choctaw Nation in Indian Territory, where his father had been an army contractor and sometime storekeeper, had landed him with his nickname. He was white, his parents were white, his hair was dark brown not black, tousled not straight, and his eyes were as blue as a Swede's. He was working on his first mustache and trail beard. For all that, he was still "Choctaw" to everyone in this outfit.

His real name was Calvin Taylor but he couldn't remember the last time anybody had called him that. Sometimes he almost forgot it himself.

He was gangling, as his weight had not kept pace with his latest spurt of growth, taking him to six feet. He was still a virgin, although how he was mystified him. He'd come close to losing that burden a number of times. Some girls and women involved on those occasions had told him he was handsome.

Finn lit his quirley. "I see them Mexicans is still with us."

"Huh?"

"I figured they'd have ridden off by now."

"Maybe they're going to stay with us all the way to Tucson."

Choctaw felt thirsty. Reluctantly, he got out from under the wagon. He walked a few yards over to a clump of prickly pear and nicked some pads off with his clasp knife. He rubbed the pads against the sand, wiping off the vicious fur of spines. Choctaw wounded the pad with his knife and sucked.

And tasted dust. The flavor of a bull-whacker's life. After a while, food, drink, and cigarettes all tasted of dust.

Still . . . it was better than going home. He'd take dust, thirst, and heat any day, rather than return to his pa. He felt a free man here. Dirty, tired, and frightened sometimes, but free.

That was an illusion, of course. He was no longer a prisoner of his father but of Schmitt and Gottlieb, freighters of Prescott. They shackled him with five dollars and ninety cents a week and two greasy meals a day, and for that he night herded their oxen and took care of Evil Jenny, his mule, and the other just-as-evil mules, and labored to get the wagons across the Ninety Mile Desert and make eighteen miles a day doing it, so that Schmitt and Gottlieb showed a profit.

Finn asked him, "You figure them Mexicans is what they say they is? Prospectors?"

"Why shouldn't they be?"

"My pa says you can never believe a greaser."

"What about Luis?"

Luis was the assistant wagon master, and hailed from Sonora. An agreeable, humorous man, though he'd give you hell if you fell down on your job.

Finn filtered smoke down his nostrils. "I don't mean Luis. I never think of him as a Mex. He's more like a white man. No, I mean these new fellers."

"What do you think they are?"

Finn shrugged. "They could be *bandidos* or something."

Choctaw shaped his own quirley. "Maybe somebody should drift over to where they are and listen in on 'em."

"You mean spy on 'em?"

It was Choctaw's turn to shrug.

Finn gave him an alarmed look. "I wouldn't do that, Choc. Might be risky."

"Why?"

"You might end up with a knife in your back. My pa says them spics are terrible knife people."

Choctaw sneered at the fear in the other boy's face. "I ain't scared of no Mexican."

Choctaw walked off. He didn't actually

know where he was going, although he *was* heading in the general direction of the Mexicans' campfire. But he wasn't really planning to spy on them. That was just big talk . . .

He glimpsed a bosky of mesquite trees on a low hill nearby. His belly was starting to ache for breakfast. Choctaw strode over and plucked some beans off a tree, chewing a few, taking the edge off his hunger. He gazed at the land around him.

A landscape unlike any he'd ever seen, or imagined. Along all horizons were a run of purplish mountains. Strange bare mountains without trees, their edges sharp as knife cuts against a hot blue sky. Below the mountains lay the desert, rusty earth streaked with the green of mesquite, and studded with cactus. That included the ones Mexicans called saguaro, standing like bullet-headed giants, arms raised in surrender.

Choctaw heard voices.

Lower and softer than Anglo voices, and talking in Spanish. Choctaw moved into the grove of mesquites. He stared through the screen of branches and slowly made out, at the base of the slope before him, the Mexicans sitting around their campfire. Or at least three of them. Then one got to his feet and strode about.

This man was something to look at. He wore a large felt sombrero, bell-bottomed leather chaps with buttons all down the sides, and a short, winged, olive jacket. True, his clothing was scuffed and faded, but he was still a *charro,* one of those Mexican cowboys.

Choctaw heard a small noise behind him, stones rustling underfoot. He turned.

The fourth Mexican stood facing him.

Choctaw recalled Finn saying, about these newcomers, "They could be *bandidos.*" Easy to think that about this man. He was clean-shaven and very hard looking, with high, powerful cheekbones pushing forward, his nose flattened against his broad cheeks. His face might have been formed out of sun-darkened rock.

Something else Finn had said: "Spics are terrible knife people." Choctaw remembered that too. Because the Mexican stepped forward and, sure enough, there was a knife in his hand.

# CHAPTER TWO

Choctaw tensed. He poised on the balls of his feet, ready to meet the other man's attack. He stared at the knife in the Mexican's fist.

It was a Bowie, with a blade eight or ten inches long.

Choctaw started to imagine what a massive piece of steel like that would do to his guts, buried up to the guard and churned around. As he did so, the Mexican smiled.

But it was a surprising smile. Not the leer of a killer. The smile of someone trying to be friendly. Then the Mexican did something else that surprised the Anglo boy.

He went down to one knee. He knelt by a prickly pear. With the murderous knife in his hand, the Mexican nicked off some pads. He popped one in his mouth, chewed, and said, *"Hola, amigo."*

When Choctaw merely stared, the man asked, *"Hablas español?"*

Choctaw *did* speak Spanish, something he'd picked up on his travels out here, but he found he couldn't answer; he stood tongue-tied.

A voice behind him called something.

He turned and saw the other Mexicans had spotted him. They stood, staring up at him. Charro asked (in Spanish), "What you got there, Hairy?"

Hairy rose to his full height. He kept his pleasant smile as he replied in the same language. "I caught this long streak of *gringo* piss spying on us."

"Spying on us?"

"It's all right, he doesn't speak Spanish."

Hairy's nickname was obviously a joke, as he was the only one of the Mexicans not sporting a beard or mustache or both. He went on, "He keeps snooping round us, maybe I'll collect on *him.*"

Charro asked, "That son of a whore? Not worth it. He'd only fetch a boy's price."

"I don't think so. He's what, nineteen or twenty? Right color too."

"No, Hairy. The color's right but nothing else is. It's got to be straight."

Whilst Choctaw was trying to puzzle out what the hell these men were talking about, Hairy stared at him directly. Still speaking in Spanish, and still smiling, he said, "Go couple with one of your stinking cows, American filth."

Choctaw felt his cheeks glowing. One of the other Mexicans laughed and blew Choctaw a kiss. He called, "Yes, go fuck yourself."

The boy's face got warmer. Any second, Hairy would spot he could understand Spanish after all, and then what?

So Choctaw smiled weakly, turned, and walked away. Laughter followed him and his face burned some more.

By the time he reached the teamsters' breakfast fire, the heat had left his cheeks, but his arms trembled slightly and his hands were still clenched in fists of rage.

Approaching the bullwhackers sitting around their fires, it occurred to him how they all looked pretty much the same. Sun, dust, and wear had battered the color and shape out of their clothing. It had done the same to Choctaw's shirt, denims, and slouch hat. Nobody shaved on the trail either, so every face sported mustaches and trail beards — except Finn. Whatever facial hair he'd managed to grow was too pale to show.

The teamsters ate bacon and beans off tin plates, swabbing all up with sourdough biscuits and hanks of bread. Choctaw joined them, sitting next to Finn. As he ate, his anger and humiliation slowly eased.

Nobody said much, not even John Shadler. They didn't even start up the perennial argument over which were better for hauling, mules or oxen. It all boiled down to mules were faster, oxen were cheaper.

It stayed fairly quiet until Shadler was rolling his first after-meal cigarette. As he did so, the wagon boss observed, "Them fellers over there." He glanced towards where the Mexicans were camped. "I looked up the river canyon while there was still light last night. Didn't see no dust. If they did come that way, there should've been some. I did see dust off southeast though."

Danny McClure scratched his beard. "Southeast?" McClure was an Ulster Irishman with a throat-tearing accent, a voice that mostly burst violently and harshly from him. He was a short, powerful man with carroty hair and a handlebar mustache that aged his hard face. He had an arrow wound above his left eyebrow. It had happened many years ago, for the scar tracing the passage of the arrowhead was almost invisible now.

Shadler drank coffee from a tin cup. "Yeah. Round about the north end of the Pinaleños. Like maybe a party their size'd make."

24

"That's Indian country. Gettin' down for Cherry-Cow country."

"Yeah."

Ike Kirby said, "They'd be crazy, prospecting down there."

Dutchy asked, "Why should zey lie aboudt idt?" Dutchy had one cheek buckled from the kick of a mule. That slightly muffled his voice. It was sometimes hard to understand him, anyway, through the gutturals of his accent.

Shadler crimped a wry smile around the cigarette in his mouth. "Maybe they didn't lie about it. Maybe they didn't make any dust coming down the Gila."

Finn wondered, "Then what was that dust over east?"

There was a lull in the talking. Sidelong, trying not to be obvious about it, Choctaw watched John Shadler.

The wagon boss was like something out of a Beadle and Adams dime novel to him. A man with his own legend. They said Shadler had fought Indians and hard eggs across the Southwest; that he'd been a scout for the army and a guide for emigrant wagons; a Ranger and a shotgun guard for a stage line; even a policeman once, in a town up in Kansas, where the good citizens were nervous about the influx of Texas cowboys.

Even if you discounted most of that, (and Choctaw wanted to believe it all) you could see he was a born wagon master. Sometimes he would ride out of sight of the wagons on his near-white hinny, Magnolia, scouting alone for miles, looking for water, the best trail, signs of danger. Choctaw could imagine how much guts that took.

Choctaw watched how Shadler smoked a cigarette and copied him. He noted the way Shadler rode Magnolia and tried to sit likewise on Evil Jenny. Shadler turned a silly-looking mule into a noble mount, just riding Magnolia the way he did.

The wagon boss wasn't a showman. Long hair and fringed buckskins weren't his style. His coppery hair was cut short. His skin was freckled, almost brick-colored from the sun. Against his red flesh his eyes were a cold gray-blue. Shadler's mustaches were long and wide, a darker red than his hair. He wore a rusty trail beard.

The wagon boss dressed simply: canvas jacket, denims, Texas hat. His only vanity were his moccasins. Real Cherry-Cow mocs someone had told Choctaw. The deerskin boots would have climbed to the thigh if Shadler hadn't furled them back at the knee.

Shadler carried one pistol in his army holster, the butt turned in against his ribs.

The pistol was a Starr double-action army .44. Schmitt and Gottlieb had ensured every man in the outfit without a rifle of his own received a Spencer .52 carbine, the sort of gun Choctaw once dreamed of owning. But now it was a Yellow Boy he wanted, because that was what John Shadler carried. There was nothing Choctaw wanted in the world more than a Starr double-action pistol and a brass-faced Yellow Boy Winchester. Except, perhaps, a pair of Chiricahua moccasins.

It was Choctaw who got the discussion going again. He said, "You notice them Mexicans' horses? They're all ganted and their gear scratched up. Like they've been pushing hard through rough country."

Horn Miller made a dismissive noise. "This is *all* rough country, kid." He sounded like someone stating the obvious to an idiot and Choctaw felt embarrassed. What Horn seemed to be implying was: *Don't join in with the man talk until you're old enough.*

But then Shadler said, "Choctaw's got a point. Why would anyone drive their horses hard through this country 'less they had to?"

"They're just some spics." As Horn spoke heat touched his cheeks. He looked embarrassed and glanced around, perhaps realizing he'd just insulted Luis. But the as-

27

sistant wagon master wasn't there; he was off somewhere attending to his duties.

Choctaw found he was grinning like a Cheshire cat. Shadler had complimented him on making a good point, and in front of all the others. And with the only thing he'd said.

Finn asked, "You don't figure they're *bandidos,* or bad men on the run, do you?"

Horn said, "Even if they are . . . four men ain't gonna jump thirteen. They ain't gonna do that." He spoke with confidence. But then he glanced around, and his voice, when it came again, was considerably less sure. "Are they?"

28

# CHAPTER THREE

After breakfast, the outfit started moving south again.

Like Finn, Choctaw expected the Mexicans would leave them. It was sixty or seventy miles to Tucson. A horsebacker could make that in a day, or a little more, whilst the outfit would probably be four days getting there. But to his surprise, the Mexicans tagged along. Maybe protection was more important to them than speed. This worked both ways, as their company meant four more guns in the outfit's defense.

It became sickeningly hot. Men, horses, and oxen suffered, plodding through their own dust. Mules appeared unperturbed. It was generally believed among the outfit that mules wouldn't break sweat amidst the fires of hell.

The heat made skylines pitch and heave like restive oceans. Mirages flaunted at the edge of vision. Now and then a scrap of reality gashed the shimmering haze. To their left, the teamsters sometimes glimpsed mountains marching south, parallel with them.

The outfit made eighteen miles that day before night camping. Choctaw and Finn drew night herd once more.

After the wagon master, the night herders had the most dangerous job in this outfit. Elsewhere on the frontier it might have been the safest. John Shadler said some Indian tribes, like the Cheyenne, were loath to fight at night. But Apaches had no such inhibitions. If anything, they preferred night work.

Finn and Choctaw rode their mules the hundred yards to pasture. There was another full moon, giving too much light.

Finn rode a mule called Daisy. Choctaw suspected his friend had been around mules a good deal from the way he handled her. All that Choctaw knew about Finn was that he hailed from East Texas, though farm boy was written all over him, from his deeply freckled arms and face to his slightly stooped, plow-driving walk. He'd handle mules well but it was a different story with guns. Finn treated the carbine as an extra limb, dangling carelessly from him. It was now pointing in Choctaw's direction.

"Hey, Finn," Choctaw protested. "Point that thing someplace else. I ain't no Indian, you know."

The other grinned. "Or some Mex bandit."

Choctaw made a discovery. "I forgot my rope."

"You better go get it," Finn declared unhappily. The other boy could understand that. He wouldn't like being left alone out here either, a sitting target in the moonlight for any hidden enemy.

Choctaw dismounted and walked back through the camp. He walked as quietly as he could. It didn't take much in the way of noise to startle the oxen and then you might have a stampede on your hands.

He found his rope in the trailer and set off back the way he'd come.

Choctaw thought about the Mexicans. Sure, they'd laughed and sworn at him, and made him feel like a damn fool. Hairy had scared the hell out of him, with that knife in his hand. And that other talk — about how the color of something was right but it needed to be straight. What was that all about? But, at the same time, they'd taken him for nineteen or twenty, and he was really only seventeen.

Choctaw halted.

He listened.

What was he listening for? He reckoned he must have heard something out of place in the desert night, something that didn't belong. What?

The outfit's mules and the Mexicans horses were restless in their corrals.

After weeks of night herding, Choctaw was familiar with the noises animals made once it was dark. *These critters sounded like something had spooked them.*

Of course, it could be nothing — they spooked easily. But for all that a coldness settled in Choctaw's stomach. The flesh on the back of his arms, his neck, even his ears, prickled. He knew that wasn't just the chill of the desert night.

It was fear.

Choctaw told himself: settle down. A man could spook just as easy as a horse, and for the same fool reasons. All it took was a little too much imagination, jumping at shadows, overreacting to some stray noise. Before you knew it, you'd fired your gun, and then you'd have a stampede on your hands.

The boy kept listening. He strained his ears and there didn't seem to be one sound in the whole Territory of Arizona. Just a pool of icy silence stretching to those black mountains running their saw edges under

32

the paler darkness of the sky.

And then he heard a foot scuff against the ground.

It was on the far side of the corral where the horses were penned. Probably the horses heard it too. They made more restless noises, coughing and whinnying and shuffling their feet.

Choctaw told himself it was probably the night guard prowling.

But if it wasn't . . .

Choctaw decided he'd go on a little detour on his way back to Finn, swing a loop around the horse corral, just in case anything was wrong. What would be the harm in that? He realized his finger was tensed on the trigger of his Spencer. Jumpy as he was, he might shoot first at whatever showed before him, and then find he'd shot the night guard. He eased his finger off the trigger and let the carbine rest against his leg.

He started walking.

Ahead of him was a stretch of particularly thick blackness, like the gaping mouth of a trap. He halted. Gazing into that maw, part of him recoiled from going there.

Choctaw snorted at his own skittishness, acting like some kid scared of the dark.

So he stepped forward confidently. He even pasted a smile on his face. He plunged into the darkness of shadows.

And almost walked into someone.

A black man-shape.

And then moonlight touched the face and he saw it was Hairy.

Choctaw flashed an instant memory. Hairy saying: "Go couple with one of your stinking cows, American filth." His hard laughter. The knife in his hand.

Choctaw acted without thinking, swinging out wildly with the butt of the carbine. He caught something solid. Hairy grunted and spun away, going down on one knee. Impetus carried Choctaw forward. He tripped over the kneeling man and plunged headlong. He managed to turn in falling and struck the earth on his back.

He rolled over, losing his grip on the carbine. As he scrambled up, Hairy lunged at him. The man lifted his right hand, made into a fist.

Choctaw punched first. He swung a roundhouse right against Hairy's side — and struck something like a tree. Pain stunned his arm. The Mexican punched back, a right hook that caught Choctaw on the chin. He knocked the boy from his feet.

Choctaw wasn't sure what happened next, except he was facedown on the ground, dust and blood in his mouth. Bright lights flashed in his eyes, the world rocked about him, went black and then returned to exploding color. He rolled over.

Hairy stood over him.

Slowly Choctaw clawed to his knees. His jaw was numbed like it was broken and blood leaked from his mouth on to his chin. He knew he couldn't take another punch like that.

Much later he found he was standing and was surprised his opponent had allowed this. Instead of wading in, kicking and gouging, Hairy was tugging something from his belt. His knife!

Choctaw felt terror. He hurled himself at the Mexican. Hairy grabbed the boy's wrists and toppled backwards, yanking his opponent towards him. Landing on his shoulders, Hairy hooked his feet into Choctaw's stomach and kicked upwards. The boy catapulted forward, half-somersaulted in the air, and struck the ground on his head.

He lay on his back inspecting the night sky dispassionately. It seemed a very confused sky, the moon and stars playing mischievous games, changing places with each other, just to tangle him.

From somewhere he found the strength to get to his knees. A metal plate was being hammered inside his skull. The clanging filled Arizona.

Choctaw stood, swaying. His head seemed to crack open with pain and he cried out.

Figures bulked before him. Hairy was one of them, the Bowie in his hand. It looked like Hairy was being restrained by some of the others. The boy felt a welling rage. He took one rubber-legged step towards his opponent. A hand seized his shirt front. Choctaw arched against the grip and cried, "Get your fucking hands off me, you fucking —" and the man who held him flung him backwards.

Choctaw glimpsed his face as he sailed helplessly backwards. It was John Shadler.

The boy fell, sprawling.

A man sat on his chest and laid a hard palm across his mouth. Shadler had flung him down with force enough to drive all the wind he had left from his body. Choctaw lay motionless under his captor, calmly watching the stars play leapfrog and wishing they'd quit their crazy antics. Then he was no longer anchored to the earth, the man who'd held him down hauled him rudely to his feet. It was Danny McClure.

Choctaw understood. The bullwhackers were afraid the stock might run, so they'd silenced him. Most of the outfit stood about. He was pleased to see that Finn wasn't one of them.

A bull lowed in the darkness.

He felt relief, knowing at least he hadn't stampeded the herd. That would have capped everything.

John Shadler wanted to know what had happened. He spoke Spanish, but haltingly.

But, as it turned out, Hairy spoke pretty fair English. He said, "This crazy kid jumped me."

Shadler told him, "Hold it down."

The Mexican glared at the wagon boss. But when he spoke again, after a minute, it was in a whisper. "That kid hit me with his rifle butt."

Choctaw opened his mouth to protest; just in time he remembered to whisper back. "What you expect, coming at me out of the dark so sudden —"

Hairy sneered.

"Anyway," Choctaw asked, "what was you doing sneaking round there?"

"I wasn't. I went for a leak and was just cutting back through camp."

"Like hell you was."

"Crazy kid."

"And then you tried to Goddamn murder me!"

The last few words, Choctaw forgot everything and shouted.

McClure gripped his Spencer in both hands, leveling it across his body. There was no mistaking his intent. He was poised to club the boy down with the butt of his carbine, rather than have the oxen stampede.

John Shadler said, "You keep your voice down, boy, or I'll shut your mouth for you."

Choctaw blinked. He stared, first at Shadler, then at McClure. New emotions writhed in him. In that instant he hated John Shadler; he hated the Irishman waiting with his rifle to smash him down. And Choctaw hated himself. For, inexplicably, tears had filled his eyes. He had betrayed himself. Not only had Hairy whipped him in a fight, now he was going to cry like a baby.

Choctaw couldn't let anyone see him with tears in his eyes. He walked off a ways, stepped behind a wagon, took the rag that passed for a handkerchief from his pocket, and swabbed his eyes dry. Then he went over to the lead wagon, passing Horn Miller and Ike Kirby. He knew from the way they fell silent at his approach that they'd been talking him down. Not only had he broken their much-needed sleep, he'd been whipped by a Mexican.

They could sneer all they liked. Choctaw had been in a roughhouse or two and knew a tough man when he met one. When he thought about Hairy's knife, that snarling length of blue metal, he got queasy with fear again. He'd been in plenty of fistfights, but this was the first time anyone had pulled a knife on him. *The first fight where someone was fixing to kill me.*

Choctaw was sitting on the tongue of the lead wagon, morosely shaping a cigarette and rubbing at his jaw, which was starting to ache like hell, when John Shadler came over.

Shadler demanded, "What the hell you think you're playing at?"

Choctaw thought: *All right mister high-and-goddamned-mighty wagon master, you and your outfit, you and Schmitt and Gottlieb, you can all go to hell.* He opened his mouth to tell Shadler this.

But then Shadler said, "You know, you're a damn good bullwhacker, Choc."

Choctaw blinked and stared. Shadler's words left him more dazed than Hairy's punch. He realized he was gaping like a fish. The wagon boss went on, "Too good a mule hand to let himself get killed by some rough customer like that Mex."

"Huh?"

"Think about it, Choc. If they is *bandidos,* what's to stop 'em slitting your throat, dragging you out into the desert, then saying the Indians done it?"

"I never thought —"

"Well, start thinking. You got out of that scrimmage without getting a knife in your ribs. You might not be so lucky next time."

Still dazed, Choctaw asked, "So you're pretty sure they're *bandidos*?"

Shadler made an exasperated sound. "Dunno. But they're *something*. Not just some sourdough prospectors, the way they act."

"How do you mean?"

"The one you tangled with — he said he was going for a leak? He wasn't. He was doing a little guard duty of his own. Taking a walk around the camp perimeter."

"How'd you know that, Mr. Shadler?"

"I been watching 'em. And I saw that feller go for his little night stroll, and followed him. No, Choc." Shadler leaned towards the boy, like a conspirator taking another into his confidence. "If I was to call it, I'd say they're acting like fellows with somebody on their trail. If anyone was after me — say, some kind of posse was breathing down my neck — I might act like they're doing."

"Yeah?"

"Not that I ever had no posse on my heels,

40

you understand?"

Choctaw smiled. "Sure."

"Ain't you on night herd?"

Choctaw returned to Evil Jenny. There was another dazed smile on his face, he knew. Today he'd been beaten and punched in a fight. Threatened with a knife. Laughed at, insulted, and humiliated. At the same time John Shadler had called him "a damn good bullwhacker" and "too good a mule hand."

Which made it, he reckoned, just about the best day of his life.

# CHAPTER FOUR

Next morning the outfit covered another eight miles before making their late morning camp. This was where the main road to Tucson was joined by the military road to Camp Walsh, a cavalry post about twenty miles east.

Here the wagons sat, coiled once more into a defensive circle. Nearby a long wash sloped down to a creek a few hundred yards away. A lick of sand-clouded water you could cross in ten strides, and never get more than knee-deep.

Inside the wagon circle teamsters ate breakfast. After eating, they kept busy, silencing axles with grease, fixing gear. Some saw to the stock, the oxen unyoked and turned out to graze. As they'd been night herding, Finn and Choctaw were allowed to rest further, maybe sleep off their morning meal.

Choctaw lay in his blankets under the lead

wagon, with his head on his saddle. But sleep wouldn't come. It was too hot, or there was too much white glare off the face of the desert, or something.

Finn wasn't even trying to rest. Instead he sat a few yards away, out in the sun as usual, even though it was shaping up to be an even hotter day than yesterday.

Finn said, "I can't wait 'til we get to Tucson. I keeps thinking about them whirligo women."

Choctaw said, "My pa always told me to steer clear of bad women. And I never done nothing my pa told me. Except get out."

Finn looked troubled. Choctaw smiled at that. The two boys felt differently about their respective parents. Finn still got homesick. He became vaporish, thinking of his ma and pa. Choctaw decided Finn was a mama's boy.

Choctaw eased his head down against his saddle. Carefully. His jaw was now numb from Hairy's punch. It would probably sprout a dandy purple bruise. His head ached where it had struck the earth and there were dull bands of pain across his neck and shoulders. When he remembered the fight, how effortlessly the Mexican had whipped him, his face grew warm with embarrassment. But as well as pain and humiliation, he felt guilt. It could be he'd overreacted last night, attacking a man about some entirely innocent business. After all, he *had* struck first, lashing out with his rifle butt when Hairy appeared out of the dark before him. But then Choctaw remembered Hairy's knife, the ten inches or so of blue steel the Mexican was fixing to bury up to the hilt in Choctaw's guts. His charitable thoughts towards the man vanished.

One of the Mexicans appeared, leading two horses. It was Charro. The Mexican filed past, heading down into the wash, presumably taking these animals to water. The horses he led were a coyote and a bay. Choctaw liked the look of the bay, a handsome animal with three white socks and a star. He was envious. He wished he was riding a horse like that, instead of some silly mule.

Choctaw made another attempt to sleep. And couldn't. Why not?

He realized it had got quite noisy in this neighborhood. A cactus wren racketed in the mesquite, a tiny bird with a voice like gunfire. There was a quail whose call you heard a lot out here, and it was a damn irritating one, a run of about four whoops that came around again and again. That quail was calling now. Mules brayed and then bulls joined in, lowing and grumbling. Choctaw got back down into his blankets, cradling his head first on his left arm, then on his right. He told the animal kingdom: "Please let me sleep, you noisy bastards."

Then he must have slept after all, for the next thing he knew he was blinking awake, sitting up. Another noise had startled him back to consciousness. A foot, crunching gravel nearby. Choctaw sat up, one hand flapping towards his Spencer.

A great disc loomed between himself and the sun. A sombrero.

Standing over him was Luis. The assistant wagon master asked, "You been sleeping, kid?" He grinned. "Dreaming about all them bad women you're gonna to call on in Tucson?"

The Mexican tilted his back against the trailer wagon, fashioning a quirley. He passed the makings to Finn, who sat nearby.

Choctaw imagined he'd only dozed ten, fifteen minutes. The sun was a hair nearer its zenith. Charro must have finished watering his two horses as he was coming up the wash towards them, leading both animals. Choctaw glimpsed further movement. A man riding his mule in a slow circle around the oxen, a rifle laid across his saddle. The New Orleans Frenchman, Eduard, day herding the stock. He passed from view behind the wagons.

Choctaw got to his feet, wondering what was wrong, knowing something was.

He couldn't hear that noisy wren or the whooping quail. A lot of the racket that had been going on only minutes earlier seemed to have ceased.

Finn said, "I hear tell, in Tucson, they don't tell time by the clock. It's all first drinks time, second drinks time . . ."

Choctaw was about to ask Luis, "Why you figure it's gone so quiet?" when he noticed Charro, toiling along the wash, halt. The Mexican stood, gazing around him.

Finn asked, "True what they say about them whirligos, Luis?"

Choctaw looked for John Shadler and couldn't see him. The only movement he caught was the nervous bobbing of a white-winged dove atop a cactus, building its nest.

He saw more movement, a skipping blur in the tail of his eye. A darting jackrabbit. But this critter did a strange thing: it halted, sat trembling, then shot off into the brush. He noticed a small bird swooping towards a clump of cholla hover, then veer away.

Luis grinned around the smoke in his mouth. "Whirligos? They eat you alive, them whirligos, kid."

The white-winged dove flared from its perch, the sun glinting on its wing tips.

Choctaw asked, "Hey, Luis, why you figure it's gone so —"

Luis jolted backwards, slamming against the trailer. He dropped like a puppet whose strings had been cut, landing on his rump, his back against the wheel. His shirt front was all bloody and his head nodded forward. Dust erupted, billowing around him.

There was the sound of a shot.

# Chapter Five

*So that's what Arizona looks like,* Choctaw thought. *I never looked at this country so close before.*

He was examining it closely now. Nose and lips were splayed against Arizona.

Something gnawed into his right thigh. Twisting his head downward, Choctaw bumped his chin on the mouth of the Spencer.

He decided he didn't know what was happening, but whatever it was, it was crazy. Why was he lying atop a loaded weapon? Why was he pressed so flat against the earth?

And what was all that screaming? Why didn't somebody stop it?

Could it really have been a gun that went off, just then? And could Luis really have been punched backwards before it, as if a halter around his neck had been yanked?

Choctaw decided the sun had finally touched him.

The boy lifted his eyes and saw the upper was splaying away from the sole of Luis's boot. He hadn't noticed that before. He could see it now because Luis was sitting against the trailer wheel, the soles of his feet pointing towards Choctaw, his head bent forward. He might be asleep but for the blood all over his shirt front.

Choctaw had never seen a dead person, killed by violence, before. He knew he was looking at one now.

He gazed past Luis and saw a crazed mule wheeling inside the corral. McClure plunged forward, seizing the animal by its collar and in the tail of his eye Choctaw glimpsed another burst of movement.

A swirl of dust in the wash.

Charro was trying to position himself between his two horses. Both animals were panicked, hauling on the reins. They screamed and made some of the terrible racket that was going on.

One of the horses broke free. The coyote. The animal fled, drumming towards the herd. Beyond was pink fog, streaked with movement, rocked with noise. The oxen were stampeding.

The bay reared. Its rump cannoned into Charro's back, driving him to his knees. He sprawled facedown and the horse bolted.

John Shadler yelled, "Cover him, damn you!"

Shadler's Winchester opened. He was lying, facedown, firing over a wagon tongue. Five, six, seven shots. They must have missed Charro by a hand span. They passed over him into the chaparral, one shot low, spurting sand, the rest thrashing the brush a foot above ground level. Another gun opened, a Spencer, and another.

Charro staggered upright.

"Use them guns!" Shadler roared. "Cover him!"

Choctaw pulled his carbine into his shoulder and stared along the sights. But how could you shoot something you couldn't see?

Charro was running upslope, his elbows pedaling at his flanks like a trained sprinter, his face contorted, his mouth gulping.

Guns blasted.

The runner pivoted forward. He somersaulted and crashed across stones. Dust steamed over him, thinned. Charro sat up. Then slowly he nodded forward, as if anchored to this place by a desperate weariness. His arms trailed across his thighs.

Someone was shouting.

It was McClure, calling, "Help me throw these mules."

Dimly Choctaw recalled he was the mule handler with this outfit, alongside Finn. Where was Finn?

It was taking Choctaw three times as long as normal to do anything. Either thinking or moving. Revolving his head on his shoulders, when his head weighed heavy as a tombstone, he looked behind him. He couldn't see Finn anywhere.

McClure yelled, "Damn ye, Choc! Help me!"

The Irishman flailed amidst a cloud of mules. They kicked and swirled about him, braying and squealing.

Evil Jenny lunged for a break in the wagon circle. Choctaw ducked out from under the lead wagon and grabbed her collar, dragging his weight down on it, anchoring her. Something whipped viciously at his right shoulder and the animal arched its spine and lashed out with its forehooves and screamed. A thousand pounds of mule exploded against him, muscle and bone and snapping teeth and flying iron-shod hooves. The boy hooked one arm around a hind leg and his shoulder punched the mule's off flank. He slammed Evil Jenny on her side, tying hind legs together, then looping the same rope around her foreleg cannons. Choctaw swore grimly throughout this operation, and when it was done, he was wet with fear and sweat. And then he had to do likewise with Finn's mule.

Now all the loose mules were thrown and tied. Choctaw crawled under his trailer.

Screaming went on around him. It wasn't the mules, they had mostly quit after being thrown, though the kitchen wagon team, still in harness, set to bawling frantically when a gun went off.

It was a man screaming. It came from under Dutchy's wagon where the Mexicans had sheltered. One of them had been hit in the first volley and had been screaming ever since.

Choctaw was unnerved. The screams went right through him, drilling into his head, his teeth, his bones. He wondered: *If I'm hit, will I scream too?*

His arms shook, and fear filled his belly and mouth like poison. He knew he was teetering on the edge of panicking, of maybe even turning coward. Maybe in a second, he'd fling himself facedown on the earth and hug it close like a small child burying himself in his mother, wanting to hide there forever. Or maybe he'd lose his head entirely and run screaming out into the desert.

McClure called, "You done well, kid. Now look to your guns."

52

To himself the youth said, *Yes, sir, Mister McClure. If I can keep my hands still long enough, that is. What makes them shake like that?*

Choctaw tried to close his ears to the screaming, concentrating on the priming and loading of the weapon in his hands as if it were the only thing that could ever matter. As he worked a strange thing happened. A wonderful sense of calm eased over him, as if in mechanical actions and automatic thinking there was some release from terror and bewilderment. He'd finished, the Spencer was checked, ready and loaded, and his hands were no longer in rebellion. They were nearly as steady as they normally were.

John Shadler told the whole outfit, "You see something, shoot at it."

Choctaw gazed into the near distance, now writhing in the mad haze of noon. And saw nothing. Idly he wondered what he was looking for.

There was an angry buzzing, like a tarantula hawk wasp, and an object lay quivering on the sand, nine inches from the boy's face.

He squinted at it. It took him a minute to make sense of what it was.

It was an arrow.

A short and wicked thing, no more than a yard in length, with three blurring flights at its tail. The head was a sliver of chipped quartz, fiendishly barbed.

He now knew his enemy. An enemy infamous far beyond the limits of their own savage country.

*Apaches.*

John Shadler called, "Everybody keep your heads down and stay calm. These scuts ain't gonna rush us, and they can't hold us for long. Pretty soon somebody else'll be coming along this road. Maybe the army. Then we'll be out of it."

That made sense, Choctaw thought. Yesterday they'd been passed by two sets of travelers. But the day before, he remembered, they'd seen no one. As for the army . . . Choctaw hadn't seen a soldier in weeks and Camp Walsh was twenty miles away.

It seemed everybody had gone to ground (that is, hid themselves under the wagons). The screaming ebbed. The charro sitting in the wash began to call something in a bleary, drunken voice. Choctaw couldn't tell what he was saying.

Choctaw had fought Indians all his life. Mainly he'd fought them in the canebrakes behind his pa's store, hacking notches out of the gnarled cottonwood switch that passed for his deadly Kentucky rifle. Back then he was Kit Carson and any movement out there — the trembling of a sumac bush, the shiver of post oak branches — were Blackfeet, trap-robbing savages; only Kit Carson spotted them first, and then, the dead shot turned them into another notch on his butt stock, as he made another good Indian. But there'd been no trembling fingers to master then, or airless lungs to pump. No dizzy mind to control, no throat fiercely dry with fear. And he'd spotted his enemies easy enough. Here, he couldn't see one of them.

Choctaw tried to get some kind of fix on time. How long since he'd been lazing against the wheel, (where the quartz-tipped Apache arrow now lay) discussing saloon women with Finn and Luis? A century?

He could see Hairy's bay horse. The animal had snarled its feet in its lines and stood in a mesquite grove, a couple hundred yards out.

Choctaw glimpsed movement and pulled the butt of the Spencer into his shoulder. He squinted down the sights, framing slithering movement. His finger was poised to clamp on the trigger.

Two facts registered.

One: a good Indian-killer squeezed a trigger, instead of jerking it.

Two: he was a finger squeeze away from shooting one of his own side.

The crawling man was one of the Mexicans, bellying forward under the trailer of Dutchy's wagon. The wheel masked his upper body, then he crawled further and Choctaw saw it was Hairy. It must be the broken-cheeked man, or the other Mexican, who was wounded.

Hairy knew what he was doing. As he snaked along on elbows and belly, he held the muzzle of his rifle clear of the ground, keeping it free of dust. Now, behind an off-wheel, he eased to one knee and lifted his weapon.

He swore.

The rifle spun out of his hands. Hairy sat, clutching his right thigh and the arrow thrusting out of it.

Choctaw scanned the brush. Seeing absolutely nothing. Haze made a mockery of vision. It was like looking at the landscape through a pane of water-smeared glass, or a film of rippling liquid. What you saw trembled and danced about and sometimes stretched like yeast. Even when the haze cut out, and the desert lay before you in sudden, startling clarity, you still couldn't see a damn thing. The Apaches hid too good.

The invisibility of the ambushers made

them somehow more terrible. There was an Apache close enough to drive an arrow into Hairy's thigh — yet the desert out there might have been peopleless.

Cursing and flopping on his rump, Hairy thrashed his way out from under the wagon, back into the corral.

John Shadler yelled, "Well, shoot at them bastards!" A few hopeful Spencers barked. Dutifully, Choctaw let off his first shot in anger, doing his bit for Schmitt and Gottlieb and the defense of the outfit. He fired carefully into nothing.

An Apache shouted at them from the chaparral. He was calling in what sounded like rage. Guns tried for the hidden voice without result. At first the words meant nothing to Choctaw, until he realized the Indian was calling in Spanish. Yelling something about Mexico, or Mexicans.

The disembodied heckling ceased abruptly. There was a burst of gunfire from the Apaches. Shots fairly peppered Dutchy's wagons, wood erupting in a rain of crazy splinterings. The Mexicans stayed flat under them.

It came to Choctaw that the Mexicans were drawing a disproportionate amount of fire. What had that Indian been yelling?

Out in the wash Charro began to moan

deliriously.

From where he lay, Horn Miller asked, "Why don't they just finish him off?"

McClure answered. "Not Apaches. That'd be too easy."

John Shadler put in, "They'll leave him as bait, to draw us out. Then they can get some more white-eyes."

Miller observed, "Cunning bastards."

Dutchy said, "Zey haf the devil's cunnink."

Miller said, "Least he ain't their prisoner. You know what they do to their prisoners."

Choctaw had heard plenty about what Apaches did to their prisoners, of the myriad fiendish ways they might torture a man, usually involving knives white-hot from the fire, and attention to a man's privates in particular . . .

Now Ike chipped in. "I could always plug that greaser, put him out of his misery."

Shadler called, "Put up that rifle, Ike. I'll take care of that Mexican, if anyone has to."

McClure declared that the sun would soon kill the Mexican, anyway.

Choctaw thought about the Apaches. About how little firing they'd done so far. And what about all that yelling and war-whooping Indians were supposed to do? There'd been precious little of that. The boy had heard about a hundred Indian fights, the question being: what to believe? Some claimed there were thousands of Apaches, armed with Spencers and Henrys. Others said the widely scattered bands totaled only a few hundred warriors, largely dependent on bows, lances, and antiquated smoothbore muskets.

Whatever their numbers and armaments, most commentators agreed that Apaches were primarily sneak fighters, hit and run guerrillas. They favored quick ambushes of small parties. They rarely engaged large bodies except in considerable strength. Not that there was much comfort in such knowledge. To tackle seventeen well-armed, well-defended men so openly, the Apaches must be in large numbers out there.

There was another burst of enemy fire.

A mule fell, screaming.

The animal was the nigh pointer on the kitchen wagon. It lay, kicking, deadly hooves lashing at its running mate, iron shoes flying at the wheelers and the swing team, at all it could reach. There was chaos in the team. In a moment there would be crippled mules alongside the wounded one.

Dutchy stopped that.

The Dutchman sprang to his feet, walked three paces to the mule's side, and shot it in the head with his Spencer. The blunt head slammed against earth, the animal kicked once and was still.

In the same instant, Apache guns crashed. This was what they were waiting for, a target. But Dutchy was ducking quickly back into cover. Almost quickly enough. Then he was spinning around and going down. Giving a high, piercing scream of pain.

John Shadler yelled, "Shoot, for Christ's sake!"

Spencers opened up, the bullwhackers aiming at smoke and flame flashes in the chaparral.

For a moment Choctaw was frozen. It was unimaginable, that thorny, feisty Dutchman, hard as rawhide, screaming his pain like a woman. Yet even he had screamed.

The boy came out of his daze. He grabbed for cartridges in his belt; then, in the tail of his eye, he caught more movement. A tiny flicker of color near the bay horse.

Haze was warping vision once more. A few paces to the rear of the horse, he saw a pillar of shimmering brownness. The haze lost some of its strength and this brownness became a man, crazily proportioned, no body, all arms, legs, and head. The curtain of haze was ripped aside and Choctaw could

60

see him clearly.

An Apache, not much more than two hundred yards distant.

A shortish man with skin of beaten copper, naked but for a kilt of some pale cloth, baggy knee-high moccasins. His mane of blue-black hair fell to his chest, bound with a thick scarlet rag at the temples. This man had thin arms, a broad, powerful chest, and his face was wide-mouthed, all hard angles. He held either a quirt or a rope.

Choctaw fixed the man's deep chest in his front sights. Even the sweat glazing on his bare ribs was telescoped cruelly into focus. Just a squeeze on the trigger and he was Choctaw's first good Indian . . .

Choctaw jerked the shot.

And missed.

Missed the man clean and nicked the horse. The bay ran.

Choctaw swore at himself. *Goddamn it, squeeze the trigger, don't jerk it.*

He levered the Spencer, thumb-cocked the hammer, and fired. Again, too quickly. The Apache lunged forward, and haze claimed him again. He became wildly elongated, a streak of weaving darkness. Choctaw caught the dim running shape in his sights. *Squeeze the trigger, don't jerk it.* His finger took its time now, coiling the trigger.

But his target vanished, as if the earth had sucked it under.

A man squirmed under the wagon at Choctaw's left. McClure. He yelled, "Choc! Keep your head down, for Christ's sake!"

The youth obeyed. He saw a bullet or bullets had splintered the wagon bed above him, and another arrow lay snapped on the earth by the rear off-wheel. It was strange. Whilst firing at the Indian he hadn't realized he'd been under fire himself.

McClure declared, "I seen you shooting."

Choctaw was about to confess miserably: "Yeah, if you call that shooting . . ."

McClure said, "Good shooting, Choc. You stopped that savage from getting that horse."

"I did?" the boy muttered. The Irishman seemed to take that as a statement of fact.

The two teamsters lay, watching and listening. It was quiet again. And then the wounded Mexican, lying under the wagon, began to scream once more.

# CHAPTER SIX

McClure and Choctaw listened to the Mexican scream.

Choctaw tried to will him to silence. Find some guts, he told him. Take it like a man. The boy glanced at McClure. The Irishman's face was grim; he chewed at his lower lip.

Choctaw asked, "Dutchy hurt bad?"

"Aye. Wrist all smashed to Jayzus."

The other spent a moment digesting that. Then he asked, "How many we lost so far?"

"Well, Luis — and Eduard."

Choctaw realized he hadn't thought of the New Orleans Frenchman since the fighting started. "Eduard?"

McClure nodded grimly. "Hit him on the first volley. Shot him off his mule."

"Dead?"

"Fair shot to pieces."

"Jesus."

"Aye. Those bloody, murdering sons of

bitches."

Choctaw ought to feel bad about another of the outfit being killed. The fact was, when it came to Eduard, he found it hard to feel anything. Most of the bullwhackers he'd known were close-mouthed, but Eduard particularly so. He saved up most of his talk for the salty tirades he'd launched at his mules. Choctaw didn't guess he'd ever spoken more than half a dozen sentences to Eduard, or vice versa.

McClure said, "And one of those Mexicans is hit pretty bad." As if on cue the man he was talking about let out a high, jarring scream. Both Choctaw and McClure flinched. The Irishman said, "That poor bastard there. Finished if you asked me. Bullet here —" He touched his groin.

Choctaw grimaced. "And that *charro* too."

"Huh?"

"The Mexican in the wash."

The boy drank from his canteen, splashing a little water onto his hands, also onto the barrel and breech lock of the Spencer. He asked, "Hey, Irish, why do you figure them Mexicans is drawing so much fire?"

When there was no reply, he turned his head and saw McClure crawling off behind another wagon.

Mercifully the wounded Mexican stopped

64

screaming. A thick silence descended.

Time dragged. The desert broiled in afternoon heat, bleached in haze. Choctaw had assumed Charro was dead, but about two hours after noon the man began to shout unintelligibly in a rasp of a voice. He shouted for some minutes.

Ike thrust his head out from under his wagon and declared, "I figure them Injuns is gone." He climbed to his feet and grinned. Shadler told him to get flat and not act like a damn fool. Kirby said, "I tell you they're —" and a shot came. Ike hurled himself facedown.

But the shot wasn't for him. It killed a mule in the mess wagon team.

Shadler gave a cry of frustration. "The hell with this. McClure! Choctaw! Over to me!"

Choctaw was surprised to hear his name called. But when McClure crawled over to where Shadler lay, under Miller's wagon, Choctaw crawled after him. As he made his way along, on his belly, or on his knees and elbows, being careful to keep the muzzle of his Spencer out of the dust, he wondered why Shadler hadn't called for Finn. He was a mule handler too.

A couple of yards along he found out.

Finn was lying on his side, his face pressed to the earth.

At first Choctaw thought his friend was dead. Then he saw a pulse working quickly in the boy's throat, and his tongue move around his lips, his mouth gaping. He was staring into the earth and trembling all over.

Choctaw asked, "Finn, you hit?"

Finn's stare moved and found its way to Choctaw's face. There were tear stripes rilling the dust on his cheeks and tears in his eyes. But what Choctaw saw mostly in the other boy's eyes was fear.

It was an ugly thing to see. It put a sour taste in Choctaw's mouth. Partly it reminded him of his own fear, when the firing had started and he was down hugging the earth just like Finn was now. It reminded Choctaw of how near to turning coward he'd been. And partly it was such a disfiguring thing, robbing a human being of any kind of dignity.

"Finn?"

The other looked once more at the earth, and seemed to try and burrow himself deeper into the sand. He made small whimpering noises.

Choctaw's mouth twisted in contempt. He thought: *you yellow, gutless bastard, Finn.* He opened his mouth to say that. Shadler called, "Choc!"

Choctaw twisted around and saw Shadler

66

gesturing him over.

He forgot his friend, the yellowbelly whose guts had run out, and moved to the wagon boss's side.

Shadler crouched down, back of Miller's wagon, his Winchester laid across his knees. "Choc, I want you and McClure to throw the kitchen wagon mules."

"Yes, sir."

Shadler started to say something and then paused. He gazed off, lifting his fist to his mouth and chewed at one knuckle. He returned his hands to the Winchester, flexing and unflexing his fingers. He seemed to have forgotten the boy crouching by him, then he said, "Them red bastards ain't content with running off our oxen. Now they're amusing themselves picking these mules off one by one. So we'll hog-tie 'em. You two go in quick and get the job done and we'll cover you. All right?"

"Yes, sir."

Shadler glanced at Choctaw. The tension in him seemed to ease, he even smiled a little. "You ain't short on guts, are you, boy?"

When the other didn't answer, Shadler went on, "Not like —" He gazed off, towards Finn Choctaw supposed. The wagon master's lips twisted in contempt.

"How's Dutchy?"

"Dutchy?" Shadler looked startled. Anguish showed in his face. He seemed to be thinking hard about the question. But when he spoke it wasn't to answer. "Get ready. You and McClure don't move until we start firing, then —"

Shadler's gaze switched from Choctaw to something past him and his eyes showed alarm.

Choctaw turned. Finn had risen to his feet. The boy stood, gaping, in a pantomime of astonishment. Choctaw wondered how long Finn had been standing there, looking as silly as that. He was mouthing words, but too low for Choctaw to hear. Now Finn stepped forward. A somnambulist, he walked calmly past the mule teams on the kitchen wagon, sleepwalking out into the desert. Choctaw thought: *Where the hell's he going?*

McClure called, "Come back, kid!"

He sprang to his feet and lunged after the boy.

Choctaw didn't think. He went after Finn too.

Shadler called, "No, Choc!"

Only twenty paces from the cover of the wagons, a long, gradual slope started. Finn paused atop this slope, staring down. At the bottom of the slope was a wall of chaparral where the Apaches hid.

Standing there, Finn couldn't have presented a bigger target. But no shots came.

Still calm and unhurried, he began to descend the slope.

McClure got to him, grabbing his shoulder. But Finn twisted violently, and McClure slipped and went to one knee. Finn staggered forward and then broke into a half-run.

Choctaw reached the top of the slope. Behind him he heard someone — Shadler? — yelling "Come back, Choc!" and "Crazy kid!"

Choctaw plunged down the slope. Finn glanced back and saw him in pursuit. He yelled something and started running hard.

The other boy put on a burst of speed. Finn started to weave and Choctaw lunged forward, diving and tackling Finn about the waist. Finn went down and Choctaw pitched past him, plowing into dust, which burst around him, enveloping him. He coughed against it and rolled out of it and slithered downslope and fetched up on his back.

Finn sat up. Two men crashed down the slope towards him — McClure and Shadler. Finn scrambled to his feet and the others seized him by both arms. Finn yelled and fought them. There was a struggle and then Shadler stepped back and raised his fist and drove a straight-armed punch against Finn's jaw. There was the meaty smack of impact and the boy dropped like he was poleaxed. The men took his arms and began to drag him upslope.

Choctaw remembered where he was. He got to his feet in a hurry and lunged after Finn and his rescuers.

There was a whistling sound in the air.

Something like an iron band caught him across the chest and he was yanked off his feet. He hit on his rump with force to jar his teeth and then found himself being dragged backwards, dust boiling around him.

The dragging stopped. Choctaw saw there was a rope across his chest, pinning his arms to his sides. He glanced behind him and saw the rope, lying slack now, running on into the wall of brush. He switched his gaze forward and glimpsed Finn's rescuers halfway up the slope. He cried, "Mister Shadler!"

John Shadler glanced back. Alarm showed in his face and he called something. Choctaw opened his mouth to yell and there was another, stronger yanking on the rope and he was whisked backwards once more. He

70

glimpsed the rope behind him pulling taut and the wall of chaparral hurling towards him. He was fairly flying along, his rump bouncing and scraping over the earth and then the open sky and the open world vanished and brush was a roof over him and all around him, and he was crashing through it, over rubble, through dust and thorns and cactus and God knows what. Vegetation whacked at him, thrashed him, and ripped him.

And then he juddered to a halt.

He was under open sky again, dragged clean through the chaparral. Dust settled around him where he sat. He coughed and blinked against it. There were dim shapes behind the dust, and, as it thinned, they became men.

Short and middle-sized men with very dark skin, men in shirts and breechclouts, long black hair falling to their shoulders and chests, bound in head rags. Men with weapons in their hands — rifles, bows, lances — and the white gleam of paint on their dark faces.

Choctaw stared at them helplessly. Terror filled him like a load of icy water, anchoring him to the earth.

This couldn't be happening, he decided, it couldn't be real.

Yet it was.
The men around him were Apaches, and he was their prisoner.

# CHAPTER SEVEN

Choctaw's eyes went to the rope looped around his chest, following it as it ran through the circle of Apaches standing around him to an Indian mounted on a pony. The rope was tied to the pony in some way, which was how they'd managed to drag him along so quickly.

He could see cuts, scrapes, and patches of blood all over him, but he was too dazed and numbed to feel much. He coughed against dust thick in his throat. The boy was soaked in sweat and drained of strength. When an Apache crouched behind him and twisted his arms behind his back he couldn't resist. He felt rawhide sear his wrists as his captor bound them. The binder twisted a stick in amidst the rope. He grunted a few words, his voice deep in his chest. The other Apaches laughed.

The rope across Choctaw's chest was lifted from him, but replaced an instant later by a rawhide noose around his neck. The captive was jerked roughly to his feet. His legs felt like rubber and he swayed. But before he could fold to the ground his captors broke into a run, one of them yanking on the rope. Choctaw ran with them, somehow staying upright. But his short boots couldn't find the same purchase on broken ground as the Indians' moccasins. He fell and was dragged. He seemed to bounce and plow through a world of blinding, choking dust.

And then they halted.

He looked up from where he lay. His captors surrounded him. But at first, he ignored them, because he was starting to feel his hurts. Choctaw ached as if he'd been thrashed all over with clubs. He burned with many cuts, including a deep gash on his knee. He'd scraped flesh from his legs, his back, his ear and elbows, and all those places stung like hell.

After a time, he came out of feeling just pain and gazed at the men standing around him. He counted eleven. He guessed he'd stand half a head taller than any of them. Stocky, powerful men in their twenties and thirties. Not in feathers and buckskins like savages in Beadle and Adams, nor yet the Choctaws he knew from home, who dressed like white men and had plenty of white blood in them, who drawled English like Arkansas farmhands.

These men wore scarves around their heads, or rags across the temples, or let their hair fall in strong manes to their chests, or lower, unbraided. They wore long-tailed shirts, smocks, crumpled boots, thigh-length moccasins. He was surprised to see one man sported a brocaded vest, almost colorless with wear. Most seemed to have painted their faces in the same startling way — a horizontal slash of white paint splitting the cheeks, running from ear to ear across the bridge of the nose. They bristled weapons — bows, lances, muskets, knives, clubs. Only one held a modern weapon, a Henry carbine. They looked a combination of pirate and tramp. At the sight of them, Choctaw's blood ran cold. Except in his wrists, where his blood pumped with a slow, nagging fury.

What had he been thinking, running out into the desert just to save a worthless coward, someone better left to the Indians? He must have been crazy. And the gutless yellowbelly was safe now, back inside the wagon defenses, whilst the man who'd tried to save him was a prisoner of the most terrible hostiles on the frontier.

And everyone knew what Apaches did to their prisoners.

Choctaw became aware that something of an argument was going on amongst his captors, several Indians talking at once in grumbling-in-the-throat voices, the words short, guttural, fast-dealt. The dandy in the vest lifted the knife in his hand, gesturing with it towards the captive, shouting something.

The boy was hauled to his feet and stood swaying on weak legs. The vest wearer advanced on him, knife raised.

Choctaw waited to be butchered.

The Apache waved the knife under the prisoner's nose, shouting into his face. The boy was startled by the hatred in the moist black eyes, the same hatred warping the man's features. Hatred even shook in the heavy voice, almost as if this savage was capable of knowing the same fury, loss, and depth of feeling as a human being. The Indian was yelling, *Mi mujer! Mis hijos!*

Choctaw felt almost weightless with terror. If it wasn't for the rope around his neck, he was sure he'd lift gracefully to the horizontal and drift off towards the mountains like a trailing cloud.

The other Apaches crowded about him. They continued shouting, at him, at each other. One of them spat in his face. Someone swore at him in thick-tongued Spanish. He heard the vest wearer, again crying, *"Mi mujer! Mis hijos!"*

A man stepped between Choctaw and the others. He asked the boy, *"Hablas español?"*

Choctaw attempted to speak but couldn't. *So it's true after all,* he thought, *you can be speechless with fear.* The Apache must have realized this. He turned away from the captive, dismissing him. Another man pushed the boy in the chest. Choctaw retreated four staggering paces. A foot hooked behind his ankles. He landed on his rump with force enough to jar his teeth. Some of his captors laughed.

Choctaw heard an animal snarling. Rather, a man snarling like an animal. He realized that this sound writhed in his own throat, he was the snarling animal. He twisted one leg under him and sprang upright, charging them, all of them.

A ring of jeering brown faces bobbed around him and there was more laughter. They retreated before him. His actions were stupid and profitless, he knew, why give them a show, but he didn't care. The boy found his voice, emitting a stream of obscenities that were childish and useless in his own ears but he didn't care about that either. *Get them mad enough,* he thought, *they might just kill me quicker.*

One man wouldn't be drawn. He struck the boy across the forehead with the butt of his quirt.

Choctaw fell to his knees. Thunderclaps crashed and echoed between his ears and splintered lightning flashed across his vision.

Two Indians took his neck rope and climbed upslope. Choctaw was hauled upright once more. He felt blood on his face, and his right temple, where the quirt had struck him, pulsed with fierce pain. The youth stumbled dizzily uphill after his captors.

The slope ended. Beyond, there was eye-stinging sky, in which a single cloud floated. The Indians kept back of the skyline. They had different plans for him. His captors slid behind him and one of them prodded him forward with the point of a lance, nine feet of ironwood tipped with a rusting bayonet. The youth cringed back from the skyline. The wagoners would shoot at anything that popped up into view. Choctaw might even get himself picked off by John Shadler's Winchester . . .

The lance point jabbed him again. A hand grabbed his hair and wrenched. From behind, a lifted knee rammed with shocking force into the boy's testicles. He grunted and found he'd staggered upwards, was skylined.

An Apache took a firm grip of the rope, a yard behind Choctaw's head. This man was up on the skyline too but a pace behind the captive. He was careful to keep the prisoner before him as a shield. He shouted something over the boy's right shoulder.

Choctaw squinted westward. When the haze shifted, he could make out the corralled wagons, about three hundred yards distant. Slowly, he came to understand his captor's halting Spanish. The man was yelling, "Give us the Mexicans! Give us the Mexicans and we'll give you the Anglo!"

There was a pause whilst the Indians waited for a response. When none came, the Apache began shouting the same again, and the feeling of this-is-the-last-time-I'm-saying-this-next-we-quit-fooling-and start-work-on-the-boy in his voice reached the captive. It seemed to rob him of the last of his courage. Choctaw opened his mouth. He was going to yell, "For Christ's sake, give them what they want! Don't leave me to them!"

He never spoke.

Something drove into Choctaw's back.

The boy was knocked headlong.

He somersaulted. He fell ten feet through air and struck the slope and bounced raggedly and somersaulted and bounced again and rolled and kept rolling. The gradient pitched steeply downward. Dust fumed over him. Then the plunging slope eased off; he skated yards on his chest, and sledged to a halt.

A single gunshot was fading into silence.

Choctaw recognized the bark of a Winchester.

He wrestled over onto his back. His fall had spilled him a hundred yards below and fifty yards ahead of the ridge. A dozen yards below the same ridge the Apache spokesman lay, facedown.

Dazedly Choctaw came to understand what had happened.

There had been a shot from the wagons. Damn good shooting. The Apache had been shot out from behind his prisoner. He'd fallen against Choctaw and both of them had been knocked downslope.

At least there was one good Indian out there.

Except the Indian wasn't dead. As Choctaw watched, the man staggered to his feet, hands clasped to his side. He couldn't have been hit too hard as he broke into a stumbling run. He went upslope, bent over, zigzagging as he ran.

There was more firing from the wagons. Spumes of dust fountained on the slope about the veering runner, but he made it to the ridge, and vanished beyond.

Using his knees Choctaw struggled upright. He wasn't sure what had happened or was happening, but a miraculous fifty yards had opened between his captors and himself. Even the rope that had tethered him like a horse hung limply about his neck. *All I've got to do now is run to the wagons. Run two hundred fifty yards with my hands tied behind my back. And not get killed in the process.*

Choctaw ran ten yards before he lost balance, tipped forward, and sprawled headlong in a bed of thorns. As he writhed clear an Apache bullet drove sand into his face. He squirmed upright and began running again. Rifles cracked, bullets yowled around him. After another twenty paces he realized he was sprinting in the wrong direction, his path angling away from both Apaches and wagoners. He veered back on course. This time the trailing rope fouled his legs and he crashed down on sand.

Someone — John Shadler — was yelling, "Stay flat, Choctaw! Stay flat!"

81

Through sand and bloody teeth Choctaw said, "Yessir, Mister Shadler." The boy wasn't listening to Shadler, only to his terror. It was crazy fear that got him to his feet, willing him to movement, driving him onward through the final two hundred yards. Terror spurring him on, his heels had wings. Choctaw found there was no trick to running with your hands lashed behind you. He was a hundred yards out. Bullets sang by his ears. Ahead, sharpening from haze to reality, the string of Murphy wagons juggled on the heaving skyline.

Between one stride and the next, he went down.

His chin struck the earth. Impact seemed to shake the teeth from his head. He laid his battered face against the sand and didn't move.

Not for a very long time, as far as he could tell. A dozen lifetimes seemed to elapse, crawling by with tortured slowness. But eventually he did manage movement.

Choctaw raised to a sitting position and, using his knees once more, he stood.

The instant he put his weight on his right leg, pain such as he'd never known shrieked through this limb. The leg buckled under him and he fell. The pain was blinding, and he screamed.

He lay on his back. He saw his right leg was bloody from hip to foot. Pain shot through it again in a surging jolt. He felt another outcry welling in his throat and wanted to bite his sleeve and gag his mouth, but he couldn't, his hands were bound behind him . . .

From the direction of the wagons dust boiled towards him. The dust sprouted heads, arms, legs. McClure, Horn Miller, and John Shadler, dashing to the rescue. A scene straight out of Beadle and Adams. Choctaw laughed harshly at such nonsense. And then he screamed again.

Miller and the Irishman grabbed Choctaw under the arms. John Shadler stood clear. Choctaw heard the crackle of Indian rifles. Shadler sank to one knee, shouldered the Yellow Boy and levered, and triggered four shots as fast as one into the desert.

The boy's rescuers hoisted him, McClure lifting the youth's uninjured leg. They swung him up above waist level and ran for the wagons. He was flung about like a rag doll, and he yelled and swore at this rough handling.

Twenty paces short of the wagons, Horn went down. The charge piled on top of him. Choctaw's damaged leg bounced against the earth and he'd screamed out, but he could manage little more than a cry.

Shadler called, "You hit, Horn?"

"Just burned me."

Horn made it to his feet; the mess untangled itself without any more than one of the rescuers stamping on the man they were rescuing. McClure leading, they carried Choctaw to the wagons. John Shadler covered the retreat of the heroes with his Yellow Boy, all but emptying the magazine in the last dozen yards.

As he reached the wagons, Shadler gave a sudden gasp.

The beautiful Yellow Boy spun end over end from his fingers and lay with its brass face fouled in red dust. Shadler sat carefully, his hands pressed to his side, to the dark, widening stain there.

It was Horn Miller who called, "Boss!"

Hold it!

## CHAPTER EIGHT

This long night was ending. First light showed behind the mountains to the east.

Finn blinked weary eyes and stared into paling darkness. He said, "I can see something out there."

Two men were riding unhurriedly towards the wagons. Both were in shadow, then, as the night softened, black fading towards gray, they gained shape and detail. One rider astride a mule. Another man on a gray horse. The mule rider was a squat figure in a pale shirt. Finn glimpsed a dark copper face, high-boned cheeks, the jet flash of hair. A head rag banded his temples. There was a cold blaze of silver in his ear.

*An Indian.*

Finn lifted his Spencer but someone beat him to it; from the wagons a rifle crashed.

The mule reared and spun. The rider clung aboard. The other man urged his horse forward, yelling, "Hold it! Hold it!

Hold it!"

Finn heard McClure say, "Missed the fucker." There was metallic clacking as Spencers were cocked.

The horsebacker's voice came again. "Hold it! Hold it! We're white men!"

Horn Miller shouted, "All right, hold it! Who's out there?"

"White men!"

"Yeah? What sort of white men?"

"Arizona Volunteers."

"Then who's that Injun up there?"

"Scout. Friendly."

There was a long silence. Then Miller called, "That Jack Adams?"

"That's me."

Horn yelled, "Bring your people up, Adams!"

Hooves clattered. Ghostly horse-and-rider shapes paled from darkness, filing through the gray half-light. A considerable number of them. Short of the wagons, they began to dismount. Some of the wagoners ran out to them, beating at themselves with their hats, pumping hands, slapping backs. Finn heard whoops and cheers. Somebody fired his rifle into the air. Horn Miller and McClure got into an impromptu dance, knees flying chest high, their elbows sawing away like a pair of fiddlers. Their stamping raised a lot of dust.

Finn approached Adams, who sat rubbing the cramp out of his legs. Under his slouch hat his black hair tangled to his shoulders. He wore a mustache and a full black beard too, so not a lot of his face was visible. Two cartridge belts made an X pattern across his chest. He asked Finn, "Hey, sonny, you got a jug anywheres?" Adams spat tobacco juice at a rock. "I come a long ways dry."

Finn shook his head. "Liquor ain't allowed in this outfit."

"Who says?"

"Schmitt and Gottlieb."

"Schmitt and Gottlieb? Sanctimonious bastards. We saved their Goddamn wagons, didn't we?"

Adams stood and showed he was a very tall man, maybe six four. He crossed to the wagons. They'd laid John Shadler on a blanket under his trailer.

Adams peered down, squinting out of eyes that had done their share of squinting, to judge from the mesh of lines about them. "John Shadler, ain't it? He dead?"

"I got a jug," Shadler told him. His voice was a bare whisper. It hurt Finn to hear that, the wagon boss broken and diminished by pain like any other man.

Adams stooped to listen.

Shadler went on, "I got a jug. In my possibles bag. Seems like a good time to get her out."

"You is a Christian man, Shadler. You hit bad?"

"I was lucky. Bullet went right through. I ain't gonna die."

Adams said, "I'll send a coupla men on to Camp Walsh, to fetch the army sawbones."

Finn wandered over to the Arizona Volunteers. There were about forty of them. Some shaded up under their horses. Others sat and kneaded the cramps out of their legs. The bulk of them appeared to be Mexicans, wearing serapes, wide-brimmed hats, and cotton pants that might once have been white. A volunteer swept his sombrero from his head and beat at the dust on his shirt with it. Lank blue-black hair fell to his chest. Curious, Finn studied the faces of his rescuers.

"Jesus, mister," Finn told Adams. "Half these fellers here is Indians."

Adams scratched his beard. "Sure. Fact is, you don't find too many white men with the stomach for this business. All of those hypocritical sons of bitches in Tucson. Screaming all the time about cleaning out the Indians. But how many'll stick their necks out and do anything? Ask 'em to leave town and come out here in wild country and suddenly they's otherwise occupied. So a man has to trail over all hell and creation with Goddamn spics and Indians for company." Adams drank from Shadler's jug. "Them's Papago Indians. Sometime we use Pimas, Maricopas, Yumas, Navajo — any breed of red nigger. I'd side with Old Nick hisself, if it'd kill Apaches."

Adams returned Shadler's jug to its owner, who said, "Glad to see you, Adams." Finn had a strange notion; he didn't believe Shadler meant what he said. He sensed a tension between these two men.

Adams said, "I guess that's your oxen out there, scattered all over the place."

"Yeah. The Apaches stampeded 'em."

"Want us to help you round 'em up?"

"We can do that. But thanks anyway."

"We been chasing Cherry-Cows. They hit a ranch and run some horses off the Papago reservation. Chased 'em six days, never saw a one o' them varmints. Only their dust." His eyes slid back to the jug.

"Finish what's in there."

"Obliged, Shadler." Adams took the jug back. "I come a long ways dry." He drank, sighed, and wiped his mouth with the back of his forearm. "Looks like this bunch you tangled with pulled out in the night."

Shadler coughed and lay back, his bloodless face stiff with pain. Adams asked, "You sure them Apaches ain't killed you?"

"I ain't gonna die. Not yet. I've got some scores to settle first."

"Scores?"

"With those red bastards out there."

From very far away Finn's voice asked, "How is it, Choc?"

Choctaw tried to say, "Hurts like hell." But he couldn't speak, his throat was on fire.

Choctaw opened his eyes. He was startled to see gray sky behind the mountains, tinged with red. It was dawn, he had slept the night through.

He raised his head and saw men near the wagons, with mules and horses. The men were strangers to him.

Finn said, "Help's come, Choc."

Choctaw wanted to say "That's good," but he couldn't speak.

He felt the slow, throbbing anger of his leg. He remembered the warm, secure place he'd been, until he opened his eyes and reentered a world of pain. Time inched past. He listened to the breathing of the horses and the shuffling of their feet.

Choctaw heard wagoners yelling, cheering and whooping. It all seemed a very long time and a long distance away.

An image flashed before his eyes. He saw a Winchester spinning and falling and laying its golden-brass face in the red dust.

Choctaw began to cry. Tears seared deep acid rills down his cheeks.

He listened with horror to the choking, sputtering noises he made. He couldn't remember the last time he'd wept this hard. Not since his mother died? Maybe not even then. But he was helpless to stop. The celebrating wagoners made noise enough to rock the desert. But all Choctaw could hear were his own sounds of anguish.

■ ■ ■ ■

# PART TWO

■ ■ ■ ■

PART TWO

# CHAPTER NINE

*What I need,* Lieutenant Austin Hamilton told himself ruefully, *is a damn stiff drink.*

Private Sean Kenney gazed blankly at the commanding officer of Camp Walsh. He displayed no interest in what was happening to him. Kenney might have been a length of sweat- and dust-soiled blue cloth, dangling limply from a hook before the lieutenant's desk.

"Stand up straight, Kenney," Sergeant Tyson growled. He put the emphasis on the surname, making it clear this was a personal thing between them.

"Kenney," Hamilton declared, "You are a disgrace to that uniform."

"Yes, sir."

"You are a disgrace to the Third Cavalry and to the whole United States Army, Kenney."

"Yes, sir."

Nature had not blessed Private Kenney.

95

He was snub-nosed and buck-toothed. His eyes were insolent. They were very narrow set, and there was a slight cast in them, and nobody would have trusted them.

Hamilton laid his hands on his desk. "What I'd like to do, Kenney, is to inflict upon you the worst punishment I can think of, which is to ensure you serve every minute of your enlistment at this Godforsaken outpost. Unfortunately, that's beyond my authority."

"Yes, sir."

"Tomorrow, Kenney, you will spend running 'round the parade ground from reveille to taps. Carrying a forty-pound log. The rest of the week you'll be chopping logs. Next week, kitchen police. And fourteen nights in the guardhouse."

"Yes, sir."

Tyson blurted, "Lieutenant, all respects, sir, what this scut needs —"

"That'll do, Sergeant."

"Yes, sir."

Hamilton saw argument building in Tyson's face. Hamilton said, "Dismissed."

Tyson and the prisoner exited. Hamilton stared bleakly after them. He fingered the stubble on his throat, then kneaded the loose flesh above his Adam's apple. He declared, "That damn Tyson — you see the look he gave me? I'll bust *him* next, if he doesn't watch out."

He was talking to Pat Scanlon, post surgeon.

Scanlon chewed one wing of his handlebar mustache. "He's a good non-com, Austin." Scanlon was years from the old country; there was little brogue left in his voice.

"It's a personal thing with him and Kenney."

"Kenney's no damn good."

"No-good civilian, maybe. He won't be the first no-good civilian I turned into a good soldier."

"That shifty-eyed son of a bitch?"

"I can make a soldier out of him, Pat. You can't Tyson's way. He'll hang Kenney up by his thumbs. Well, the next thing you know, Kenney'll desert. And maybe stick a knife in Tyson on the way out. Then I've lost two good soldiers."

"Well, I'm not saying you should let non-coms —"

"Paddy, don't tell me how to run this post. I don't tell you how to cut off a man's —"

Hamilton pinched a finger and thumb together at the bridge of his nose. He closed his eyes. A voice in his head told him: I shouldn't have said that. I'm tired.

Shame touched Hamilton. Scanlon was

tired too, with better reason. Only an hour earlier the surgeon had rasped a bone saw through a man's arm, severing the limb at the elbow.

"I'm sorry, Pat."

Furnishings in the office ran to two mesquite chairs, a plank bench, and two bare tables. One supported a half-full bottle and some glasses; the other, smaller table served as a desk. Hamilton crossed to the larger table. He poured two fingers of mescal into each of the tooth glasses.

"Drink, Pat?"

The surgeon nodded.

Hamilton drank slowly. Scanlon drained his glass in one swallow. In the guttering lamplight his face became a sheet of blood. Hamilton probed the coal-oil flame of the lamp with his cigar, drawing until the stogie took.

"Goddamn," said Scanlon.

"Have another," Hamilton invited.

Scanlon shook his head gently. He could quench his pain, at least temporarily, with a single drink. Hamilton envied him that. Sometimes the lieutenant felt a store full of mescal wouldn't ease the demons riding him. He tipped the bottle again, for himself.

"The Dutchman?"

"Too early to say."

"The others?"

"The kid'll make out. He's young. Tough. A kid like that can drink up a lot of hurt. One of the wagoners pushed some tobacco through that hole in his leg. That's their idea of how to cleanse a wound. Providing that doesn't kill him, he should be on his feet again in a day or two."

"The Mexican?"

Scanlon studied his empty glass. "Had it. God knows why he isn't dead yet. You know what those savages stuff in their guns. Bullets made out of scrap metal, tin cans all hammered together. When it hits, it spreads out like shrapnel. Shredded his intestine. Anyway, if the lead doesn't kill him, peritonitis will."

"Hard man to get drunk?"

"Who?"

"The Dutchman?"

"Did we properly anesthetize the patient, do you mean? Well, he finished the bottle. Private Krautz sat on his head while I sawed off his arm."

"Jesus."

"Jesus Christ, Austin. That's who the Dutchman kept calling on. Can't say I noticed Him helping any."

"I sent Primitavo and a detail to scout their trail."

"They want a company on their trail, not a scout and detail."

"I can't send soldiers I haven't got."

"Tell that to those wagoners."

"No doubt I'll have to. You're starting to sound like that damn Tucson newspaper."

Hamilton glimpsed an instant derision in the other man's eyes. Scanlon looked old, he thought. Hamilton wondered if his friend was ill.

Scanlon moved towards the mesquite door. "Good night, Austin."

"Good night, Pat."

Scanlon's dragging steps crossed the parade ground. You couldn't mistake his footfall.

Hamilton tossed back his drink and felt slow liquor flame briefly inside him. Too little fire, too soon spent. Hamilton relit his cigar and crossed to the doorway. He looked out on Camp Walsh. Hamilton knew better than to stand there, holding the lamp. Some *bronco* Apache lay out there, perhaps, waiting for the evening the white-eye chief forgot and targeted himself in the doorway, with a lamp in his hand. The commanding officer of Camp Walsh was in mortal peril a dozen yards from his own bed. That was the extent to which the military controlled the area.

The sky was a stormy emerald tonight, a drowned vastness above blue-black mountains. Myriad stars pitted the night. Here and there they glinted.

Hamilton saw Scanlon enter the post hospital, which was a sagging, low-roofed adobe, like all "permanent" dwellings at Camp Walsh. A sadness for both of them touched him but Hamilton knew it was mostly self-pity. Scanlon was once his best friend. He had been the one man on post Hamilton could talk to, which is what the lieutenant wanted more than anything else. A weakness, he knew. Commanders lived in isolation.

He groped for his Hunter watch, somehow reading the tiny face in the icy moonlight. Fifteen minutes to taps.

The buildings of Camp Walsh were blotches of darkness on the paler gloom of the night. Dwellings were grouped on all sides of a rectangular parade ground: adjutant's office, post bakery and guardhouse, the commissary and the quartermaster's storehouses, the sutler's store. Officers' quarters faced the men's barracks. In back of the quartermaster's and commissary were the blacksmith's forge, the cavalry stables, and some corrals.

As was usual with frontier forts and

camps, there was no wall, fence, or palisade around these dwellings. Walsh might have been any meager Arizona village but for the scattering of army tents there, and Old Glory hanging limply at its flagpole on the parade ground.

Under the mountains the coyotes were baying. They sounded like men under torture, deranged, no-longer-human creatures in their final agony. Hamilton had listened to coyotes before, in other shabby camps along the frontier, calling over ground as tenuously held, and from darkness as malevolent, as that at Camp Walsh. But this place was different. Something was waiting for him here. His Scots grandmother, or Scanlon's mother, they would call what he was feeling premonition. He didn't know what it was. Only that it *was* here. Out with the coyotes in the darkness.

Hamilton closed the door and walked towards his desk.

There was a small mirror hanging from a nail on the wall. Hamilton paused by it and studied himself.

Medium height, medium build. Thirty-seven years old and tired as hell but oddly enough that didn't seem to show in his face. Hair dark brown, retreating now up the high forehead that was a feature of Hamilton males. Wide, fine mustache. A woman had once said he was "almost handsome" — the one woman he'd almost married. What was most noticeable about his face, he wondered? His gray eyes, especially against his Arizona tan? The firm set of his mouth, maybe indicating a confidence, perhaps even an arrogance, he didn't feel?

Hamilton returned to his desk. He spread the map on the table before him, pegging glasses at each corner. The map showed the Apache country. It was six years old, thus badly out of date. A rash of settlements had flowered where the map showed nothing. Army camps had been abandoned as the theatre of Indian operations shifted. Camp Walsh was marked, but then it was Fort Breckinridge.

Pouring over this map was a ritual with Hamilton. He enjoyed it, because it took him nowhere. He need make no decisions. After hours of scrutiny, the riddles the map held would still be unresolved. The cartographer had provided only a mystery.

Apacheria ran from San Antonio, Texas, to the Rio Verde, here in Arizona. It embraced parts of Arizona, New Mexico, Texas, and a couple of northern Mexican provinces. Not that this was continuously Apache country. The Apaches existed in pockets throughout this immensity, usually in remote mountain strongholds. They were land pirates who lurked, watching the roads, the widely scattered ranches, mines, and settlements for easy plunder. For a decade the army, plus civilian militia like the Arizona Volunteers, had made war on them.

In some areas, the bands had started to surrender. In New Mexico Apaches had gathered at Cañada Alamosa, Fort Stanton, and other agencies. Some other Apaches were camped peacefully along the White River. But there were at least three concentrations of hostiles left in Arizona.

Hidden along the upper Verde were the so-called Tonto Apaches. Hamilton's information was that many of these Tontos weren't even Apaches, but renegade Yavapai, Walapai, or Yuma Indians. In eastern Arizona were hostile bands of Pinal or White Mountain Apache. Southeast of Walsh the Chiricahua Apaches, under their chief Cochise, had their mountain strongholds. Usually the Chiricahuas directed their efforts at the country south of Walsh, raiding deep into Mexico. The Tontos wouldn't come as far south as Walsh unless fleeing pursuit. But the Pinals regularly raided and plundered the area. Hamilton guessed the Pinals were responsible for three quarters of all local trouble. Already talk had it that Cochise and his band had waylaid the freight train. Hamilton thought it was more likely Pinals.

What was happening was hard to pin down. Every year the army proclaimed victories and lengthy counts of hostile dead, yet depredations continued. The toll taken by the hostiles was equally vague. Hamilton speculated on average *broncos* killed one Anglo a week and had done so for the last ten years, but it was possible they had killed two Mexicans for every Anglo. Nobody really knew what was going on south of the border, except that the Indian situation remained "very bad."

No one knew, either, the Apaches' real condition. You rarely saw hostiles before battles, or even during them. After, you might see a dead one, all his secrets sealed within him. What was happening amongst them, how did they think, feel? How many were left? How many warriors were there, and how well armed? How near defeat were they? Ten years of constant attrition had gradually squeezed them back into the wildest and bleakest mountains. How much longer could they hold out?

Hamilton lifted the bottle. The red liquor blazed in the coal-oil light. Smoky shapes writhed behind the thick glass. He made a decision. He slammed the bottle back onto the tabletop. It was no answer, only damn rotgut.

One day, Hamilton thought, a resounding silence would crash down over this wilderness. For weeks, months afterwards, frightened miners, settlers, and soldiers would continue leading their gun-clutching, ambush-conscious lives, until finally they realized what the new silence portended: the last hostile had been slain, still gripping the country in his dying spell, as the Apaches held it captive now, with the mere fact of their existence.

# CHAPTER TEN

The two riders halted their mules. They could see beyond the ridge, without framing themselves against the skyline. Finn was looking east, into the valley. Down there, tallowy lights glimmered amongst gray smudges on the darkness — the buildings of Camp Walsh.

McClure was looking west at the mountains, at their back trail. To his way of thinking this was a perilous time in a journey. A weary traveler, coming in view of his destination, naturally relaxed, believing himself already home and safe. Then *they* would strike. *They* knew how men's minds worked.

"Finn," McClure announced. "You away over that ridge, I'll cover you. I come over, you cover me."

"Yessir." The boy flapped around in the darkness for his Spencer. He'd forgotten where it was. McClure decided the boy was a damn fool with guns. The only thing he was an asset with was mules.

They crossed the ridge without incident and Finn kicked his mule into a little speed down the far slope. McClure told him to pull in his animal. They were challenged by a sentry who was so frightened he stammered in German, forgetting his English. A corporal appeared. He was Scots-Irish. He pointed out the corral, the commanding officer's quarters, and the post hospital. After seeing to the needs of their animals, the two bullwhackers entered the hospital.

They waded into a sallow, coal-oil gloom. In the center of the room, a weary-looking soldier scrubbed a long plank table. McClure recognized the post surgeon, Scanlon, buttoning on his army jacket. Scanlon asked the newcomers, "And who the hell are you?"

McClure told him, "We're from that freight outfit that got hit."

"I remember — I spoke to you."

"That's right. We seen the wagons get to Tucson, then came back here."

"Any more trouble?"

"No."

"You made good time. I suppose you want to know about your friends?"

"Yes."

The surgeon waited a moment before speaking. "I have to tell you the Mexican's a goner. Be lucky if he lasts the night, the way he's breathing."

"I didn't mean the Mexican."

"The kid? He's okay. Be up and around in a day or so."

"That's good. What about Dutchy?"

"Dutchy? You mean the German?"

"Aye."

"You friends of his?"

"Aye."

"I'm afraid I had to amputate his left forearm."

Scanlon caught the look on McClure's face but chose to ignore it. A silence thickened around him as he finished buttoning his tunic.

McClure fingered his mustache. "You said that wouldn't be necessary."

"I said I *hoped* it wouldn't be necessary. But you can't predict with that kind of wound. The flesh either heals, and you leave it, or it goes rotten and you have to amputate. There was nothing else I could do."

"How's Dutchy making out?"

"He's survived the operation. That kills half. We can only wait and see."

"You said —"

"I know what I said, mister."

"Can we see 'em?" Finn asked.

"You won't be able to see the German.

He's . . . under sedation."

"Can we see Choctaw?"

"All right. Why do you call him that?"

"What?"

"That heathen name. He isn't an Indian, is he?"

"It's a nickname. Like they call me Finn, only my name's Phineas."

"If you say so. I've no business treating Indians."

"He's not an Indian."

Choctaw lay on a straw pallet on the floor of a narrow box room, robed in an army blanket. A kerosene lamp standing on a stool nearby provided dim lighting.

The boy looked up as the door opened and visitors entered: Finn, McClure, and Scanlon. The surgeon said, "Fifteen minutes only, gents," then left.

Finn asked the patient, "Do it hurt much?"

"Itches like hell."

McClure asked, "You hear about Dutchy?"

Choctaw nodded.

McClure said, "Those murdering red bastards."

Finn blurted, "Hey, Choc, you hear what we found out? About them Mexicans?"

"What about 'em?"

"What one of those Mexicans had hidden in his saddlebags."

"Which one?"

"Scar-face."

"What, they was bandits after all? They had stolen gold hidden in them saddlebags?"

"No."

"I know. Some miner's poke, some prospector they'd robbed —"

Finn smirked. "Scalps."

"Scalps?"

"Six Apache scalps."

"Why the hell should they want Apache scalps?"

McClure said, "Money, that's why. Down in Mexico they've started paying bounty on Apache scalps again. Hundred dollars for a buck's scalp. Fifty for a squaw. Twenty for a kid."

Finn added, "They calls it 'Apache ranching.' Seems the usual thing is to get a bunch of the varmints to come in and parley. Liquor 'em up. When they're good and drunk —" Finn chopped a hand sideways, signifying finish. "Do it all the time in Mexico. 'Paches don't never seem to learn. Maybe they're more interested in getting aholt of whiskey than in their own skins."

Choctaw nodded.

"Anyway, our Mexicans didn't do it that way. They went out in wild country looking for Indians. Maybe pickings are getting scarce. Got six scalps, anyhow. A man, a woman, two gray hairs — old man and woman that is — and two kids."

McClure said, "You remember you said their horses looked all beat up."

"Yeah."

"Well, you was right. A war party must've got on their trail. Reckon they run over all hell and creation trying to dodge them Indians. Then they run into us."

Choctaw thought back. Some things were now becoming clear. Why the Mexicans had been so nervous. Remarks they'd made which he hadn't understood at the time made sense now. Hairy saying, "I'll collect on *him.*" Another saying: "He'd only fetch a boy's price." They'd been joking about claiming bounty on him. When they'd said, "right color" but "it's got to be straight," they were talking about *his scalp.* He understood now why the Mexicans had drawn so much fire, why the Apaches had wanted to trade him for the Mexicans; even that Indian crying *"Mi mujer! Mis hijos!"* — "My woman! My children!"

112

Finn said, "Six less of the vermin, any-how."

Choctaw declared, "So that's why those Indians jumped us. Sure. You notice how they mostly shot at them Mexicans?"

"I didn't notice that." Finn laughed. Then the boy's face warmed, and he looked at his toes. Even his ears colored.

Choctaw was pleased to see that. He'd not forgotten how Finn had played the coward.

McClure shook his head and turned his hat in his hands. "Naah, Choc."

"Sure. What other reason would they have to jump us?"

"Reason? You got to understand, kid, Apaches don't have no reasons to do noth-ing. They're not full humans — they're savages. You see the things I've seen, and then you'd know. Apaches kill because that's how they are — that's their nature, just like a rattlesnake's got to bite, or a wolf's got to pull down a sheep. It's their instinct."

"But they said they only wanted the Mexicans, that they'd trade me for —"

McClure made an impatient sound, and breathed hard through his nostrils. But his voice, when it came, was even and con-trolled. "So why'd they kill Luis, if they were only after them scalp-hunters?"

" 'Cus he was a Mexican too. They took

113

him for one of them. That's why —"

"Goddamn you, Choc!" Choctaw flinched at the anger in the other man's voice. Heat flushed the Irishman's face. "Talking about how Apaches have *reasons.*" His lips twisted the last word contemptuously. "That's Goddamn Indian-lover talk! Apaches got no reason for nothing! No reason to live, even!"

McClure was shouting. In normal conversation he sounded like he was calling hogs. Now his voice rocked the tiny room as he bellowed full blast. "They jumped us 'cus they was Apaches! Doing the only thing Apaches know! Stealing and murdering! Murdering good men!"

McClure seemed to realize he was shouting; he broke off abruptly. There was a long stillness. Choctaw felt startled and embarrassed. He looked at the floor, not wanting to meet anybody's eye. After a time, he noticed the others were doing the same, as if this floor had all of a sudden got mighty interesting.

The Ulsterman turned his hat in his hands some more. Then he spoke in the smallest voice Choctaw had ever heard him use. "I'm going to see the commanding officer."

McClure departed. Choctaw and Finn listened to the silence he left behind.

Choctaw let out tension he hadn't realized

he was feeling in a long sigh. "Well, he sure —"

Finn exclaimed, "Hey, I forgot!"

"What?"

"I got somethin' to show you. Newspaper clipping. Out of the Tucson newspaper. Can you read, Choc? Want me to read it to you?"

"I can read."

"Yeah? I thought you'd never been to school."

"So?"

"So how come you can read?"

"My pa teached me. Made me read a lot. The Bible, Shakespeare, and such."

"Shakewhat?"

"Shakespeare. You won't never've heard of him."

"My pa never stood by book learning. Said you couldn't fill an empty belly with books."

"Wished I'd had your pa. Mine made me read 'til I was sick of it. What's in this newspaper? Am I in it?"

"Shall I read it to you?"

"I can read." Choctaw grinned nastily. "You figure I can't read, dontcha?"

"You can read, go ahead and read it."

"I figure I can read better than you, Finn."

"Oh yeah?"

"Am I in it?"

"You're the one so good at reading. Go ahead and read it and see."

Choctaw glared at the newspaper. He scowled.

"Ha." Finn smacked his thigh with his palm. "If you can read so good, bigmouth, what's the headline say?"

"It says — 'Finn has a face like a mule's ass.' "

Finn snorted a crowing laugh. "I figured you couldn't read! Your pa teached you. You brung up among them Indians and all, how'd you ever learn to read? Never was no Shakewhosit either. Want me to read it to you, Choc?"

Choctaw leaned forward and punched Finn in the chest. It was what he'd been saving his strength for. The other kept his grin, but Choctaw knew he'd hurt him with that playful jab. Which had been his intention.

Choctaw said, "The headline says *'Doing of demons.'* "

He read:

*Three men have been slain in the latest outrage perpetrated by the Apache Indians.*

*On February 3, hordes of these incorrigible savages ambushed a Schmitt and*

Gottlieb freight train on the Camp Walsh Trace twenty-one miles west of infantry camp. The number of savages was estimated at upwards of two hundred, and they were led by the infamous Cochise, chief of the Chiricahua Apaches; the same Cochise that only last September was declaring how much he desired peace with his "white brother"; the same Cochise whose savage followers murdered no less than twelve citizens in an eleven day period last August. The only peace we would offer the "great chief," and all the devils he leads, is eternal peace under the sod, even to the extermination of every buck, squaw, and papoose in the Apache tribe.

. . . One estimate puts loss amongst the savages in the fight as fifteen to twenty buck Indians killed and many more wounded. We can be sure they were severely punished.

. . . Where, pray, was the army we pay so dearly for? How is it the savages can lay in wait for a train along a main thoroughfare, in full daylight, and hold this artery of communication for a whole day?

Each week, as President Grant and his "society of friends" extend the olive branch to the savage murderers of our citizens,

*the Indians grow bolder and more destruc-*
*tive. We can only hope the truth about the*
*bestial nature of these fiends is com-*
*municated to the president before we are*
*all murdered in our beds and entire coun-*
*ties depopulated . . .*

Finn asked, "Did you know it was Cochise as jumped us? Christ! We even heard
of him in Texas. Two hundred of them
devils. Did we kill that many of 'em? We
must've killed a couple each, huh? That's
what it says in the paper."

Choctaw drew the newspaper from his
face and stared at it in cold anger. Nothing
about his exploit, putting himself in danger
trying to help another fellow, even if that
fellow was a worthless coward . . . or John
Shadler's shot that set Choctaw's rescue in
progress, a shot that was already becoming
legendary . . . shooting the Indian out from
behind Choctaw at a near-impossible distance. They didn't need to swell the Indians'
numbers, or bring in Cochise, or invent
dead Apaches, when they had that to report.
It was things like that had made Kit Carson
a legend.

Choctaw said, "My name ain't in it."

Finn said, "Mine ain't either."

Choctaw sneered. "Why should it be?

Everybody knows you played the —"

Scanlon announced, "Nine fifteen, gents. I want my hospital back." He stood in the doorway.

Finn said, "I'll go take a look at the mules."

Scanlon told him, "Watch you don't get shot by one of our sentries, son. One of the damn fools nearly took a shot at me when I was walking over here."

Finn told Choctaw, "I'll be around a few days, I guess. I'll come see you tomorrow."

Finn left.

Scanlon asked Choctaw, "How is it, kid?"

"Itches like hell. When can I get up?"

"If you've got any sense, you won't stir for three days at least. As you haven't, I guess we can find you a switch to hobble around on tomorrow."

"I'm sick of being a Goddamn crip."

A look of annoyance crossed Scanlon's face. After a pause he told Choctaw, "You'll keep that leg. Whether or not you limp on it, depends on how fast you try to do things."

"What about riding?"

"You've got to relearn how to walk, first. You wouldn't want to end up . . . how did you put it? A Goddamn crip?" He smiled sardonically. "Here, hit that." The surgeon tapped his own right shin. "Go on. Hit it."

"Jesus."

"That's cork, son. Genuine Portugee cork. Left my real leg at a place called Gettysburg. Why'd they call you Choctaw?"

"That's where I was born. Choctaw Nation. Indian Territory. My pa was an army contractor there." When he saw the look on the surgeon's face he protested, "I ain't no Indian. Folks was white." He pointed at himself. "Blue eyes, see?"

"So you was raised up among savages."

"Lots of white folks around too. Soldiers, agents, traders and such. Anyway, the Choctaws ain't anything like Apaches. They're pretty near white men. That's what they're called: 'civilized Indians.' Is your whole leg . . . cork?"

"Just below the knee. Minié ball whisked it off in a flash. I walked ten yards before I realized it was gone from under me."

"Hell."

"You believe that, son?"

"Yes, sir."

"Well, you shouldn't, it's a damn lie! There was a Union general, he got one leg blown off at Antietam, so they gave him a cork one. Damn me if that wasn't blown off at Chickamauga. You believe that, son?"

"No, sir."

"You should, it's the truth! Roll back them blankets, let's have a look at that leg."

Scanlon examined the wound dispassionately. He shook his gray head. " 'Civilized Indians.' "

Choctaw sat up. "You hear that?"

"These ears aren't cork, son, just the leg."

"That was a shot."

## CHAPTER ELEVEN

McClure said, "I'm from that freight outfit that got hit."

Hamilton looked up from his desk. "I remember. Can I offer you a drink?"

"I want to know what you're doing about it."

"All I can."

McClure was an Ulsterman, Hamilton judged. The teamster asked, "Which is?"

"I sent a scout and detail out."

"Jesus Christ!"

Hamilton almost smiled. "What would you suggest I do?"

"Get your soldiers off their backsides. Kill some Indians."

"Which Indians?"

"Any you can find! That's your job, ain't it?"

"Let me tell you what my job is, mister. I've got to maintain this post, to protect all white citizens in this corner of the territory, to administer law where there is no civilian law. I have to protect friendly Indians on their agencies, to keep open all lines of communication. And pursue offensive actions against hostiles whenever the opportunity offers."

"Well, don't the —"

"And to do that I have one hundred and twelve men. Oh, and two civilians."

"Hell, I thought you'd at least brass it out. But you plain admit it. You can't do your job. All right. There's the Arizona Volunteers —"

Hamilton snorted. "Volunteers!"

"At least they kill Indians —"

"I came across a camp your volunteers had been through. They killed Indians all right. The one's too old to run away, or too little. Infants with their heads bashed in. Old women raped and killed. A baby thrown in the fire. Your heroic Arizona Volunteers."

"It's mostly the tame Indians that do that. Anyway, it was the Volunteers that saved us from Cochise and his cutthroats, wasn't it? Where was the army all that time? If we'd've waited for your —"

The shot came then.

McClure moved first. Before Hamilton was halfway out of his seat, the Ulsterman was at the door and had opened it a crack.

123

A Colt pistol had come from somewhere into his hand.

Hamilton came around the table behind him. He called through the crack in the door, "Corporal of the guard!"

Sergeant Tyson's voice came from the outer darkness. "Two Indians out here, sir."

McClure squeezed past the door and Hamilton followed. Men were gathered in a circle of lantern light, by the corral.

There was a boy amidst the soldiers. Hamilton seemed to remember him from McClure's freight outfit. The boy was white-faced and shaking.

"What happened here?" Hamilton asked.

Tyson pointed with his carbine. "The boy here —"

McClure asked, "What happened, Finn?"

"Jesus . . ." the boy stammered. "I was just looking over the mules when they seemed to jump out of nowhere. 'Fore I knowed it . . ." He was opening and closing his mouth like a landed fish, as if he'd just been sick and was working himself up to it again. Tear stripes made dogleg patterns across his cheeks. Hamilton saw the gleam of new tears on them. He smelt vomit on the boy's breath.

An Indian girl stood in the center of the circle. She wore a knee-length garment of pale buckskin and was barefoot. The girl looked around with the fearful expectancy of a trapped animal. Her mouth was open. Her teeth seemed very white against the darkness of her skin.

Another Indian girl sat on the earth. Her eyes were closed, and she gave short gasps of pain. The girl held her left arm across her body. The arm was covered in blood, the blood covering the front of the shift she wore.

Hamilton asked Tyson, "Apaches?" but it was the unwounded Indian girl who said, "Apache," and nodded gravely.

Hamilton said, "Sergeant, double the guard. And put another man on the corral. Where's Robertson?"

A private told him, "Up at the hog ranch, most like."

"Somebody go get him."

In the tail of his eye, Hamilton saw McClure lift his pistol and point the weapon at the unwounded Indian girl.

Hamilton asked, "What are you doing?"

He saw McClure wasn't listening. He was aiming his pistol like a man in a trance, a man closed off from anything outside himself. McClure wasn't here and now; perhaps he was days back, with his friends being killed and wounded around him, and

Apaches firing from the chaparral.

Hamilton said, "Put that gun up, mister."

McClure snagged his thumb over the pistol hammer and eared it back. The top knuckle on his fist whitened.

"Put up that gun or Sergeant Tyson will shoot you."

As Hamilton spoke, his words mocked him. Tyson wasn't going to shoot a white man to save an Apache, not even an Apache girl. And there was nothing Hamilton could do about it. The canvas flap of his pistol holster was snapped down. By the time he could unsnap it . . .

Hamilton's mouth was dry, and he felt sweat on the palms of his hands. An orchestra started warming up inside him — an orchestra of nerves humming a jangled, discordant music, all the notes harshly out of tune. He decided he'd let himself get way out of shape as a soldier, mentally and physically. *The next time I walk towards a gunshot,* he told himself *I'll make sure my holster is unsnapped.*

He heard Tyson say, "Put it up, mister!" and then the sergeant cocked his Springfield carbine.

Time seemed frozen for a few slow heart-beats. There was a long pause before some-thing changed in McClure's face. The Colt

126

seemed to get looser in his fist. Almost nonchalantly, he returned the weapon to his jacket pocket.

McClure stepped towards Hamilton. The latter braced himself. He could hear the man already: *"Who are you soldiers paid to protect, the whites or the Indians? Indian lover . . . Squaw lover . . . red-nigger lover . . ."* He wasn't prepared for what the teamster did.

McClure spat in his face.

Spittle went into his eyes and mouth.

Hamilton felt his cheeks burn. He was conscious of a dull ache in the small of his back, and behind his eyes. He lifted his hand and carefully wiped the spit off his face.

McClure turned and walked away.

Hamilton saw white, staring faces all around. Lantern light had bleached out all features, except the eyes. He told the faces, "Get the girl to the hospital."

Scanlon was among the onlookers, glaring stonily. Hamilton wondered if Scanlon would balk now and declare, *"I've no business treating Indians."* Hamilton didn't know how he'd deal with that.

But Scanlon nodded stiffly, and a private took the wounded girl by her uninjured arm and moved her towards the hospital. She was only about five feet tall, a plumpish figure under the deerskin garb. Her hair came halfway down her back. The other girl was taller and slimmer. Hamilton couldn't help noticing how her dress pushed up at the front, where her breasts would be.

Hamilton asked, "Where's Primitavo?"

"Begging the lieutenant's pardon," Tyson said diplomatically, "You sent him to scout that war party, sir."

"That's right, I did. All right, sergeant. Thanks for your help just now."

"It's all right, sir."

"And find an extra duty for the sentry on the corral."

"Begging the lieutenant's pardon . . . these devils move like ghosts, sir."

"Even so, his job is to make sure no one gets past him."

"Yes, sir."

"Where the hell is Robertson?"

When no one answered him, Hamilton walked over to the post hospital. He watched Scanlon clean and dress the Indian girl's wound. He was surprised at the gentleness with which he worked. The surgeon washed the blood from his hands in a tin bowl of water. "She's lucky. Bullet missed the bone."

"Pain don't mean the same to them," Scanlon's orderly commented.

Hamilton doubted that. At times the girl drew trembling lips back from her teeth. Once she gave a low "aaahh" of pain, but he would agree she'd been trained not to cry out. The other girl watched, her face drawn in concern. Once she reached forward and squeezed the other girl's unwounded arm. She seemed to have forgotten her own terror.

He caught a smell of her: a smell of mesquite smoke and old buckskin and the sharp tang of bear grease. She'd used the grease to pomade her hair. He tried to ignore the fact that she was a comely girl. Only fifteen or sixteen but full-breasted and shapely. To take his mind off that he noted how a livid scar, white as bone, raked her forearm from wrist to elbow.

Robertson entered.

Angus Robertson was in his late forties, Hamilton guessed, but looking older. A faint burr when he said his *r's* reminded of the Scotland he'd left many years ago. A middle-sized, leathered, squint-eyed man with thinning sand-colored hair and wisps of beard and mustache. He had a peculiar voice — an up-and-down voice that was sometimes low and sonorous, other times a querulous singsong. One story blamed his vocal impediment on an Apache arrow that had

clipped his windpipe; another to a hangman's rope he'd deserved, but had survived.

Robertson asked, "What's this, Lieutenant?"

"That's what I want you to find out."

Robertson talked to the unwounded girl
in Apache. To Hamilton it sounded a harsh
language, full of short grunts and choking
noises. The Scot moved his hands as he
talked.

He told Hamilton, "This is Alope. The girl
got shot is her sister, Klea."

"Are they Apaches?"

"Sure."

"What kind?"

"If it don't beat all. Say's she's one of the
People Who Live by the Black Rocks. The
Aravaipas."

"Who are they?"

"Sort of kin to the Pinals. Didn't figure
there was any Aravaipas left. I heard most
of 'em got massacred years back, by the
Arizona Volunteers, or run off and joined
with the Pinals. 'Tain't so, she says. A whole
band of 'em been up north. Says" — he
grunted an Apache word — "heads 'em up."

"In English, Robertson."

"Coyote."

"Never heard of him."

"That's just one of his names. Course he's

130

got two or three others. Anyway, Coyote sent in these women 'cus he heard the white men wouldn't hurt them."

"What's he want?"

"He's been up on the White River Agency with his band, but he didn't like it up there, and he's tired of war. So he decided to take what's left of his people back home, make peace with the white man and never break it."

"Fine. Where's home?"

"The Place of the Black Rocks."

"Where's that?"

"Just about here, Lieutenant."

"And where's this Coyote now?"

"Pretty close, she says. Waiting for your word he can come in. Seems he's heard the *nantan* — the white chief — is a kind man, with good thoughts towards the Indians."

"I'll be damned! How many in his band?"

"It ain't much of a band. Maybe two hundred altogether."

"Two hundred! That's enough to be going on with."

Hamilton rubbed his throat. "All right, Robertson, I guess you've earned yourself a drink. Corporal, put the two girls in the starve-out, and put a sentry on the door."

Hamilton stepped outside. Scanlon followed him out.

Hamilton stood and listened. He heard night noises, beetles and crickets rustling, and then coyotes yowling in the hills.

Was that the something waiting for him in this place? A coyote? A two-legged one?

Scanlon asked, "What are you going to do, Austin?"

Hamilton shrugged. "Like the Mexicans say. *Quién sabe?*"

"Huh?"

"Who knows, Paddy? Who knows?"

# CHAPTER TWELVE

Late the next morning, Hamilton was inspecting the horses in the post stables when Robertson approached. The scout told him, "Lieutenant, I just been talking to an Indian on the sentry line."

"An Apache? An Aravaipa?"

"Name of Zele. Says Coyote is off a ways, waiting for your word he can come in and palaver."

"Why doesn't he just come in here and talk?"

"He doesn't trust Americans."

"The hell he doesn't."

"Mangas Coloradas came to talk peace with the army. So did Cochise. Both of 'em was arrested. Cochise got away but Mangas was murdered."

Hamilton rubbed his chin. "This Indian still at the sentry line?"

"Yes."

"All right. Get back to him. I'll be out in

a few minutes."

Hamilton summoned a guard. "Sentry, give my compliments to Second Lieutenant Riordan. Ask him to report to me at my office at once, in full uniform."

"Yes, sir."

Hamilton went to his headquarters and changed into his cavalry shell jacket. He considered strapping on his saber but guessed Coyote would see it for what it was — a useless affectation.

Hamilton walked to the sentry line, where Robertson was talking to an Apache. Scanlon was there, also. The Indian was a middle-sized, potbellied man in cloth shirt, knee moccasins, and short cloth kilt. His chest-length hair was bound with a thick red rag. He was unpainted but his very dark skin flashed with sweat.

Robertson told Hamilton, "He says he's going back now, to tell Coyote we're willing to talk. They'll make a call like a screech owl, then Coyote'll meet you by those three cottonwoods out there. You can bring one other with you, but no more."

Scanlon frowned. "Sounds damn fishy to me."

Hamilton said, "I guess now's the time to test out my theory — that Apaches are human beings too."

"Human beings commit murder every day, Austin."

Hamilton smiled a very little. "That's reassuring."

"Don't go out there."

Hamilton nodded to Robertson. "Tell him I agree."

The Apache walked off. About a thousand yards east of camp there was a clump of three sun-withered cottonwoods. Beyond, the flats rippled in haze; the mountains trembled and stretched their peaks against the sky. Hamilton checked his pistol. He studied the trees and the thousand yards to them.

Presently, Robertson observed, "That sounded like a screech owl to me."

"Will you come with me, Robertson?"

"I guess I'll have to," Robertson said unhappily.

"No, you don't have to."

"You'll need an interpreter, won't you?"

"You'll get yourselves killed," Scanlon declared.

"Let's hope not." Hamilton brushed a little dust off his right shoulder. "If you're right . . . Riordan will take command. Try and keep him from making a damn fool of himself, Pat."

"If anything happens, get off a shot. We'll

come running."

"All right. Thanks Pat. Are you ready, Robertson?"

Robertson nodded. The two men walked out to the cottonwoods.

They crossed unshaded ground and both men sweated. They sat in the meager shade the trees offered. Robertson passed his canteen and Hamilton drank gratefully. He gave up trying to see anything through the haze. He lifted his wrists before him and stared at them until they stopped trembling. He thought of the one woman he almost married; other women he should have bedded; and one man he ought to have killed. If he got out of this without getting a dozen arrows through him, Hamilton decided he would look up that gentleman . . . and some of those ladies.

Robertson was sweating badly. Hamilton suspected he'd been at the bottle last night. Hamilton felt sorry for Robertson. He wondered what strange fortune had brought him to this place.

Hamilton turned his head and stiffened and said, "Jesus!" very softly.

Two Apaches stood a dozen yards away. They might have dropped from the sky, for all the noise they'd made.

Robertson said, "Keep your hand away

from your gun, Lieutenant."

Hamilton settled his hands carefully at his sides. He remembered Sergeant Tyson's words: *These devils move like ghosts.*

One of the Indians lazed a Springfield carbine across his arm. The other held a lance drooping a white eagle feather. The rifle holder spoke to Robertson and the scout replied. The Apache grinned. It was a gap-toothed grin, for a pair of his front upper teeth were missing. He was a paunchy, moon-faced young man. A long club of very white, polished bone hung by a thong from his wrist.

"This'n's Klosen — means Rope," Robertson said. "He's a wild one all right. See that club he's got there? Know what that's made of?"

"Some sort of bone."

"Thighbone of a man."

Hamilton said, "Oh."

"The other's Coyote."

Coyote was a stocky man of middle height with a square, handsome face. His mouth was wide and humorous. In his dark brass face, his eyes were nervous and intelligent.

Coyote dressed like any other Apache. He wore a filthy white shirt, knee-length kilt, high moccasins. His only vanity was a sliver of turquoise that hung from the claw necklace on his chest. The chief wore an improvised buckskin gun belt and holster, a pistol on his left hip. The grip had been broken and was tied with a strip of leather. Coyote trapped the lance clumsily against his body with his left arm. A chalky scar divided this arm from elbow to wrist and the flesh had wasted around the scar. Hamilton guessed the whole limb was stiff from the wound.

For a moment Coyote and Hamilton studied each other. The Apache's eyes followed every movement. Hamilton suspected the Indian was as tense as a cocked pistol.

Coyote spoke to Robertson. "He says we can talk better in the shade."

The four men sat in the shade of the cottonwoods.

Robertson said, "He wants us to smoke."

Hamilton nodded. In his mind there was a tableau of painted and feathered Indians sitting gravely at the first Thanksgiving with the Pilgrim Fathers. He expected to see the chief proffer a splendid ceremonial stone pipe; instead, Klosen rolled four *macuche* cigarettes, the sort Mexicans smoked sometimes.

"Tell him I'm the soldier chief," Hamilton said. "I want to hear what he's got to say."

Hamilton and Coyote talked whilst Robertson translated.

Coyote said, "This valley is our home. My father, and his father before him, hunted and grew corn and roasted mescal here." Hamilton knew the mescal Coyote referred to was a fruit eaten by the Apaches, not the drink. "Then the Anglos — the whites — came one night. The Anglos and the Mexicans and the Papagos. They killed our women and children. Since then, we can go no place but the Anglos shoot at us. Our young men are brave, but there are too many Anglos, with too many guns.

"We've no blankets left to keep out the cold, or cloth to cover our bodies. The children are down to eating pine nuts and skunk cabbage roots. The women cry. The young men are angry; they say they'll fight the Anglos until they die. Some of the people have gone a little crazy, maybe. They say better for us to kill our women and children, then ourselves first, before the Anglos do it."

Hamilton asked, "Why don't the Aravaipas go to the White Mountain Agency? Many White Mountains Apaches are there, living at peace with the white man."

"That's not our country," Coyote replied. "They aren't our people. We are at peace with them, but we've never mixed with them. Here there's mescal summer and winter. At the White Mountains there is none, and without it we get sick. Some of our people have been at the White River Agency but they weren't happy there. Now they all say 'Let's go home and talk with the soldier chief. Let's make a final peace and never break it.' "

Klosen asked, "What does the soldier chief say?"

Hamilton stood. He turned and walked a few paces.

Robertson joined him. "What will you do?"

"I don't know. Can I trust them?"

"Your guess is as good as mine."

"Dammit, Robertson, I need to know."

"I can talk Apache. That don't mean I can read their damn minds."

Hamilton scowled. "I've no authority to let Indians stay here. Then again, if I don't, they'll just scatter back into the mountains. It might be years before they come in again."

"Your decision, Lieutenant. I wouldn't like to make it."

"Goddamn it," said, Hamilton. He ran a hand through his hair. "Tell Coyote he can bring his people in. He can stay here, under my protection, until I receive further orders."

"How do I translate that?"

"The best you can. Just don't make him any wild promises, for God's sake."

Robertson talked to the Apaches. Klosen flashed his broken grin. Coyote looked puzzled, then openly relieved. Hamilton found the change of expression on his face almost touching. The chief smiled slowly, like a man who'd long since forgotten how to smile. He took the lieutenant's hand and shook it, grinning. Despite himself, Hamilton grinned back and felt silly because of that.

Coyote picked a fist-sized rock from the ground. Robertson said, "It's peace, now. You have his word on it, which he'll keep until this rock melts."

"Until the rock melts?"

"He'll gather his band and bring 'em in as soon as he can."

Coyote let the rock fall. Abruptly, he and Klosen turned and walked off into the haze.

Robertson said, "Well, it's done then, Lieutenant. Finished."

Hamilton stared doubtfully after the two Apaches. He nudged Coyote's rock gently with the toe of his boot.

# CHAPTER THIRTEEN

Robertson reined in his gray horse at the top of the slope. "Down at the bottom, past them big rocks, we'll see O'Brian's place."

Choctaw leaned forward in the saddle of his sorrel gelding, a horse he called Red. He moved carefully, because his wounded leg was troubled with little sharp pains. It was worth bearing, if it meant being on horseback and no longer nailed to the earth.

Both men rode downslope. They came in sight of O'Brian's Station. A low, flat-roofed adobe, an outbuilding. A large, pole-gated corral with three high adobe walls. The corral was roofed with branches so that the horses moved across shadow-barred ground.

"I can't see anyone," Choctaw said.

"You won't. O'Brian'll be indoors, watching. He won't show himself until we're up close."

Nor did he. The two riders were a hundred yards from the main building before

O'Brian walked out of the adobe, a rifle in his hands. They rode up to him slowly. O'Brian was a tall, slender man with fair skin that was peeling badly. His fine blond hair was a colorless blaze in the sun. His mustache made a pale strip along his top lip.

Robertson asked, "How's doin's, Ed?"

"Robertson."

"This is Choctaw. Choctaw got an Apache bullet in the leg few weeks back."

"Hell." O'Brian nodded towards the corral. "Throw your horses into the corral. Then we can get out of this sun."

"Obliged, Ed."

Choctaw followed Robertson into the main building. It was sparsely furnished, and the floor level was two feet below the ground level outside. A couple of ollas of water hung from the ceiling, to let the room cool. There was a plain plank table and two benches.

O'Brian asked, "You boys want eat?"

Robertson answered. "I got a side of bacon in my saddlebags there."

"Fine. You fancy a knock first?"

O'Brian produced a stone jug. Robertson drank, then O'Brian, then Choctaw. "Christ, mister!" Choctaw complained.

O'Brian asked Robertson, "Shot by

Apaches you say?"

"Cherry-Cows. Where's Felipe?"

"Got sick, so he went into Tucson. Company was supposed to send me a relief, but they ain't yet."

"How long you been by yourself here?"

"Ten days. Seems more like ten year. I like to went crazy. Every night I've had the same dream. There's Apaches all over, painted up to hell and yelling, then those *broncos* haul me over this table. Then Cochise himself comes in through that door and stands there, a-looking down."

Choctaw managed to speak. "I'm surprised you've got any throat left, drinking this stuff."

Robertson said, "You've got to let it grow on you."

O'Brian asked, "You hear about Ben Price?"

Robertson nodded.

Choctaw asked, "Who's Ben Price?"

Robertson told him, "Price worked at a swing station, just like this one, up on the Gila."

O'Brian said, "Last fall, Apaches raided the place. Left Price out in the yard in front of his station. Sharpened a wheel spoke and stuck it through his guts. Pinned him to the ground. Lit a fire on his belly. Cut his eyelids off. Cut his penis off and stuffed it between his teeth. So I heard. Benny Price was a friend of mine."

Robertson said, "I knowed him too."

O'Brian shook his head slowly. "Old Ben Price. Not bin a day since that happened, I ain't thought about it. I tell you, I can't remember what it's like, to eat proper, or digest food, or sleep with both eyes closed. There's only the bars on that door between me and the whole damn Apache tribe."

"Why'n't you come into Tucson with us, Ed?" Robertson asked.

Choctaw drank, then wiped his mouth with the back of his wrist. "I thought we was too close to Tucson for Apaches."

O'Brian said, "It is thirty-six mile. I've been here eight months and they've been at the horses three times, the bastards."

"You must've got a few of them then?"

"Two times I never heard 'em go. Woke up in the morning and the corral was empty. Took the whole bunch without making a sound. The other time, Felipe heard 'em and took a shot at 'em. Damn fool couldn't hit the side of a mountain. He shot one of the company horses instead, and the Indians got the rest."

Choctaw drank from the jug, grinned, and said, "Them at Walsh's friendly, anyhow."

145

"Huh?"

Choctaw saw Robertson trying to ward him off with a look, he didn't know why; he wanted to tell O'Brian that not all Apaches were to be feared. "Two hundred of 'em."

"What?"

"Army's got a whole band of 'em, camped peaceful at Walsh."

"Two hundred of 'em! At Walsh! That's only twenty mile!"

"It's all right. They're friendly."

"Friendly? How'd you know? Two hundred of 'em. Jesus Christ! What's the God-damn army doing about it?"

Choctaw ignored Robertson's scowl. "Why, the army's protecting 'em."

"Protecting 'em!" O'Brian stood so abruptly the plain plank bench went over.

"Sure."

O'Brian walked a dazed circle around the room. He hung his head in disbelief. Choctaw thought O'Brian looked funny. He reached for the jug again. "This stuff does grow on you, you're right."

"How many soldiers at Walsh?" O'Brian asked.

Robertson told him, "About a hundred."

"A hundred! So how the hell do you watch two Indians with one soldier? Jesus Christ! If they're so peaceable, how come they ain't

146

at the White Mountain Agency?"

Things were getting too confused for Choctaw. He took another drink.

O'Brian declared, "That crazy army! Protecting Indians! It's us they're supposed to protect. What do we pay taxes for?"

"When did you last pay taxes?" Robertson asked.

"I would if anyone asked me to."

"You'd have to tell 'em what your name was in the States first."

Choctaw expected O'Brian to reply "So would you," but he didn't. Perhaps he'd heard that story about the hangman's rope.

"You want to eat yet?" O'Brian asked. His eyes slid back to the jug. "Or shall we drink up a bit more appetite?"

Choctaw rolled onto his back and groaned. He lifted his hands to his forehead and pressed back the throbbing there. After a while he sat up and winced with pain.

Choctaw swore, rose unsteadily to his feet, and looked around for water. O'Brian dozed in a rope hammock in a corner of the room. The boy couldn't see Robertson. Light in the room came from the kerosene lamp on the table.

Choctaw stooped, lifting the stone jug, and found it was empty. He remembered what had awakened him and stepped towards the door. He recalled O'Brian saying: *There's only the bars on that door between me and the whole Apache tribe.* He found his Spencer carbine, stepped out through the doorway, and pulled the door closed behind him.

The night was as black as a cave. The sky was a shade paler than the mountain darkness below it. Choctaw could just discern the saw teeth where mountains and sky ran together. He swore softly at the pain in his head. He unbuttoned his jeans and urinated against the wall, sighing gratefully. His voiding, and the breaths he took, made the only sounds in the darkness.

Choctaw buttoned up his fly. Flesh crawled on his back and arms and he wondered at that. He seemed to have sobered, all of a sudden. The pounding in his head eased to a dull aching he could almost forget.

In the corral a horse whickered.

The boy stepped towards the door, opened it a fraction, closed it, and sank on to his haunches outside. He put his back to the wall and the Spencer across his knees. He sat on the earth and felt the still-warm dampness of his urine under one buttock.

Choctaw heard faint noises across the

darkness, horses moving restlessly in the corral. He studied the corral until he could see the horses tossing their heads. He remembered his own red gelding was in that pen.

Choctaw's hands started to tremble, and his head began to hurt him again. His heart grew faster and larger in his chest and throat. His ears were thick with the slow pulse of blood.

There was a flick of sound in the darkness, a pistol shot ahead. Choctaw pushed to his feet, and took a long step towards the sound. His eyes hunted the darkness. In his left ear he caught a soft brush of movement.

He realized his mistake. He'd stepped away from the wall, his back was unprotected.

Choctaw whirled to his left, half around. From the blackness before him loomed a thicker blackness. He saw the flash of metal.

Choctaw didn't think to fire. Wildly, he lashed out with the butt of the carbine. He struck bone. A voice gasped, almost in his face. Choctaw was spun around with the blow. His foot tripped on something and he pitched headlong. He grunted as he struck the earth, the weapon trapped beneath him. He rolled.

Sobbing for air, the boy got to his knees.

149

He lifted the Spencer. A darkness reared over him, a figure cut out of the night. Choctaw pointed the Spencer at it and fired.

The recoil knocked him onto his back. The gunshot seemed to rock the night. He coughed on powder smoke and writhed over onto his knees and felt the wall with his shoulders and squirmed his back up against it.

A corral pole fell, ringing. Horses screamed. Choctaw saw a horse vault the gate bars. The animal swerved off into dust. Behind the noise of horses, he heard men yelling. All the horses seemed to be piling from the corral. He glimpsed an Apache running through the dust. All at once the man was gone. Dust bloomed over everything, then it was thinning, and he heard the fading drum of hooves.

As Choctaw sprang to his feet a gun seemed to go off in his face. He heard the bullet tear into the wall behind him and ducked, stinging eyes blinded. Very close he heard O'Brian swearing. From the ground Choctaw yelled, "Don't shoot! Chrissakes! It's me! It's me!"

Choctaw blinked furiously until he could see again. The night was graying about him. He made out the corral, seemingly empty, pole bars slanting into the ground. O'Brian, standing out in front of the adobe. The mountains, and under them, a pale surf of dust. The horses. As he watched their dust wrinkled into further distance.

A few yards to his left, towards the outbuilding, there was a loose shape on the earth, the sprawled bulk of a man. Choctaw's first good Indian. Choctaw took a few strides towards his victim, changed his mind, and turned towards O'Brian. As he stepped by the fallen man, he knew he'd made another mistake. A voice in his head told him, *I never checked if he was dead.*

The boy twisted, trying to fumble his Spencer from his right hand to his left. The man was no longer prone, he was kneeling up. There was a cold gleam of metal in his hand. Choctaw spun, tripping over his own feet. He cried out as he fell, as if the knife was in him already.

He struggled onto his back. He'd lost his carbine. He sat up and saw the kneeling shape leaning towards him: a black, faceless creature with a knife swinging at the end of the outreaching arm.

There was a burst of gun flame and the shape was knocked flat. It lay on its back with its arms outflung. O'Brian stood over the man on the ground, fumbling with his rifle. He dropped the weapon, and pulled a pistol from his belt. His thin, fair hair was awry, and his shirttail was out of his pants. O'Brian fired his pistol into the darkness on the ground, and again, before his pistol misfired, and then jammed.

A man was half-running, half-staggering towards them. Choctaw saw it was Robertson.

"Where the hell you been?" Choctaw demanded, pushing himself to his feet. "Mister Goddamned Indian scout?"

Robertson stared at Choctaw like a man in a trance. His hair was loose and his bald crown shone pinkly.

Robertson turned and walked towards the corral. "That's four times, Ed."

"The bastard's paid for it this time," O'Brian declared. He laughed shakily. Choctaw saw the man was white-faced and trembling. The boy realized his own arms and legs were shaking. His wounded leg ached, and he felt very tired.

The Indians had driven off all the company horses. But they hadn't taken Choctaw's sorrel, or Robertson's gray horse. Robertson had hobbled them and maybe the Indians hadn't time to cut the hobbles.

"We'd better get back in the house," Robertson said.

"Those devils is long gone, like them

152

horses. How many you figure?"

"Three or four. You never know with Apaches. When they find out they're one down they might swing back and try another lick at us."

Choctaw stared down at the dead Apache. As far as he could judge the Indian was a young man, in his twenties. He lay on his back with one leg bent at the knee, doubled under him, and his arms flung wide. All his wounds appeared to be in his chest and the front of him was covered in blood.

There was no peace in the dead man's face. He'd died with his eyes wide open, and his mouth drawn back in a cry of pain. A line of faded scarlet paint ran across the broad, bronzed cheeks.

"Pinal, most like," Robertson observed.

Choctaw told O'Brian, "I'm beholden to you."

"Huh?"

"You killed this Indian."

"Well, let's say we both notched him. You nailed him, I finished him. Died hard, didn't he? A hundred dollars' worth of Indian there, kid. Fifty dollars each, huh?"

"Fifty dollars?"

"Hundred dollars for a buck's scalp down in Mexico." O'Brian spat on the corpse. "You ain't so much now, is you, Mister

Indian?" He produced a knife from somewhere and knelt by the body, one hand reaching down for the hair.

"Well, Choc, how does it feel?" Robertson asked.

"Huh?"

"You've killed a man. You and O'Brian between you. How's it feel?"

Choctaw rested another glance on the dead Apache, watching O'Brian working with his knife. He didn't know that he felt anything at all.

# CHAPTER FOURTEEN

Next morning, the eastbound stage arrived at O'Brian's Station.

The stage slewed to a halt in a fog of its own dust. Dark with lather, the four team horses bowed their heads. The reinsman pushed down the brake lever and climbed from the box. The messenger remained on the coach, a Winchester in one hand and three pistols through his belt.

The reinsman beat at his canvas jacket with his sombrero. He was pink and gray all over with dust. He stared at the corral, empty but for Robertson's and Choctaw's horses.

O'Brian told him, "Apaches."

Choctaw walked towards the stage, feeling the knots and bumps of the earth beneath him through the soles of his Apache moccasins. The messenger watched him. Most of the stage guard's face was lost in mustache and beard under his pulled-down hat brim. His eyes, startling blue against the tan, followed the boy.

The coach was a mud wagon, with canvas sides and top. The only passenger climbed out by furling back the canvas curtain, hooking his legs over the side of the wagon bed, and dropping to the ground. He gave a low sigh of pain as he did this, and his mouth creased with the same pain. He lifted a hand and pressed it against his right side.

Choctaw said, "Mister Shadler."

John Shadler smiled, though even that hurt, Choctaw guessed. Shadler's eyes narrowed as he smiled. "Choctaw. Hell kid, how're you? How's the leg?"

"Not bad, sir."

"Now don't start a-sirrin'. You and me's in the same outfit. I'm pointing towards Walsh myself. To see Dutchy. How was he, last time you saw him?"

"Not so good."

Shadler's smile faded. He gazed at the corral.

O'Brian told him, "Apaches run off the horses last night. Choctaw got those moccasins off the Indian he killed."

"You killed one of 'em, Choc?"

Choctaw replied, "Well, O'Brian killed him too."

Shadler pursed his lips thoughtfully. "Well,

156

you killed him, and O'Brian killed him. 'Pears like you kill Indians by committee around here."

Everyone laughed, including Choctaw, who wasn't sure what a committee was.

The messenger climbed from the stage. "You pepper one of them scamps, kid?"

"Me and O'Brian 'tween us."

The messenger grinned a yellow-toothed grin. "Where is he?"

"Who?"

"The dead Indian?"

"We lugged him off into the brush back there."

"Then I think I'll go and pay my respects to the dear departed."

"Might run into some of his friends, come back to pick him up," Shadler cautioned.

"Maybe. Pity. I'd like to piss on that bastard's grave. I ain't never seen a dead Apache."

"I got the scalp inside," O'Brian said. "If you want to look at it."

"So you tangled with 'em again, Choc," Shadler declared. "Seems like they're following you around."

"Hope not," the boy said, and men laughed.

"Carry on like this, you gonna end up like the next Kit Carson or somebody."

It didn't seem possible that John Shadler could have said that. Choctaw became a weightless thing, something that could float on air effortlessly. He felt a grin spread out across his face as far as it would reach.

Robertson came from the main house. He smiled at the stage crew but when he saw Shadler he halted and his smile vanished. He and the wagon boss studied each other.

Shadler kept his grin, but there was no warmth in his eyes. "Well, Robertson," he asked, "you kill any Indians last night?"

Choctaw grinned. "He was just sleeping off the whiskey."

Robertson turned and walked back into the house.

The reinsman said, "We'll rest these horses here for a few hours, then move on to the next station."

"Watch yourselves," O'Brian advised. "That raiding party might still be about."

"What about you?"

"I'm going into Tucson with Robertson and Choctaw. There's no horses left to guard and I sure ain't stayin' out here by myself."

O'Brian led Shadler, the messenger, and the reinsman to the main house. Choctaw unyoked the team, let the horses cool, then watered them. He thought about John

158

Shadler's words: *you gonna end up like the next Kit Carson or somebody.* How did he know Carson had been Choctaw's hero all his life? The boy grinned in a way that was probably foolish, but no one could see him so what did it matter?

When it came to heroes, there was no doubt who came second only to Carson. A real-life hero he'd seen in action. Charging out to rescue that gutless wonder Finn. Then leading another charge to rescue Choctaw himself, calmly covering the retreat, as if the Apache bullets whining past his ears didn't exist. Making that shot, that great shot, picking off the Apache who held Choctaw prisoner . . . then, even though hurt bad, he hadn't turned himself over to the army doctor at Walsh, unlike the other wounded. No, first he'd seen the wagons safe to Tucson, even with a bullet through him. Only then had he let a sawbones tend him. There was a hero for you.

The boy heard a small sound and turned. As if his thoughts had called him up, John Shadler was there.

"Come here, boy."

"Yes, sir . . . I mean, Mister Shadler."

"That Indian you killed. What you shoot him with?"

"With my Spencer. O'Brian finished him

off with his handgun."

"You got a pistol of your own?"

"No, sir."

"I bet you're itching to see Tucson."

"Hell, yes. I ain't been near a town since
—"

"Tucson can be a rough town. If you stray into the wrong quarters. Where I figure a young feller like you'll be pointing pretty soon."

Choctaw grinned.

"You need a weapon about you, to protect yourself in spots like that." Shadler drew something gleaming from his jacket pocket, a bar of hard sunlight. He put the bright thing into Choctaw's hand. "This is for you, kid."

The pistol was a Starr double-action army .44. As Choctaw turned the gun against the light, the metal changed from mist gray to gray blue to deep blue. His fingers closed around the short cedar grip and a dizzy feeling rippled through him. The beauty of the weapon seemed to tie a fair-sized knot in his throat.

"Mister Shadler —"

"Every dead Indian . . . ." Shadler began and then halted, as if searching for words — or perhaps pain was troubling him again. His mouth tightened and he swallowed.

"Well, there's damn few white men got the guts to fight 'em, more's the pity. Then there's some like Robertson . . ."

"What's wrong with Robertson?"

"Why, nothing," the other replied. " 'Cept if there's one thing worse than an Indian, it's a white man who squaws with 'em."

"Mister Shadler, I can't —"

"Sure you can." The wagon boss slapped Choctaw on the left shoulder. "You aim to get a few more red devils with this pistol?"

"Yes, sir."

Shadler seemed to be hunting for words again. He stared. His eyes were brilliant in his stark face, but it was the brilliance of fever. The boy shifted uncomfortably. Shadler turned and walked back towards the adobe. Choctaw gazed after him a moment, then looked again at the weapon in his hands.

# CHAPTER FIFTEEN

Choctaw found a dish-shaped rock in the shade of some palo verde trees, sat on a rock, and rolled a quirley. Nearby O'Brian crouched over a skillet, frying their late afternoon meal. Robertson sat on the earth a few yards away, pulling off his socks. The scout swore loudly, then drew his left foot close to his face for inspection. "That's some blister," he observed.

Near where Robertson sat, collected rainwater dripping from an overhang had formed a tiny pool. The scout rolled his trousers up to his knees and shuffled on his rump over to the pool. He lowered his bare feet into the gray water, which just covered his ankles.

With the unlit cigarette in his mouth, Choctaw reached for the matches in his vest pocket. Instead, he lifted the pistol from his jacket pocket and turned it in his hands, for only the tenth time that day.

Robertson told him, "You're supposed to be keeping watch, boy."

"You said we was too close to Tucson for Apaches."

"Should be able to see town from up ahead, there."

Choctaw rubbed his leg, which had begun hurting again in the ride from O'Brian's Station. "You keep watch. You're the great Indian scout."

"All I am is a man with a blister on his foot, size of an egg."

Choctaw took his only handkerchief from his pocket and with the one corner that was still half clean rubbed the grip of his pistol, where there might have been a smidgen of dust.

"You sure you got that shined up enough?" Robertson asked. "No doubt John Shadler told you to get some more Indians for him with it."

"What if he did?"

Robertson grunted with sarcasm. "John Shadler."

"Don't you be running down Mr. Shadler. He saved my life."

"Did he?"

"Sure. When that Indian had aholt of me, and his knife up against my throat. I'll never forget that. Just about to slit my gizzard and

Shadler picked him off. Missed me by a whisker and shot that red devil out from behind me. At who-knows-how-many-yards range."

"Sure he did."

"Everybody knows he did. Who else could make a shot like that?"

"Yep. I reckon Shadler must be Dan'l Boone and Davy Crockett and Kit Carson all rolled into one. And a bigger hero than any of 'em."

"He made that shot, and then he come and saved me. And got hisself bad wounded doing it. Sure he's a hero."

Robertson gave Choctaw a pitying look. "I bet if John Shadler told you to flap your arms and fly to the moon, you'd have at it. If he told you to go up to Cochise's camp and wipe out the whole Cherry-Cow band single-handed. Wouldn't you, boy?"

"What's wrong with wanting to kill Indians? Indians killed some of my friends. They damn near killed me. Twice."

"As I heard it, the Chiricahuas was hunting men who'd killed some of them. Some of their women and children that is."

"If we hadn't killed Indians this country wouldn't be."

Robertson lifted his feet from the rock pool and began drying them with handfuls of bear grass. "I suppose Shadler called me a squaw man? 'Nothing so low as a man who lies with red bitches.' Something like that, huh? Well, I did have a Yavapai woman. Lots of miners, panning for color around Prescott, when the first strikes happened, got themselves a Yavapai or Walapai squaw. But when the country got settled some, and white women started coming in, they sent their squaws back to the tribe. I didn't though. That was my crime. Miners who'd been with half the squaws in Arizona, they got hot under their damn collars, seeing me living with just one. But, then, she wasn't just a squaw to me. The Arizona Volunteers —"

Robertson stared off at something, at his memories Choctaw guessed, and a look of undisguised sorrow settled over his face. "They was chasing a raiding party. Hostiles. Only they didn't look so damn far. Jumped the first camp they came across. My woman was there, visiting relatives."

Choctaw heard the catch in the man's voice and looked up. Robertson's red eyes leaked a straggle of tears across his cheek. The man mopped clumsily at his eyes and sniffed.

Choctaw felt embarrassed, and was moved, and yet he felt his mouth work itself into a half-smile of contempt. Robertson dabbed at his eyes with the heel of his palms, blew his nose on his fingers, and reached for his socks. "I heard Jack Adams was one of 'em. The only reason he's still on the Earth is 'cus I can't prove it."

Choctaw shook his head slightly. "I don't understand this business at all. You say one thing and John Shadler says another."

"There's no rules about this business." Robertson finished pulling on his boots and rose to his feet. "Except the Indians have to lose."

"Ain't it always been like that?"

"But the white man loses as well."

"I don't see how."

Robertson walked towards O'Brian. Choctaw noticed the Scot was limping on his left foot.

After the three men had eaten, they mounted, (with O'Brian riding double on the back of Robertson's horse) and rode south. A mile along the trail they halted atop a ridge.

Choctaw lifted his sombrero from his head and held it out before him to shade his eyes. He squinted. Where the mesquite ended, he saw rectangular patches of ground where folks had combed out irrigation ditches and laid neat rows of beans, melons, and squash.

A wide river mirrored the sky. Beyond the river lay a scatter of straw-thatched huts, a broken wall, long flat-roofed adobes lying like white bricks in the sunlight, a stone church tower, a speckle of small, milling shapes, more and bigger buildings then open land again, pink sand and olive mesquite and the beginnings of the mountains. Choctaw looked for more buildings and found none. What adobes and houses there were made an insignificant cluster on the limitless distance, like a rat's nest in a barn.

"Well," said O'Brian, "There's Tucson." He kicked his horse into movement.

Choctaw shook his head slowly in disappointment. The boy turned his red gelding and followed the others down the long slope into town.

# CHAPTER SIXTEEN

Choctaw stepped outside the freight office. He stood in the half darkness of the early evening. He took off his new hat and felt fine rain on his hair and shoulders.

"Spring rains," McClure told him. "They're late."

The Schmitt and Gottlieb agent in Tucson was a southerner named Gravitt. He observed, "Only the second rain this year."

Choctaw stepped back into the office and closed the door.

Gravitt poured two whiskeys and handed these to McClure and Choctaw, then poured a drink for himself. Choctaw drank slowly and carefully, not just because he wasn't much used to whiskey, but also because he didn't want to spill liquor on his new clothes. Today he'd bought himself a new outfit — a gray-blue shield-front shirt, blue bandanna, and blue denim jeans to go with his black plainsman's hat. He'd got his hair cut and the meager growth that passed for his beard and mustache shaved off.

McClure said "aaah," appreciatively. He asked, "This Old Crow?"

Gravitt drank. "Whiskey, by God. You hear something?"

Choctaw listened. He heard footsteps. There was a brisk knock on the door.

Gravitt went behind the store counter and emerged with a Remington 10-gauge sawed-off shotgun, which he broke open.

Choctaw asked, "Nervous, aintcha?"

Gravitt thumbed two fat cartridges into the shotgun breech. "Freight office gets robbed from time to time."

Choctaw dug a hand into his jacket pocket and felt the blunt grip of his pistol. Gravitt called, "Who's there?"

"Oliver Wentworth."

Gravitt tucked the shotgun out of sight behind the counter, then opened the door. An Anglo entered, and behind him, a Mexican. Gravitt addressed the Anglo. "Mister Wentworth."

Choctaw knew of Oliver Wentworth, of course. Wentworth freighted for the army, hauling in supplies from Drum Barracks in California. He was more than the local freight king, however. He was talked about as the next mayor of Tucson, or even next governor of the territory.

Wentworth was a broad-shouldered, bull-necked man of about fifty, Choctaw judged. Fierce burnsides framed a square, grim, clean-shaven face. Under his thatch of gray hair, blue eyes glittered coldly.

He wore a cape over a black broadcloth suit. Wentworth carried a brown felt hat in his left hand and shook rain from it. "Gentlemen," Wentworth said, "this is my associate Alfredo Ruiz. Señor Ruiz and I plan to open a freight line down into Mexico."

The Mexican was a slender man, a check-pattern serape over his left shoulder. He wore a Boss of the Plains hat. Ruiz had a long hound's face, thin mustaches, and beard. His brilliant eyes made Choctaw uncomfortable. They reminded him of John Shadler's eyes.

Gravitt introduced his companions. When he introduced Choctaw, Wentworth almost flinched. He asked the boy, "What kind of name is that? Choctaw? Are you some kind of Indian?"

"No, sir. My real name's —" He had to think a moment. "It's Calvin Taylor."

"Then call yourself that. That's a white and Christian name. Call yourself that, not some title befitting a heathen savage."

Choctaw blinked at the accusation in

Wentworth's eyes. "Yes, sir."

"You killed an Apache at O'Brian's Station?"

"Well, I kind of nailed him, but Ed O'Brian killed him mostly."

The anger left Wentworth's face. He flashed the thinnest, and briefest, of smiles. He shook Choctaw's hand, his grip surprisingly powerful. "Were you hurt, son?"

"No, sir."

"You did well."

The Mexican came forward and worked Choctaw's hand like it was a pump handle. He spoke in Spanish too rapid for the boy to catch, although it was clearly all praise and compliments.

"Every dead Indian . . ." Wentworth began, and paused. It was the same speech John Shadler had tried to deliver, Choctaw remembered, only Wentworth finished his. "Every dead Indian is a marker post — a milestone — on the road to the civilizing of Arizona."

Choctaw was having trouble with Wentworth's accent. At first, he'd taken him for a New England Yankee but now he suspected Wentworth might be a real Englishman.

Wentworth said, "These are sorry times, when a citizen has to take up arms in his

171

own defense, whilst an army we pay thousands of dollars for stands ineffectually by. What we need are soldiers not afraid to strike the hostiles — and strike them hard. Regardless of what newspapers back east might say. And speaking of the army" — Wentworth made a small gesture with the hat in his hand — "you were at Camp Walsh recently. Is it true what we hear? That the army's feeding and protecting a band of savages?"

"Yes, sir."

Ruiz demanded, "Why is this? Why do your soldiers protect *Indios*? In my country, when soldiers find Apaches, they kill them."

"The army's treating with 'em."

The Mexican's face hardened. "You can't treat with wild animals. Except the way you treated them."

Wentworth said, "We are all in your debt, son. Should you ever seek a change in employment . . ." Again there was the barest suggestion of a smile on his lips. "Though I'm sure Schmitt and Gottlieb wouldn't wish to lose the services of their doughtiest Indian killer. After John Shadler, that is."

"Well, Ed O'Brian killed him too."

"I'll bid you good night, gentlemen." Wentworth and Ruiz left the building.

Gravitt told Choctaw, "Got yourself a job with Oliver Wentworth, if you want it."

"I dunno. Sounds like he might speech me to death. This place really get robbed?"

"Hell, yes. In Tucson, if you don't nail it down, somebody'll steal it. There was a feller got hired to guard a store in the plaza. He was shot dead by robbers only last week. Know what the bastards was after? Coffee and sugar."

McClure reached for his hat. "Well, Choc, what you say we take a stroll into town?"

There appeared to be no street lighting in Tucson. McClure negotiated the narrow, haphazard streets by moonlight, Choctaw following. These alleys were crowded, even so late, with men, horses, mule teams, and wagons. There was a fight in progress, two men encircled by twenty or so others shouting them on. McClure announced, "This is the place, up here. The Elephant."

"The what?"

"Come on, Choc." McClure led the boy to a saloon and went inside. Choctaw paused at the entrance.

The Elephant was a low-ceilinged adobe, with rush mats over the earth floor. The bar and gambling tables were crowded with Anglos, Mexicans, soldiers. A Mexican band played *ranchera* music on fiddles, guitars, and *guitarróns.* The air was gray-blue with tobacco smoke. Pale dust, stirred underfoot, fogged the dim kerosene light. The room crashed with voices.

Choctaw looked at the women. He looked at bared brown forearms, bare feet, bare ankles and shoulders. He looked at gay shawls, vivid scarlet skirts, plunging dresses. He looked at a woman drinking a tooth glass of red liquor who threw back her head and laughed loudly. He saw women smoking cornshuck cigarettes and *cigarillos.* He was shocked. Anglo women didn't smoke — not decent ones, anyway — nor wear bright garments, nor show off their shoulders and arms and legs, nor laugh loud, open-mouthed laughter. Not in public, at least.

One girl caught his eye. She answered his stare with her own dark eyes and smiled. The invitation in her smile put a knot in his throat as large as his foot. He gaped. The girl laughed and turned back to her companions.

Choctaw made his way through the crowd, joining McClure at the bar. The Ulsterman handed him a bottle and a shot glass. "Don't spill none, mind. You want to drink it, not take a bath in it." Choctaw poured carefully but he spilled a tear of yellow liquid down the outside of the glass. He drank, coughed, laughed, and declared, "Jesus! This stuff'd grow horns on a muley cow."

"Get outside of that bottle, kid."

Choctaw remembered the girl who'd smiled at him and turned to look for her. He noticed a very tall, bearded man with black hair tangled to his shoulders. This man seemed familiar. He returned the boy's stare coldly and Choctaw glanced quickly away.

McClure said, "Over here, Choc."

Choctaw followed the Irishman into the crowd. He glimpsed familiar faces around a table: Finn, Horn Miller, Ike Kirby. Ed O'Brian was there too.

O'Brian shouted, "Here's a man as killed his Indian!"

Men started slapping Choctaw's back and shaking his hand. Proceedings began to get a little blurry; the fact that impressed itself most strongly on him was that there were plenty of drinks coming, and they were all free. He poured a stream of fierce liquor down his throat. Somewhere in there a Mexican girl squirmed on to his lap and kissed him hard on the lips, forcing her tongue inside his mouth. Choctaw was starting to enjoy the kiss when the girl sprang to her feet, laughing, and men surged around him again, with more drinks and handshakes and questions.

A man asked, "You was in that fight, out in the Ninety Mile Desert, few weeks back?"

"That's right." Choctaw slewed around, looking for the Mexican girl in the crowd, not seeing her.

"Got yourself shot, didn't you?"

"In the leg, here." Choctaw patted the wounded limb.

"Suppose you killed some Indians then, too, huh?"

The boy studied his questioner. It was the bearded, long-haired man he'd noticed before. Jack Adams, was that his name? Choctaw decided he didn't care too much for Jack Adams.

"Might have."

"I never seed no sign of it."

"Seems to me," Horn Miller commented, "you Arizona Volunteers hadn't caught up with the Indians either."

"Have before. Plenty times."

Choctaw said, "You talk a good fight, mister."

"Killed my share."

"Sure." Choctaw grinned. "Squaws and kids and old ones."

Choctaw lifted his glass to his mouth and

Jack Adams slapped at him and knocked the glass from his hand. The boy gaped stupidly, watching the glass spin along the floor. Adams grabbed a fistful of Choctaw's shirt front and pulled him to his feet. "I ain't takin' that from you, you little —"

The boy found he could hardly stand, his legs were pillars of rubber beneath him. He turned his head slowly and looked for the glass where it had rolled underfoot. Adams lifted his fist to his shoulders. Then Horn Miller, McClure, and O'Brian were between him and the boy. O'Brian shouted, "Cool off! He didn't mean nothing!"

Choctaw said, "I didn't mean nothing."

"I'll shut your big mouth!"

Adams released his hold and the boy slumped back in the chair. Adams faded into the crowd. Presently someone jammed another glass into Choctaw's hand and asked him how he'd killed the Apache at O'Brian's station. He seemed to be telling the story over and over, until he was thick-tongued with the telling of it.

A little later Finn said, "Come on, Choc." He took the other's arm and rose from his chair.

"Where we going?" Choctaw asked. His tongue seemed to get between him and the words.

"How long since you had a woman?"

"Hell, I'm drunk."

"So?"

"I don't figure my functions'll function."

It took him several tries to say that.

"You'll be all right."

Together they left the saloon.

# CHAPTER SEVENTEEN

Choctaw followed Finn out of the Elephant and the night air struck him like a club.

The boy found a wall to hang on to until the sky stopped tumbling overhead and the earth ceased to whirl beneath his feet.

Finn asked, "You all right, Choc?"

Choctaw sat on the mud. A light rain was still falling and clouds hid most of the moon. "I ain't sure," he said, and stood and vomited over his shoes and the front of his pants.

Presently Finn asked, "You okay, Choc?"

Choctaw vomited again, being careful to puke on the earth this time, and said, "I am now." He brushed some of the worst of it off the bottom of his sodden trousers. "There was a fight out here, before."

"Heard about it. Mule skinner got his eye gouged out."

"Oh?"

"Weren't much. There was a good one last

night, though. Outside the Congress Hall. Soldier got ripped up with a Bowie knife. He ain't expected to live. Come on, Choc, I got the hots for a woman."

Walking down the street, Finn told him, "I had one night before last. A Mex gal they call Little Gold Dollar. You'll like her."

"Will she like me?"

"She'll like that scalp money in your pocket."

Choctaw began to tell Finn he hadn't collected the scalp money and couldn't until O'Brian took the scalp into Mexico, but Finn was getting ahead of him, down the street. They were near the edge of the Mexican quarter. There were only a few huts between them and the broken town wall. Choctaw guessed Little Gold Dollar must ply her trade in one of those. He paused again and doffed his hat, letting the thin, warm rain course down his face. He turned and looked for Finn, and couldn't see him. It was too dark to see much, with clouds scudding over the moon.

He had to be in one of those huts, Choctaw decided, and started towards them. He heard feet turn in the mud behind him.

Choctaw looked over his shoulder. A man was approaching, faceless in shadow, over ground pocked with rain holes. Instinctively,

Choctaw felt for the bulk in his jacket pocket that was his pistol.

A cloud shifted off the moon's face and Choctaw saw this man was Jack Adams.

Adams halted.

Choctaw half-crouched, balling his hands into fists. Then he saw Adams was smiling. He stepped towards the boy, his right hand extended.

Choctaw straightened up. He felt ashamed of what he'd said, back in the Elephant. The Arizona Volunteers had saved him from the Apaches, after all. He stepped forward and thrust his own right hand before him awkwardly. "I'm sorry, Mister —"

Adams lashed out with his right foot, aiming the heavy kick at Choctaw's wounded leg. Choctaw half-turned, missing most of the kick, taking the bootheel on the thick muscle behind his knee. Both men were off-balance. Choctaw steadied first and let fly a right-handed punch. He felt the impact to his shoulder.

Adams was jolted backwards; he kicked out one foot and sat on his rump in the mud. Pain twisted his mouth and his eyes were dull with surprise. He swore, and, after a minute, rose slowly to his feet.

Pain was shooting through all of Choctaw's leg. He felt the sweat of it on his face.

When Adams swung at him, he struck back, throwing all his weight behind his right shoulder. He caught Adams high on one cheek. Adams grunted and jerked half around, swaying, and kept his feet.

Choctaw's leg caved under him; he struck the ground hard on his right hip and side. He groaned and tried to breathe. Dimly he heard feet plashing through the mud, a man running towards him from the direction of the huts.

Adams fumbled at his belt. A knife came into his hand. Not a murderous hacking weapon as Hairy used; this was a double-edged stabbing knife, with a vicious, foot-long spike of a blade.

"I'll cut you some first," Adams promised.

Choctaw heard a crack, something like two flats of wood being slapped together. The knife spun into the mud. Adams fell to his knees, clasped both hands to his head, and keeled over sideways, lifting both knees and curling them into his body.

Choctaw looked up, expecting Finn, and saw Angus Robertson standing over him, a pistol in his hand. Robertson asked, "This bastard stick you?"

Choctaw got to his feet and rubbed at his leg. Adams sat up. He took one hand from the side of his head, looked at it, and swore.

Robertson said, "Well, Adams, it's been simmering long enough 'tween you and me. Let's have it out now. Get your gun and get to work."

"I ain't heeled!"

"You're a liar!"

Adams climbed slowly to his feet. He kept his left hand pressed to the right side of his head. "You squaw-humping bastard," he told Robertson. "You red nigger-loving bastard. You'll be round the front of me next time, you red nigger-lover."

"Any time."

"Next time I see you, I'll kill you," Adams said. He glanced across at the boy. "And you too."

Robertson and Choctaw watched Adams weave a slow path back into town. Robertson was shaking, his face warm with anger. "He was heeled, all right."

"So why didn't he shoot it out?"

"He ain't one for face to face. Bullet in the back's more his style. That or a defenseless woman."

Choctaw said, "You better watch out then."

"What about you? Anyway, the day I worry about the likes of him ain't dawned yet, and never will. What was you doing out here?"

"Me and a friend was after girls."

"Girls? Didn't your ma tell you what you'll catch off them women?"

"Well, what was you doing in them huts?"

"Never you mind, sonny." Robertson eyed the boy disgustedly. "You look like you've been drug behind a team of horses."

"I only got these clothes today," Choctaw said, and laughed.

Robertson laughed also. "You got a place to bunk, Choc?"

"Schmitt and Gottlieb freight yard."

"In the rain? I found a *jacal.* Two or three other fellers bunking there. Room there for you to spread your blankets, if you want."

Choctaw was tired, his head ached, his leg hurt fiercely. Right then, Little Gold Dollar was the last thing he wanted. "Least I'll be out of the rain."

Robertson turned and walked back towards town, with Choctaw limping painfully after him.

"Tucson used to be a right lively town," Robertson observed. "Wild. Back at the start of the war, I remember, it was packed full of hard cases. Most of 'em had run out of California, ahead of a lynch rope." He smiled. "They say that about me, I know, but it ain't true. It's a dull town, now."

Choctaw thought of the mule skinner with

his eye gouged out and the soldier ripped open by a Bowie knife. He remembered the guard shot for a supply of coffee and sugar, and the slim dagger in Jack Adams's fist and the man's promise: "Next time I see you, I'll kill you." Choctaw said, "Too damn lively for me."

# CHAPTER EIGHTEEN

Choctaw woke to the clamor of many voices. He sat up, threw his blanket from him, reached for his boots, and upended them. He shook his boots and a spray of tiny crawling things fell, spiders and centipedes and mites that scuttled away from him as fast as their many legs could carry them. The boy stood and shook out his blanket and other little creatures fell and raced away. Then a red and black scorpion, as long as his hand, dropped, writhing, and fled also, its stinger aloft.

Choctaw dressed slowly in the closed-in heat of the adobe. He walked around the bodies of the other men sleeping on the floor of the *jacal.* He peeled back the steer hide door and stepped into the cruel, bleaching light of the new day.

He'd slept late, he judged it might be eight o'clock by the sun. A few hundred yards away, on the edge of the plaza, a noisy crowd was gathered. A wind sifted fine dust across everything, blowing hard enough to sway mesquite post fences and dim the sun. The dust stung his eyes and tasted gritty in his mouth.

Choctaw went around to the back of the adobe and urinated, standing with his back hunched against the wind. He found a well and hauled up a bucket and ladled tepid, alkali-streaked water on to his face. He was surprised he didn't feel worse but guessed the throwing up had let some of the poison out of him.

The wind eased and the sun struck through. Choctaw saw Robertson and Finn approaching.

Robertson grinned. "How's the head? Number 1 hat size?"

Finn asked, "What the hell happened to you last night?"

"I got sidetracked."

"You mean you never had a woman?"

Choctaw felt some jealousy. "Maybe I did, maybe I didn't. How was Little Gold Dollar?"

Finn scowled. "It was more like twenty cents' worth, last night. I got some good news for you, you lucky bastard."

"Oh?"

"Gravitt says you can keep the company

Spencer. A reward for killing that Indian."

"Hey!"

"And there's more. Wentworth and Ruiz, they put up the money for that scalp. Gravitt's holding fifty dollars for you, right now."

"Jesus!" Choctaw sat on the edge of the well. He grinned at the world in general.

Finn looked smug. "Pity you won't have time to spend it."

Choctaw's grin slipped.

"We're pulling out in the morning, Choc. Got a freight to Yuma. We got to start loading this afternoon. We gonna end up in California, maybe."

Robertson shook his head. "That's a hard run to Yuma."

Finn asked, "Indians bad?"

"No. Fact is, you ain't likely to meet a soul the whole two-hundred-odd miles. That's the hottest, driest, meanest stretch of desert on God's earth. Hell on earth, more like." Robertson pulled at his nose. "Only thinking about that run gives me a thirst. Let's go drink some breakfast."

"Not me," Finn declared.

Choctaw said, "Maybe you got an itch in the pants, after that twenty cents' worth."

Finn blushed. Choctaw jeered, "Twenty cents' worth," and slapped Finn on one cheek. The two boys ducked and circled around each other, trading half punches. Choctaw wanted to catch Finn with a real punch, like the one he'd landed on Jack Adams. It might take away some of his jealousy and frustration at not having had a woman, and his resentment at having to drive mules over the hell-on-earth desert to Yuma. But Finn pulled away, laughing, before Choctaw could rock him with a really good one and said, "I'll see you later, Choc."

Choctaw followed Robertson across the plaza. He saw the crowd was watching a cockfight.

As they passed the Elephant, which was still doing a reasonable business, Choctaw asked Robertson, "Ain't we going in here?"

"That's the sort of place a rattlesnake'd be ashamed to take his mother. I know a better place up here — the Lucky Strike."

The Lucky Strike was a model of the Elephant, only smaller. It held a few early (or late) drinkers, but no women. The bar dog was a huge, sad-faced man with an eyepatch. A red beard curled to his chest, as if to compensate for his baldness. There was a glass on the counter at his elbow, with a pistol hooked into it.

The giant eyed the newcomers mournfully. "What'll it be, gents?"

189

Robertson bought a bottle of mescal and poured it into two glasses.

"Breakfast," Robertson said, and emptied his glass in one.

Choctaw took his time drinking. On the wall behind the bar someone had scrawled in chalk: REMEMBER TO WRITE TO MOTHER. SHE IS THINKING OF YOU. WE PROVIDE WRITING PAPER AND ENVELOPES FREE, AND HAVE THE BEST WHISKEY IN ARIZONA.

Robertson refilled his glass. "Tell me about yourself, Choc."

"What is there to tell?"

"You a runaway from home?"

"I was fifteen when I left home. My ma died and there was no living with pa after that. No living with that evil-tempered bastard." He studied his glass a moment. "So I lit out. Went up to Caldwell in Kansas. Hired on to freight outfits and such and worked my way out here."

"Any Indian doings?"

"Folks told me I was due to get scalped lots of times. Cheyennes was out there, waiting to get me. Or Kiowas or Comanches. Or maybe Utes or Navajos. Never saw a wild Indian. Only a few tame ones that came to beg. Then I came to Arizona. Since then I've fit half the Apaches in creation, I

190

got shot, and everybody and his mother-in-law's been trying to stick a knife in me."

"Well, there shouldn't be any Indians on the way to Yuma. Just a long, long, dry. Still . . ." Robertson lifted his glass. "You like freight work?"

"Not hardly."

"Then why do it?"

"What else is there to do?"

"You ever shoot for the pot?"

"Some. Why?"

"Good pay for a post hunter at Camp Walsh. Army's crying out for 'em."

Choctaw coughed over his mescal. "Walsh! I ain't going to Walsh. You fixing to get me killed, Robertson? I've seen enough Apaches."

"I figured you'd seen — and smelled — enough mules."

"I ain't anxious to lose my scalp."

"Apaches don't scalp Anglos. Just Mexicans, sometimes. That's 'cus Mexicans put bounty on 'em."

"Well, that's nice. The Apaches won't scalp me. They'll just kill me."

"I'm not saying it ain't risky. Walsh is a long ways from anywhere and damn close to the Apaches. You need to watch out, sure, if you want to draw your pay each month."

Robertson drank, adding, "Good money, mind."

"It wants to be."

"On that Yuma trail, eggs come out of the hen hard-boiled. There was a soldier died at Yuma, went straight to hell. Few days later his ghost came back, trying to steal some blankets. He said hell was too damn cold after Yuma."

"Shut up, old man." Choctaw drank his mescal. "What is the pay, anyway?"

"Fifty dollars a month. And, if you call me old man again, I'll hang your tripes out to dry from a cactus."

Choctaw nursed his glass. "Fifty dollars! Just for hunting? With that kind of money, I can do anything."

"Sure you can," said Robertson. "But only if you live to spend it."

"I'm not stupid enough to get killed while I'm drawing that kind of pay. You sure there's a job going?"

"As I live and breathe."

Choctaw slapped Robertson on the shoulder. "Settled then. Let's drink to my new career." He filled both glasses.

"What about Schmitt and Gottlieb?"

"The hell with Schmitt and Gottlieb!"

■ ■ ■ ■

# PART THREE

■ ■ ■ ■

PART THREE

# CHAPTER NINETEEN

Apaches were there, many of them. On the flat beyond the creek there must have been three hundred Indians, moving in and out of brush shelters. Half conscious of doing it, Choctaw counted each hut. He made it thirty-nine.

"Looks like there's more of 'em," Choctaw said. He wanted to sound nonchalant but his voice came out a whisper, not just dry from the thirst and dust of the trail. Fear jumped in him like little quick knives. It slowed the blood in his ears, and put weakness in his arms and legs. All of a sudden playing Kit Carson, out in the wild and lonely places, amongst the Apache, didn't seem such a good idea. It was a lot safer piking at cards in Tucson. Or even driving mules across the desert to Yuma for Schmitt and Gottlieb. Perhaps joining Robertson had been a bad mistake. The last and worst in a long line.

"Your horse is getting spooky," Robertson told him.

"Me, too." the boy said quickly, to cover the shake in his voice.

"Scared, kid?"

Choctaw began to say, "Only a little . . . it ain't much . . . ," but Robertson said, "If you ain't, I sure am."

"Yeah?"

"Just don't let *them* see it. You got to figure, half the time, they're just as scared as we are. It's when two scared critters meet up trouble starts. So, stay scared but look brave. *Comprendo?*"

*"Sí, patron."*

Robertson kneed his gray horse gently and rode down to the creek, Choctaw following. They let their horses lick at the creek, which a long-legged man could cross in one stride, then rode towards the camp.

"Those boys is playing *wap*," Robertson observed.

A small crowd had gathered to watch two men. The first man held a willow hoop in one hand, the other held a slim wooden pole. With practiced ease the man holding the hoop spun it away from him so that it rolled along the ground like a wheel. The second man flung his pole like a spear. He pitched the stick through the middle of the

196

hoop without hitting it and yelled, *"Wap!"*; then clapped his hands together in self-congratulation. The others yelled, cheered, and laughed also.

Robertson said, "Seen Apaches wager all they have on the *wap* game: horses, guns, wives, you name it. They're gamble crazy."

A half dozen soldiers stood nearby, doing nothing in particular as far as Choctaw could see. A corporal stood a little apart from the others. Robertson asked him, "More of them, ain't there?"

The corporal lifted the kepi from his head, scratched thick blond hair, and nodded. "Big bunch come in last week. Two hundred of 'em."

"Who's band?"

"Dunno. That's four hundred of 'em here, anyhow. Surrendered." The corporal sneered. "Come in to eat our rations and spy us over, more like."

"You reckon?"

"I don't know why we don't just settle these fuckers right now. Got 'em all together here, we could come around them one night . . ."

"Women and kids too, huh?"

"Sure. Squaws drop pups and nits make lice. I been out here a few years. I seen things. I ain't got nothing against a tame

Indian, wants to live peaceable. But these Apaches . . ."

"But they're friendly."

"They're all friendly when they're dead."

The scout and his companion rode on. An Apache on a silver mule rode slowly towards them, followed by a straggle of women and young ones on foot. Robertson reined in his horse and Choctaw did likewise. Choctaw recognized the mule rider as the Aravaipa chief, Coyote.

Robertson said, *"Buenas tardes, jefe."*

*"Buenas tardes."* The Apache smiled openly, showing large, regular white teeth. He was carrying a small child, perhaps less than one year old, on his lap. Under a stiff mop of blue-black hair, the infant stared out at the world with sharp black eyes. The child wore a body-covering shift of deerskin. In Spanish slow enough for Choctaw to understand, the chief said, "This is my youngest daughter."

Coyote's daughter began mewing and tasting her fingers and waving one arm, dribbling spit on her chin. Coyote smiled affectionately at the little girl. "I have another daughter, and three sons. None of them are grown yet." He pointed at Choctaw and asked Robertson, "Is this your son?"

"Son of a bitch more like."

Coyote laughed loudly and the baby looked up and began to pick at her father's bear claw necklace. Coyote moved the tiny fingers away gently and said, "He doesn't say much. Perhaps I'm speaking too fast for him. Eh, *niño*? I speak too fast sometimes."

Choctaw said, "I understand you, *jefe.*" Coyote nodded and grinned.

Robertson said, "*Niño* here got shot by the Chiricahuas. When they fought with those wagon drivers."

"Yes, I heard about that."

"Cochise's band."

"No. Cochise was in Mexico then. No, it was Chiricahuas and Bedonkohes."

In English Choctaw asked Robertson, "Who the hell are the Bedonkohes?"

"Chiricahua clan. Sort of offshoot band."

Coyote said, "Perico's band, and maybe Geronimo."

Choctaw told the Indian, "Newspapers said it was Cochise."

The Apache looked puzzled and Robertson scowled. Switching to English, he told Choctaw, "There ain't no Apache word for newspaper, idiot. Anyway, if he says it wasn't Cochise, then it wasn't." Robertson addressed Coyote. "I've heard of this Geronimo. It is said he has a big hate for

199

Mexicans."

"His attitude is the right one. Mexicans killed his whole family. Many years ago." Coyote asked Choctaw, "Where were you shot?"

"In the leg here."

"Is your leg all right now?"

"Pretty much, yes."

"Good. Let me tell you a custom of my people. When we finish a meal, we always smear a bit of grease on each leg. You want to know why? There's a story about that. A man was once very greedy. He fed his stomach and forgot to feed his legs. He got very fat. One day enemies were chasing him. He rode his horse until it dropped dead but still his enemies pursued him. He ran on, but after only a short time his legs fell down beneath him, and he and his stomach fell on top of them. 'Get up!' he said, to his legs. 'This is no time to be lying down! Get up and get me out of here!' 'We can't,'" replied the legs. 'You fed your stomach and forgot to feed us and now we're too weak.' So, since then, we always feed our legs as well as our stomachs."

Everybody grinned. Choctaw decided this was the most unreal conversation he'd ever had. What did Coyote mean by telling him a children's fable? Was he merely offering friendship, or did something deeper run underneath, that Choctaw couldn't fathom?

Coyote lifted the baby and handed it down to one of the women. One of his wives, Choctaw guessed. His other wife was there too, her arm still in the (now very filthy) bandage the army provided. This was Klea, the girl Finn had shot, that night at Camp Walsh. He'd taken Klea for plump, but now he knew she was getting large with Coyote's sixth child. Next to her was the other girl who'd come into camp to talk peace, Klea's sister, Alope. The gaggle of kids around the mule's legs were presumably Coyote's sons and other daughter.

A hand touched Choctaw's thigh, and he looked down in surprise. It was Alope's hand. She was looking at him, and speaking in Spanish, but he'd missed what she'd said.

Robertson said, "She knows a good herb, to stop a wound bleeding."

Alope said, "Wild honey's good for that too."

Choctaw started to tell her that his leg didn't bleed any more, but he couldn't force the words out of his throat. Something in the last glance she'd given him had knocked all words out of him, momentarily. He hadn't realized until then how good-looking

Alope was, maybe the prettiest girl in this bunch.

The baby started to cry. The women closed around her, moving swiftly, faces anxious. Klea lifted a blanket and pushed it into the child's face. The mother shook the infant, hard. Choctaw stared, shocked. Klea kept the blanket pressed on the tiny face and the mother kept up the shaking. After a moment the crying ebbed, and the mother began to rock the child. She closed her eyes as she hugged the little girl. She even made the same soft, cooing noises white mothers made, quieting their babies. Choctaw saw the same concern and affection on the faces of the Apaches he'd seen on the faces of white people around a disturbed baby.

The caring and affectionate faces; he couldn't reconcile them with the violent shaking, and the pressing down of the smothering blanket, he'd witnessed a minute before. The mother put the child to her nipple. Choctaw smiled and let his gaze rest on the one exposed breast. He caught Robertson's warning eye and glanced away.

Robertson said, "Well, we've got to be going now, *jefe.*"

As they left the *rancheria* behind them and rode towards Camp Walsh, Robertson said, "You want to get yourself killed, do it when

I ain't around."

"Huh?"

"The way your eyes was popping out over that breast feeding. Ain't you never seen a woman's breasts?"

"Why, sure. Plenty," Choctaw lied.

"Something you better understand. Apaches is chaste as all hell about their women."

Choctaw started to grin. "Sure they is —"

"And they don't appreciate Anglos staring at them."

"What about the way she was staring at me?"

"Who?"

"That other one. That Alope."

Robertson laughed harshly. "Staring at *you*?"

"Sure."

"You little piss ant. That's an Apache woman."

"She ain't no older than I am. Likely . . ."

"Likely she's a year or two younger. Don't signify. A fifteen-year-old Apache girl is a full-growed woman. *Comprendo?* Something you wouldn't know from your ass."

"Oh yes? What makes you think —"

"If she was looking at you at all, she was probably thinking how, if she skinned you alive, turned your skin inside out, and tanned it for five, six days, you might make a good gun cover. Or maybe a good dance shirt."

"Bullshit."

Robertson scratched his beard. "Just you go sniffing around Apache women. You'll get your throat cut in no time. Friendlies or not."

"They're rough with their kids though, ain't they? Bastards!"

"It's learning. Stopped crying right smart, you notice."

"There I was, starting to think Apaches was human beings after all. Then they treat a baby like that. Made me sick to look at it."

"Babies have to be learned not to cry. Supposing they was hid out, and enemies was near. A crying baby could give 'em all away. A crying baby could get the whole band killed."

"Jesus."

"You're going to have to learn to understand these people, if you're going to deal with them."

"I don't know if I want to," Choctaw said. "Their ways is something hard."

"That's right."

Camp Walsh was three miles from the Apache *rancheria.* As they neared the buildings, a man stepped out of the post hospital and stood in the yard. Even at a distance Choctaw recognized John Shadler.

Robertson frowned. Clearly, he didn't want to meet Shadler. "I'll go report to headquarters," he said. Choctaw nodded and the other turned his horse aside. Choctaw rode up to the hospital alone.

"Mister Shadler."

Shadler looked up. In the shadow of the ramada, his face appeared still too pale, and tired. He didn't even attempt to smile.

"Choc."

"How's Dutchy?"

As the boy spoke, he knew. He'd taken the bleak look on Shadler's face for the pain of his wound but now Choctaw saw it was a different, and perhaps worse, pain.

"You came a sight late, boy," Shadler said. "Dutchy died an hour ago."

# CHAPTER TWENTY

Robertson said, "There's a sing tonight."

Choctaw was hunkered down at the edge of the Walsh parade ground. He looked up from the quirley he was shaping. "A sing?"

"At the *rancheria*. The Apaches are having a dance."

"Why tell me?"

"You're so interested in the Apaches."

"I am?"

Robertson rubbed at his throat scar. "There'll be tiswin."

"Huh?"

"Apache beer. You coming?"

"I dunno. I don't think so."

"That Alope'll be there."

"Why tell me?"

Silence came between them. After a minute, Robertson shrugged and strode towards the post corral.

Choctaw smoked, studying the distance. Over the mountains the sky was putting on its dusk colors. Coyotes began to talk in the hills.

The boy felt sour and tired. He wanted to get drunk or have a woman or fight somebody or do something to lift the cloud over him.

Maybe Camp Walsh did this. Perhaps tomorrow he'd ride back to Tucson and sign on with Oliver Wentworth and the hell with Robertson and post hunting and the Apaches. And Alope.

This afternoon he'd been a pallbearer. He'd hated it, as he hated everything about funerals. Especially this funeral. The grave was nothing more than a slit in the earth, gouged waist deep from the flinty soil. Rocks were piled over the grave to keep wolves and coyotes at bay, because these scavengers came to root up a corpse almost before the mourners had departed. They'd put Dutchy in a coffin, despite the shortage of lumber.

The coffin had been another bad joke. It was an improvised wooden crate bearing the printed legend 40 PAIRS CAVALRY TROUSERS. A wooden marker standing over the mound read: DUTCHY KILLED BY APACHES since no one knew the German's real name.

Choctaw scowled at his memories and

flicked the remnants of his quirley at the earth. He could go over to the sutler's store. But he was low on cash and, anyway, it would be a gloomy place tonight. It wasn't just Dutchy. Word had come today of a fight with Chiricahuas in the Whetstone Mountains. Three soldiers — including a Lieutenant Reed — had been killed. The lieutenant had been at Walsh until a few months ago and had been popular with the men. One story had it that Reed had been taken wounded but alive after the fight and was tortured to death through one whole day. Stories like that were two-a-penny after an Apache fight.

Choctaw could wander over to the hog ranch. This was a space in the dust a mile or so up the creek, a few *jacals* and tents. The hog ranch provided the same goods as the sutler's — drink, tobacco, canned fruit, and meat — except the liquor was cheaper and rougher. It was rumored women were for sale too.

If he went up to the hog ranch, he'd see John Shadler, and he didn't know that he wanted to. Choctaw couldn't decide how he felt about Shadler now. The wagon boss was a changed man since the Indian fight. Almost a stranger. Perhaps both of them had changed.

He could go up to the Apache sing.

He'd been around Indians as long as he could remember. Compared to most he'd known, Apaches seemed a strange, one-of-a-kind breed. They didn't have the round-headed, Oriental look of other Indians. Maybe their ancestors were a different race, mixed in with Indians. Alope for example: Take away her dark skin and her hair so sheeny black it was nearly blue, her high cheekbones, and she might almost be a white girl. A real pretty one too.

It was easier to work out the flaws to her beauty than to list what looked right about her. He supposed her nose was a little short. Maybe her mouth was a little wide. Her eyes got real big when she was surprised or astonished, which seemed to be a lot of the time. Then she looked like a child, which she half was, being what — fifteen? Hung between girl and woman. Nothing childlike about her body though, the shape of her . . . Choctaw smiled, thinking about that. Although she was taller than most Apache girls, the top of her head only came up to the middle of his chest. She had a cute way of standing with her lips slightly parted in a smile and her eyes slightly narrowed when she was listening . . . He realized he must have been studying on Alope quite a spell, without realizing it, to notice that. He remembered her hand on his thigh, how the flesh there had almost seemed to burn where she'd touched him . . .

Choctaw smoked another cigarette without tasting it, then walked over to the corral. As he was saddling his red horse, he saw Lieutenant Hamilton emerge from his quarters and stand out front, staring into the night.

Hamilton sat at his desk and drank a tooth glass of liquor. He pushed the bottle away from him. The officer moved a dry cigar in the corner of his mouth, studying the letter on his desk.

Lifting his pen, Hamilton wrote:

*When the Indians first came in I found them still very timid. It must be remembered that the Indians have been constantly at war for many years. Some of the children had no remembrance of a time when their tribe was at peace. The transformation of them in the space of barely a month has been remarkable.*

Hamilton thought a moment. He wrote:

*I have a wonderful family out here in the desert.*

"Too damn strong," Hamilton said aloud. Jesus Christ, a wonderful family. He sounded like one of the President's Quaker friends, full of mawkish piety for the poor red man. He remembered Franklin Reed, who'd maybe died, screaming, through one whole day. Hamilton lifted his pen to strike out the words. Instead he wrote:

*These Aravaipa Apaches, especially their chief, Coyote, have won me over completely. The men, though poorly clothed, refuse to lie or steal. The women work like slaves to clothe their children and themselves. They hold their virtue above price. They desire help in learning the ways to higher civilization and I will give them this help as long as they are permitted to stay.*

*I have issued rations to the Apaches and have set them to work bringing hay to the post. I arranged a system of tickets with which to pay them, and to be sure they were properly treated I personally attended to all the weighing. I also made inquiries to the kind of goods sold to them and prices. This proved a perfect success; not only the women and children joined in the task, but many of the men. The amount that has been furnished by them in one month exceeds one hundred and fifty thousand pounds . . .*

There was a knock on the door.

"Come in."

Sergeant Tyson entered.

"Yes, Sergeant?"

"Trouble, sir."

"Oh?"

"The men have been talking. Down at the sutler's. Talking up a fight."

"What sort of talk?"

"About Lieutenant Reed — and the Dutchman who died last night. That teamster, Shadler, he got 'em stirred up."

"Did he now?"

Tyson nodded slightly. "I think some of the men . . . and some of the teamsters who just came in . . . I think they've gone up to the creek to jump the Indian camp. The Indians're having a celebrate up there."

"But it was Chiricahuas did the killing. Hostiles. Not these friendlies."

"Yes, sir."

"Sergeant, form up a guard detail. Twenty men. And ask Lieutenant Riordan to report to me immediately."

"Yes, sir."

Tyson turned and left the office. Hamilton dropped the pen and reached for his hat and pistol belt.

# CHAPTER TWENTY-ONE

The red horse pricked its ears forward, threw up its head, and snorted.

Choctaw whispered, "Whoa, boy. Hush." He knew his horse had scented Apache ponies.

The boy calmed the sorrel and sat a moment, watching and listening. A coyote yarred, the yelp dipping in and out of silence like an echo. A night breeze stirred the mesquite. It carried the smell of nopal and sage and cooling earth to him.

Choctaw spurred his horse lightly and rode on through a belt of saguaro. The land tilted away before him and he saw the Indian camp. Wickiups bunched along the creek. Beyond these huts, yellow and orange fires blazed, crossed and recrossed by shadows. He heard a low music, a formless droning that worried at the quiet.

The horse tossed its head. Choctaw reached for his Spencer, booted under his right leg. A shadow formed in the darkness a few yards ahead of him. The sorrel reared high. The shadow moved and was an Apache, lunging forward. This man seized the horse's bridle.

Choctaw swore. He had the carbine halfway out of its scabbard before he recognized the Indian. Klosen, the fat one with some of his front upper teeth missing. An Aravaipa. A friendly.

Choctaw heard his name called. He recognized Robertson's voice and saw the man approaching.

Robertson said, "I got to foller you around, to keep you out of trouble."

"It's all right, *niño*," Klosen said, in Spanish. He slurred the words. Klosen grinned and showed the break in his teeth. "I'm not going to hurt you."

Choctaw shook the bridle free. In English he said, "Try it, you bag of guts."

The Indian may have not understood the words but he took the meaning. His grin remained but his eyes narrowed.

Klosen turned and walked back towards the village. There was a weave in his stride. Choctaw now understood his thick-tongued Spanish.

Robertson said, "Let's go to the sing."

"We aren't going down there, among all

215

them liquored-up Indians, are we?"

The older man shrugged. "Suit yourself."

Choctaw followed Robertson into the Apache camp.

A crowd was gathered, watching the dancers. The dancers were in a line, shoulder to shoulder, facing one of the larger fires.

Choctaw noticed men and women paired off in this line, with the same blanket across both their shoulders. Dancing, they shuffled, stooped, knees bent. Drums thumped out a dull rhythm, with shakers and rattles and rasps as accompaniment. Something like a fiddle made a scraped keening.

From horseback Choctaw could see other dancers beyond the fire. There were two groups of them, shapes hunched in blankets. They moved hardly at all, shuffling a pace or two to each side, their heads bobbing only a little. Now, under the music, he could hear the dancers chanting to the rhythm. It looked like poor fun to Choctaw, who was used to getting his knees and elbows busy at a dance.

He dismounted and went to join Robertson. Klosen appeared, and then Coyote. The chief was dressed in his go-to-meeting clothes: a long-sleeved shirt of bleached elk skin, trimmed with squirrel tail fringes, embroidered with painted beads and shells.

A brass swastika hung on his chest. The chief rustled as he moved; there were silver bells on the toes of his moccasins.

"Hello, Robertson," Coyote said in good Spanish. He shook the scout's hand. "And your son of a bitch, here." He laughed. " 'The one who listens.' "

"I think he's frightened of me," said Klosen, grinning.

In Spanish Choctaw replied, "Like hell I am."

Coyote looked at the boy, a strange expression on his face. Choctaw had seen that look before — on the faces of people in Tucson, the night he'd arrived there. Damn it, Coyote was looking at him in admiration. In Tucson this had embarrassed him, half the time. Now he only felt confused.

Coyote said, almost apologetically, "My nephew here, he's always been a big talker."

Klosen laughed. "Have a drink, listener." He offered a clay bowl of tiswin.

"Okay, big talker."

Klosen laughed again and Choctaw surprised himself by laughing too. He drank the thin, warm beer. He asked, "What's the dance for, *jefe*?"

"For those girls."

Choctaw looked and saw the dancers on the other side of the fire were all either women or girls. Coyote explained, "We're celebrating that those girls have become women. They've traveled safely through the time when they were small and helpless, now they carry the seed of our people."

Choctaw drank more tiswin. He looked for Alope and couldn't see her. Four more dancers moved from the shadows, one following the other. Over their heads these men wore hoods of black material, tied with bands of red cloth at the temples. Feathers dipped from the red bands. Eyeholes had been cut in the hoods. These masks were weirdly ornamented with slats of paint-daubed whitewood, strange antlers rising from the dancers' heads. The dancers were naked to the waist, backs and torsos painted in white serpent shapes. They wore buckskin kilts and leggings, dyed yellow. In their hands they carried short wooden swords, painted white and marked in black zigzagging lines. The dance was some sort of fighting ritual: dancers leapt and landed crouching, and turned, slashing with their toy swords. They had strips of bright cloth and sprigs of shrubbery tied about them. Bits of metal and wood and shells hung from belts and wrists, making a rattle and a clatter. Musicians shook gourds filled with stones, or staffs hung with clashing shells or deer claws. Chanting quickened.

Choctaw felt himself answering to the insistent pulse of the music. He took another drink of the Apache beer and saw Alope moving through the crowd.

She looked to be dressed in her finest also, a knee-length dress of what might have been white moleskin, with paintings of the moon, the stars, and desert plants on it. She stopped and spoke to Klosen. What he said made her laugh, because Choctaw saw the white gleam of her teeth in her dark face. Scowling, Choctaw drank tiswin. He decided he didn't care too much for Klosen.

The drumming sounded like a steam pump going, Choctaw judged; the shakers made a hailstorm, or a high wind thrashing trees, or a string of tin cans jangling. The music and the tiswin seemed to be working on some of the dancers. They began to yell, and made wide, exaggerated gestures with their arms and legs.

Alope moved towards him through the press. She caught his eye and gave him *that* look again. This time he was ready, he looked right back. He smiled insolently and the shot came.

Alope heard the shot. She turned and looked east, at higher ground overlooking the creek bed. Choctaw looked that way also.

None of the dancers appeared to have heard. Then there was a second shot. A pistol shot, Choctaw judged. The dance stilled; heads turned on shoulders, looking upward. Choctaw's body hummed and his head sang with a sudden fear. There was his Arizona experience in a nutshell: fighting for his life with men armed with knives, and the sweat of unexpected fear. He felt for the pistol in his jacket pocket, and saw Robertson, at the eastern end of the fire circle. He joined the scout there.

He asked Robertson, "What's going on?"

"I don't know. I don't like it, whatever —" Robertson let his words fade out, because another voice was shouting out in the darkness, off east. Apaches began talking also, the men moving towards the voice, away from the fires. Over the Indians clamor, Choctaw recognized the shouter's voice: it was Lieutenant Hamilton. He was shouting, "You men there — stand still! Stand still! Now, get over here! At the double!"

Choctaw studied the darkness and made out Hamilton. Figures began to shape from the gloom, moving slowly towards the officer. Some of them wore blouses that gleamed with buttons. Soldiers.

Hamilton called down to the camp. "Robertson, you there?"

"Yes, Lieutenant."

"Tell the Indians not to be afraid. It's all right now."

"What's all right?"

"Just tell them, dammit!"

The lieutenant began to harangue the assembled shadows, his voice lifted in temper. The boy heard Hamilton shouting, "I know how some of you feel about Indians. *Any* Indians. But every damn one of you —" the lieutenant went on. Choctaw saw Coyote, looking up at Hamilton.

The boy turned his head and saw a glint of metal in the darkness. The glimmering was the barrel of a rifle, too well greased. His eye traveled along the weapon into the shadow that held it, a thickness at the base of a saguaro. The shadow was less than a dozen yards away. The man was on one knee, aiming the gun at Coyote.

Choctaw didn't seem to think about what he did next. He rested his fingers on the grip of his pistol. He took four soft paces eastward, and that put the trunk of the saguaro between himself and the rifleman. Choctaw yelled, "Watch out, *jefe*!" As he yelled, he charged towards the saguaro. He

221

yelled, "Hey!"

The man there jerked upright and ducked back behind the cactus trunk, swinging the rifle around towards the boy. Choctaw rammed him in the chest with his left shoulder, knocking the man down.

Choctaw spilled headlong, falling over his opponent, rolled clear, and came to his feet. He'd forgotten his pistol. As the man grunted to his feet Choctaw hit him, right-handed, on the chin, a punch that shocked all up the boy's arm and spun the man away and over. The man landed on a jumping cholla and swore fiercely as he tried to thrash free.

Choctaw heard a foot move tiny stones in the darkness to his right. He turned and saw a man in shadow with a pistol raised above his head. Choctaw lifted his arms to shield his head and shoulders. But the man struck at his leg instead. The pistol barrel cracked the boy above the knee — where he'd been wounded.

Choctaw fell. He screamed. There was such pain he almost lost consciousness. He went blind from it an instant. Then he was hugging the limb and rocking against the earth on his side, pain juddering through him. He heard running feet, the runners fading into the darkness, then other runners nearing.

He looked up stupidly. He was circled by Apaches, Coyote and Klosen amongst them. Robertson pushed through the crowd and stood over him, asking, "Where you hurt?"

For a time, Choctaw could only say: "Ah. Ah. Ah. Ah." Finally, he managed, "In the leg. Bastard hit me right where I been wounded."

"Now, why'd he hit you there?"

"My sort of luck." Choctaw tried to laugh but his leg hurt too much. He was about to say he'd be better off without the damn thing, but then he remembered Scanlon, and felt ashamed. He'd rather have a real leg than a cork one, even if people kept shooting bullets through it, or kicking it, or striking it with pistols. He touched the wound and felt blood.

Robertson said, "Might have opened up again."

"Shit!" Pain worked on the boy a moment, and he clutched his leg.

Coyote spoke in Apache. He leaned forward and rested a hand briefly on the top of Choctaw's left shoulder.

Robertson said, "Looks like you saved his life."

"Christ! Did I?"

"He wants to know why."

Choctaw thought. "I don't know. What the hell happened?"

"Some teamsters and soldiers from Walsh. They were gonna shoot into the camp. Hamilton got there just in time, otherwise ther'd've been a pretty fair massacre."

"Hell!"

"And you and me right in the middle of it."

After a while Choctaw found he could stand. "This ain't much. I can fix it."

Coyote spoke in Apache once more. Robertson said, "He knows a better way."

Coyote said, "Come with me, listener."

Coyote walked back to the village, the boy limping after him. Alope appeared. Coyote spoke to her briefly, then told Choctaw, "Alope will look after you."

The girl put a hand on his arm and said, "Come on." She led him through an empty part of the camp. She ducked into a wickiup, leaving Choctaw standing outside.

Inside his head his thoughts chased each other like hornets swarming. Alope reemerged and sat on the ground before the wickiup, a basket in her hand. She tugged at one leg of his trousers. "Take them off."

"What?"

"Take them off."

"Hey?"

Choctaw looked to see if anyone was watching. No one was about.

The boy removed his jeans. He hated his legs, which seemed long, thin, and pale to him, and he hated his red flannel drawers, which came almost to his knees. He supposed he looked ridiculous. Alope must have agreed, because she began to laugh.

Choctaw grinned, then he was angry, then he laughed too.

She said, "Sit down."

He sat on the earth. Alope smeared some thick honey on his wound. At the touch of her fingers Choctaw's heart leapt in his chest and sweat beaded all over him. He was back in dizzy terror. He tried to speak and couldn't. He wanted to touch her very much, but he could hear John Shadler saying something like: *If there's anything worse than an Indian, it's a white man who squaws with 'em.*" But, mostly, it was Choctaw's own fear that held him back. He sat like a man of stone. Blood boomed in his ears and his breathing seemed to roar in the silence between him and the girl.

Alope took a finger full of the honey and playfully dabbed it on his chest.

"Hey!" he said, and then remembered to switch to Spanish. "I'm not wounded there."

"Or there?" Alope asked, putting her hand

somewhere else.

Choctaw got to his feet in a hurry. The girl started laughing again. "Are you frightened of me, *niño*?"

There was that word again. *Niño*. Kid. Child. Christ, he was older than she was. "No," he lied. "No, I ain't afraid."

"Poor *niño*."

The girl stood, the basket under her arm. Choctaw stared helplessly. She turned away. *Now I make the worst fool of myself I ever did,* Choctaw thought. He slid one arm around her waist and pulled her towards him. She squirmed in his arms. *Now I make a fool of myself,* Choctaw thought, *and Klosen or maybe Coyote comes along and slits my throat.*

The girl twisted to face him. Her mouth found his.

A little later, Choctaw discovered they were down on the sand.

Alope protested. "No. No."

"Yes."

"No."

"Why not?"

"Because it's more comfortable in the wickiup."

Choctaw found she was right. There was a deerskin pallet, the bed stuffed with grass and a bedspread of bleached moleskin that

226

was soon kicked into a corner of the hut.

Sometime later, Choctaw lay with his head resting on the girl's stomach. He could smell his own sweat and the tang of the fresh mint leaves Alope had rubbed onto her nipples and on her thighs. He could hear his own panting, and the softer breathing of the girl. He was surprised to hear that. The desert night was mostly filled with sound: birds and critters about their night work, thrashers, horned owls, canyon wrens, *javelinas,* the thick chirring of crickets. But tonight, their voices were mostly stilled; there was almost silence. Tonight, even the coyotes were sleeping.

# CHAPTER TWENTY-TWO

Hamilton stood under the ramada in front of his quarters and watched the approaching horsemen. The cloth under his armpits was already warm with sweat. He rubbed a streak of dust from the sleeve of his dress uniform.

There were twenty-two cavalrymen, a lieutenant at their head. Robertson was with them, and a civilian Hamilton didn't know. The column halted at the edge of camp and formed up. The lieutenant rode over to Hamilton's quarters and saluted.

"Nelson Curtis. Out of Fort Whipple."

That was, Hamilton judged, a hundred and sixty miles north and west. "Long, thirsty trip, Lieutenant."

"Not too bad. We outfitted at Fort Mc-Dowell. That's where we picked up your scout."

"Chasing Indians?"

"No. I only wish we were. We have to

escort the commissioner on his tour of inspection of the military situation down here."

"Commissioner?"

"Silas N. Alford. Direct from Stoneman's office."

General George Stoneman commanded the military department of Arizona.

Hamilton said, "Have your men bivouac south of camp, Lieutenant."

"Thanks."

"Any Indian sign?"

"Two days out of McDowell. In the breaks of the Salt. We spotted a bunch coming out of a canyon but the devils wouldn't fight. And your scout got cold feet. I couldn't risk the commissioner's scalp, so . . . We're going down to the border and across to Fort Bowie."

"Watch out there, too. Chiricahua country."

"Huh?"

"Cochise."

"Cochise, huh? I wouldn't mind a crack at him."

Curtis was a handsome man with red-gold hair worn long, in the Custer style, down to the collar of his uniform. A wide mustache put a few years on him. He'd be in his late twenties, Hamilton judged, so old enough to have served in the war. Yet still eager for action. I've been out here too long, Hamilton decided. When was the last time I had any enthusiasm for a fight?

Curtis said, "I don't know why your scout got so leery about those Indians."

"It pays to listen to your scouts. It'd be Pinal Apaches on the Salt. Or Yavapais."

"They're all the same, if you ask me. Damn rascals, the lot of them. Sooner they're wiped out, the better."

"Have you been out here long, Lieutenant?"

"First territorial posting. I've been on reconstruction duty in Texas. I was protecting the freedmen. In other words: nursemaiding a bunch of niggers. Making sure they weren't lynched by the Texans. No job for a soldier."

Curtis turned his horse and rode back to the column. The troopers picked some ground south of camp and dismounted. They sat, rubbing the cramps from their legs.

Commissioner Alford rode over to the officers' quarters and dismounted.

Hamilton extended his hand. "Commissioner Alford. I wasn't expecting you this soon. I'll find a bunk for you in the officers' quarters, sir."

"And turn out one of your officers? That won't be necessary, Lieutenant. I've been out under the stars these last two weeks and it's been bully so far. Save for a slight disagreement with a tarantula." He smiled a brief, wire-thin smile. "A tent will do as well as a brush hut."

Alford, Hamilton guessed, was not a smiling man. In his fifties somewhere, he had a bookish, God-fearing face, dark hair frosted with gray, goatee, and small mustache. Under heavy brows his eyes were brown, stern and questioning. A lawyer's face, Hamilton decided, hard judging and hard to impress. He wore a dark gray broadcloth suit the trail had just about ruined, a short cape, and a straw hat.

Hamilton said, "My orderly'll show you where you can wash up."

"Fine."

"You'll dine with me tonight, sir? Plain soldiers fare but . . ."

"I'd be honored. Then, tomorrow, we can look at your Indians. Your friendly Indians." Again that snapped-on, snapped-off smile. "Your wonderful family."

Hamilton had a strange, empty-bellied feeling. He thought he'd struck that phrase out of the letter. It sounded all wrong, the way Alford said it.

"Yes, sir."

Alford followed Hamilton's orderly into quarters and Robertson came over. Hamilton asked the scout, "What was this band, up on the Salt?"

"Pinals, most like. We seen half a dozen *broncos*. Lieutenant was all keen to have at 'em but I didn't like it."

"Why not?"

"I don't like Apaches when they sit out in the open and let themselves be seen. Was a sight more of 'em around, I reckon. The bunch we saw took off into some rough country. Rough as a porcupine's back. Good ambush country, if there was more of them. That's what I told Mister Shavetail. He wasn't for listening but the commissioner did. They sent two riders back to McDowell to get the word along there might be a raiding party about."

"Where do you think?"

"Where will they hit? Your guess is as good as mine, Lieutenant. Raid south into Mexico, maybe. Maybe they'll cut up around here, maybe up north. Who can say?"

"I guess we'll find out the usual way."

"Huh?"

Hamilton smiled bitterly. "Afterwards."

Next morning Hamilton took Alford on an

inspection of the Indian village, then they returned to Camp Walsh. It was too hot to sit indoors, so Hamilton had a table set up under a ramada behind his quarters. They sat on benches on either side of the table facing each other.

Alford asked, "How many Indians are there, exactly, Lieutenant?"

"Four hundred and six, by my last count. Na-Han-Te brought in two hundred a month ago. Pinals. He gave up because he couldn't get the right ammunition to fit his guns. When he came in, he said, *'Demasiados cartuchos de cobre.'* 'Too many copper cartridges.' " Hamilton smiled. Alford didn't, but glared stonily. Hamilton let his smile fade. He poured a glass of water from the carafe on the table and said, "Their band had a hard winter up in the mountains. Clothing about worn out, hardly a sole on any moccasins. They were down to eating cactus fruit and acorns. Children all eyes —"

"Four hundred and six Indians. That must mean — how many? One hundred and ten or more fighting-age bucks?"

"No, sir. Eighty or eighty-five, more like."

"How do you keep track on eighty-five Indians, Lieutenant?"

"Some have gone off to hunt, or gather

mescal. In such instances, I either provided escorts, when men were available, or insisted only small parties went out. I issued them passes and monitored them going out and coming back in. I checked the amounts of mescal they'd brought in, to ensure none of the men had gone raiding . . ."

"And had they, Lieutenant?"

"No, sir."

There was a pause. Maybe Alford *had* been a lawyer in another life, the way he fired off questions, keeping Hamilton on the back foot. The commissioner observed, "You sound very confident."

"I am, sir."

"I wish I shared your confidence. Only three weeks ago, soldiers were killed in the Whetstone Mountains —"

"Chiricahuas did that — Cochise's band."

"Did they? Can you be sure none of your friendlies took part in these raids? In the past few months stock has been driven off near St. David, off the Pete Kitchen Ranch, the Papago Reservation, and elsewhere. Some teamsters were killed on the forty-six-mile trace."

"I know, sir. But some of those raids happened before Coyote came in. And there are other bands in the territory that are still hostile. I don't claim to control them."

"Question is, Hamilton, can you control these here?"

"There has been no raiding, Commissioner. I know that damn Tucson newspaper has been blaming every raid in the territory on the Aravaipas. But it's not true. These Indians merely wanted to find a place and stay there. At peace."

"At peace?"

"Yes, sir. Only the day before yesterday Coyote and some others were asking me when they could start building more permanent dwellings. I told them they'd have to wait until I heard from General Stoneman. They said, 'You know what we want. If you see him, we know you'll do what you can for us.' "

"Dammit!" Alford slammed a hand on the table. "You've exceeded your brief, Hamilton, and then some. You've gone too far!"

"I have?"

"When the Apaches first came in, you should have directed them immediately to the White Mountain Agency."

"I wrote requesting instructions, sir. After five weeks I received notice that I had sent my report on the wrong form and would I please submit it again."

"I'm not discussing army red tape. I'm talking about what you did."

Hamilton began to make an impatient reply, then held his tongue. He was tired, more worn down with this than he'd realized. But it wouldn't do to lose his temper now, he needed to make his case carefully. So he waited a little time, then said, "Commissioner . . . General Stoneman's policy is either to kill off the hostiles or persuade them to come into feeding stations, yes?"

"Yes."

"He's had precious little success in either area, would you agree?"

"Admittedly, the military results have been disappointing —"

"If we're going to defeat the Apaches militarily, we need a lot more soldiers out here."

"Or officers with more zeal."

Hamilton smiled. "Forgive me, Commissioner, but now *you* sound like the Tucson newspaper. 'What's the army doing, protecting Apaches instead of killing them?' "

"You can sympathize with them, to a degree. They see their citizens butchered —"

"Not by these Aravaipas."

"So you say, Lieutenant."

"All I know is this: Stoneman's been at it a year; a handful of Indians have turned up at feeder stations; he hasn't killed enough hostiles to make any difference; and the rest of them are worse than ever. Do you agree? In two months here, I've got four hundred wild Indians — some of them killers too, I admit that, former raiders — to lay down their arms and live at peace. Without the loss of a single soldier."

"That's not the point and you know it. You've exceeded your authority here, the authority invested in you by the United States government."

"All I did was —"

"You told the Indians they could stay where they wanted, that's what you did!"

Alford stood and walked a few paces. "The Indians have to be corralled on the agencies. What do you think would happen if we let them stay *where they pleased*? It'd create a shock our reservation system might not stand."

"I did try and persuade them to go to the agency."

"Then I suggest you try again, Lieutenant. Talk them on if you can. Force them on if you can't. I may be able to arrange extra troops —"

"If I use force, they'll feel I've betrayed them."

"It shouldn't come to that. This Coyote seems intelligent. For an Indian."

"If I try force, they'll scatter."

"So be it."

"It'll be war again."

"That's of the Indians' choosing."

Once again, Hamilton started a quick reply and paused. There was Alford the lawyer again, driving him back with questions. In reply Hamilton sounded defensive, weak . . .

Alford gazed off at the mountains in the distance, frowning. "If you regard Indians as I do, as human beings, then what we're doing out here isn't pretty. Herding people around like cattle, and penning them up on the agencies. Virtual prisoners. But it has to be done. Arizona is filling with whites. The Indian bands are surrounded. They're finished. There's no future for Indians, as Indians, in Arizona. They have to learn to live like us, or face destruction. Given the temper of the settlers out here, the only place where the bands will be safe, for years yet, will be on the agencies. If the Aravaipas run back to the mountains it'll be the end for them."

Alford poured himself some water. "You gave them a false hope, Hamilton. You let them think they can live where they choose. Well, they no longer have that right. For their own sakes, and for the safety of the

238

white population, they have to be confined on reservations. I'm not saying it's right or wrong. It's how it's got to be. We have thirty million people in this country and there are a few thousand Indians. The minority must suffer, temporarily, for the greater good of the whole."

Alford turned the glass in his hand. "However, whilst I feel you were wrong, I am willing to believe you acted from the best motives. And I can't fault your handling of a delicate situation here. What you did was expedient. Now, however, you must persuade these Apaches to move to the White Mountains. Impress on them the alternative is — there is no alternative."

"Yes, sir." Hamilton heard the defeat in his voice and hated it.

"I should be gone about three weeks. A month at the most. That'll give you time to think about how you can go about it."

"About persuading them to move, you mean?"

"Yes. I'll need two of your top strength companies."

"Sir?"

"I don't propose to traipse around the Chiricahua country with just twenty soldiers. I want to be in sufficient force to demonstrate our strength to the Chiricahuas if necessary. Not let them wriggle out of it, like those savages did on the Salt River."

"But two companies —"

"The Chiricahuas are devils. No treating with them. They'll have to be cleaned out, root and branch, I don't doubt."

"That'll leave me with less than fifty men on post, sir. We're overextended as it is, maintaining this camp, keeping the roads open . . ."

"I appreciate that, Lieutenant. As you said yourself, we are badly undermanned out here. But fifty men should be able to keep this place secure from the Indians."

"It's not Indians I'm worried about, Commissioner. There's no danger of hostiles attacking this post."

"Well then?"

"There's been talk in Tucson. All the raiding being blamed on the Aravaipas."

"You assured me that wasn't the case, Lieutenant."

"I know, sir, but . . . I'm afraid a party from Tucson might attack the Apache camp, if they knew the garrison was so understrength."

"Tucson's sixty miles, isn't it? I think you're worried needlessly, Lieutenant. Anyway, fifty men should be able to see them off."

"I hope so. Talk is . . ."

"Talk is cheap, Lieutenant."

Hamilton stood, leaning on one of the ramada uprights. "Yes, sir. But out here —" He used his fist to knead an aching in his back, "— so are Indian lives."

241

# CHAPTER TWENTY-THREE

The boy and girl lay side by side on the
sand, gazing up at the sky. Then Choctaw
sighed contentedly and turned towards
Alope, resting one hand on her bare thigh.

They lay in a shadow shaped like a giant
spider. The wide-flung legs of the spider
were the branches of the juniper above
them. Choctaw saw a red-tailed hawk on a
branch of the tree above them, bobbing its
head and preening its gray-brown feathers.
He listened to the music of running water.
There was a little waterfall nearby, splashing down to the salt lick below.

Alope sat up, carefully shaping a *macuche*
cigarette. That didn't shock him now; most
of the Apache women he'd seen smoked.
He stretched, lifted his head, and kissed her
on the left breast. She was naked, as he was.
Her deerskin shift lay some yards away. In
the westering sun, her copper body was
sometimes also golden, and her black hair

lay almost on her shoulders, because she'd loosed the figure-of-eight frame that unmarried Apache women wore, pulling their hair back on to the nape of their necks.

He lay back and chewed a *zagosti* leaf. It was getting dusky, time when animals came to water. There might be chance of a mule deer, but Choctaw decided to think about hunting later. Fairly soon, he guessed, Robertson would notice how often the boy went hunting and came back empty-handed.

Choctaw didn't care. Most of the time all he could think about was Alope. Sometimes everything about her, sometimes just her urgent body and his own fierce desire to spend himself in her.

Very often, when they were together, in these secret rendezvous places, he would say little or nothing. He would just listen as she talked, in Spanish or Apache, which he was only slowly coming to understand. But her Spanish was good, and most of the time Choctaw could keep up with it. She didn't seem to mind his word shyness, and often she talked enough for both of them. She asked endless questions, gave her thoughts on the world, told him gossip, and recounted stories of her people.

She was most way through the story about how the first of the *Tindeh* came. By *Tindeh* she meant the People, and that meant the Apaches, like they were the only real people and everybody else human-looking was just pretending at it. She'd told him this tale a couple times already, but he didn't care, he liked the story and her pleasure in telling it.

It was a long yarn about how the Apaches' mother figure, White Painted Lady — basically the first woman — had given birth to Child of the Water. (His father was either Lightning or the Rainstorm or a combination of the two.) As there were only a few human beings in the world at this time, they were being hunted for their meat by other earthly predators: snakes, various monsters, and, most particularly, the dragon, a huge emerald-colored beast.

Alope resumed her storytelling and Choctaw closed his eyes to listen. She got to the climax: the dramatic confrontation between the dragon and the last two male humans left in the world — Child of the Water and his uncle, Killer of Enemies. In this face-off, Killer of Enemies proved to be cowardly and useless. All he did was cower down. But Child of the Water stood up to the dragon bravely, for all that the great green monster towered over him.

Child of the Water loosed three arrows at his enemy. The dragon was protected by four coats of horny scales but each arrow shattered one coat, so after the third arrow impacted, the dragon had only one scaly coat left shielding him. Then Child of the Water released the fourth arrow; it penetrated this last coat, piercing the dragon's evil heart.

Instantly rain fell, lightning flashed, and thunder rolled as the Thunder People pounded their drums. The dragon gave a tremendous roar and fell down the mountains. He rolled over four mesas and fell into the bottom of a deep canyon.

Now Alope told him the moral at the end of this legend — something all good little Apache listeners should absorb. She smiled when she said this was her favorite part of the story.

"Child of the Water grew to be the first man of the *Tindeh,* who others call Apache. He was the first leader of the People and wore the eagle feathers to show his justice, wisdom, and power. With his courage, skill, and generosity Child of the Water showed the People how to live and how to look after each other.

"Killer of Enemies was a thief, greedy, cowardly, and didn't know how to live in bad country. He cultivated meaningless possessions and lived a life that was selfish, worthless, and without a god to believe in.

"It is said he may have been the first of the white men."

He reached up one hand and slowly rubbed her stomach. "You ain't so unhappy about this particular white man, I reckon."

He sat up and began to make his own quirley. Cigarette in mouth, he stood, pulling on his drawers and his jeans. He gazed at the scenery as he dressed. The land sloped away, miles of mesquite, chaparral, and saguaro melting into haze, under a sky too bright to look at. The sky was a blueness from which his eye flinched.

Arizona might belong to another time, or another world, it was so different from any place he'd ever known. Mountains miles away were telescoped hard against the eye, so it seemed you could just reach out and touch their harsh rocks. Easy to believe that dragon was hiding behind their front ranges, switching his great emerald tail and misting canyon darkness with his fetid breath. Or that the mountains themselves were dragons, frozen into bare stone.

Choctaw decided he was getting a little Apache himself, losing himself in a child's fable. The boy lifted his Spencer and tested the finger lever action and the sighting. He laced the mountains with a sham volley

246

from the empty gun. Satisfied, Choctaw grabbed an oiling rag. He felt hungry. Perhaps he would get down to some real hunting, after all. He'd acquired a taste for deer meat, the way Alope cooked it: roasted on spits over a dry cedar fire, seasoned with garlic and cloves, with red chili and pinto beans.

The hardest part, Choctaw decided, was not being able to tell anybody. Sometimes he was so full of Alope he was dizzy with her. He wanted to stamp down on Finn, smirking about Little Gold Dollar, on Robertson saying, "You wouldn't know a woman from your ass." But . . . John Shadler had said it. *"If there's one thing worse than an Indian, it's a white man who squaws with 'em."*

Choctaw scowled. He dropped the oiling rag and drew hard on his cigarette. Then he turned and said, "Hey!"

Many tiny frantic legs tickled on the back of his left shoulder. Alope stood behind him, a mesquite switch in her hand. The stick crawled with rust-colored movement. Harvester ants! A bunch of these critters had dropped from the switch onto his shoulder.

He forgot himself and told Alope, "Damn you!" Fortunately, he called in English, which she wouldn't understand. You didn't damn an Apache even if you were joking; that was putting a curse on them, which could be a deadly business. In Spanish he cried, "You know how I hate these damn things!" He started brushing ants from him whilst she stood back, laughing.

These ants could bite when you annoyed them. He swore (in English and Spanish) and brushed the last of them off, but already a few angry red bite patches showed against his flesh.

Alope leaned towards him once more, lifting the stick. He said, "Bitch!" in a language she could understand. She laughed. Earthly insults were fine, just don't bring in anything supernatural or religious. He grabbed her arm and shook it and the switch fell. Maybe he hurt her a little, but she only laughed some more (sometimes their play got plenty rough) and wrestled against him. She pushed him with one hand, hooking her leg behind his, and tripped him. He toppled backwards but managed to pull her towards him and they fell together, the boy underneath, Alope sprawling over him.

They rolled about, fighting and struggling, and then lay together, laughing.

Next they lay quiet.

He smiled at her in affection, nuzzling the top of her head. Most of the time Alope acted older than her age, so when she did act silly or childish it always surprised him a little. But maybe that's how it was with girls generally. Whereas young fellows like him never seemed to act grown up, however hard they tried.

Alope was fun to be with mostly. Except occasionally she'd go real quiet and thoughtful and sometimes go off by herself. He guessed then she was remembering how she'd lost her people when she was a child.

Alope wasn't just Coyote's sister-in-law, she was something like his ward, because her mother and father were dead. Choctaw guessed they'd been killed in the massacre by Papago Indians and Arizona Volunteers.

Thinking of that, Choctaw felt a rush of protectiveness towards her. He took her arm, pulling her to him. Maybe she mistook that for horniness, because she said "No" and squirmed against him. Because she did that, it *became* horniness. Choctaw laughed harshly and pulled her harder against him.

She twisted away. "No."

"Alope!"

"Listen."

"Alope."

"No. Listen!"

He listened and heard a thin, far-off crackling.

She said *"Besh-eh-gar."*

That was one Apache word he'd picked up. It meant gun or guns.

She brought him the ammunition belt. He fed shells into the Spencer and into his Starr double-action pistol. The distant shooting faded out. Alope started to pull on her clothes. Meantime she was looking south, towards the St. David road, so he looked that way also. After a few minutes a thread climbed from the desert haze, rising straight up against a nearly windless sky. A thin gray pillar of woodsmoke . . .

Robertson said, "Jesus."

Hamilton's mouth and throat were dry. He rubbed his hands together, his palms fluid with sweat. Behind him, mounted troopers sat with bandannas over their mouths and noses, so they looked like bandits.

Hamilton could understand the face masks. The smell came at them like flung rocks. A throat-catching, burnt meat stench, the harsh tang of woodsmoke, the sharp, biting stink of horse voidings. The horses were frightened and emptied themselves. Beside him his own horse pissed a yellow arc onto the sand.

A low fire still crackled but the wagon

hadn't burned well. Two men had been tied upside down to the wheels of the wagon, their heads about eighteen inches above the ground. Small mesquite fires had been lit under each man's head. They were white men but their heads had burned into various colors, mottlings of pale coffee-brown, grape black, and purple. Faces had wrenched themselves into something quite inhuman as their skulls exploded and their brains burst from their ears.

Two more dead men hung nearby. They'd been tied, naked, to cactus, faces against the trunks and bodies pin-cushioned with arrows. One man had something like thirty arrows in him. Their bodies had been cleft with axes. Not Apache hand axes, Hamilton guessed, but long-handled axes the Indians had found in the wagon.

Buzzards had led the soldiers to the fifth man, two miles away. The Apaches had made him run barefoot behind a horse, over bad ground, through cactus, over rock and thorns. When he'd fallen they'd dragged him. They'd lanced his body as it dragged along. It was said the Apaches had learnt this cruel sport from the Spanish *conquistadores*.

Robertson declared, "Tracks lead towards the Aravaipa camp."

Hamilton glanced at Alford. The man's face was without color, his mouth a tight, grim line.

Hamilton said, "This was your Salt River band I guess, Commissioner."

"Was it?"

"The Aravaipas had nothing to do with it."

Alford moved towards his horse and mounted up. He asked, "Are you quite sure, Lieutenant?"

Hamilton strode over to the wagon. He toed the embers of the fire, carefully not looking at the dead men. But, in the tail of his eye, he saw one man's hand, all colors from burning, raw pink and coffee and purple-black. In his death agony this man's fingers had hinged into a claw. The embers Hamilton stirred fluttered, black and gray leaves, settled, and went to white dust. His own hands were trembling, Hamilton noticed; he rubbed his sweating palms against the side of his pants.

# CHAPTER TWENTY-FOUR

Hamilton heard distant screaming.

It came nearer.

The lieutenant stepped out of his quarters. Wind slapped at his face, driving a surf of dust across the camp, making horses and mules restless in their pens. He saw a body of horsemen approaching at a canter, shapes and faces dim behind the blown sand.

There were twenty-odd riders, Company B, with Second Lieutenant Riordan at their head. The Mexican scout, Primitavo, rode at the lieutenant's side. Alongside the Mexican were two shapeless bundles in blankets. Hamilton assumed they were Apaches. One rode a mule and the other an army horse.

The company halted. The two Apaches slid from their mounts and Hamilton saw they were both women. One was a dumpy shape, her head wrapped in a cloth scarf. The other was a younger woman in a deerskin shift. She was holding a child in her arms.

Hamilton could see something was wrong with this child, the arms and legs hung limply.

The older woman was crying, *"Médico! Médico!"* The girl holding the child began to scream, and the other woman joined her. The noise they raised was fiendish; it crawled the flesh on his arms and at the nape of his neck, women crying in despair for their young. Hamilton could see the child was a boy, perhaps five or six, and his head was covered in blood.

Hamilton told the nearest private, "Get the child to the hospital."

The man gave him a bewildered look. He took the young woman's arm and stepped towards the post hospital. She broke from the soldier's grasp and ran ahead of him.

Second Lieutenant Riordan was a dark-haired young man with a scant mustache and nervous, close-set eyes. There was panic in his face. Some of that panic seemed to have reached his horse. The animal snorted, tossed its head, and shifted its white feet. Riordan said, "We saw a party of horsemen about ten miles southwest. Thirty-odd riders. White men, Mexicans, some Indians . . ."

"Indians?"

Primitavo said, "Papagos I think." He was clean-shaven, with a round, bland face.

Riordan said, "They were heading north. Then we came across those three. Primitavo talked with them."

"Well?"

Primitavo answered. "They was gathering mescal. Eight, ten miles off maybe. Somebody was to fire on them — these womans, the *niño,* an' another boy, maybe twelve, thirteen."

"Who? Who fired on them?"

"Arizona Volunteers they think. The little kid was hit. The other boy, he fire back at them — he has old gun — but he only got one bullet. Then they waiting to be killed. But whoever is shooting, they must have run."

"What happened to the other one — the boy?"

"He run off to warn other Apaches. It was Zele's kid got shot. Gonna be dead pretty soon, all top of his head blown off like that."

Hamilton said, "Orderly, get my horse. Saddle it and bring it 'round here. Lieutenant, get a full issue of ammunition to your men. Primitavo, I'll need you too. We move out as soon as I'm mounted."

■ ■ ■

On the hot stones in the fire, corn cakes were browning.

Choctaw snatched up a cake and put it in his mouth. Chewing, he told Robertson, "Soldiers coming."

Robertson sat by the same mesquite fire. He was talking to Golinka.

Golinka was an Aravaipa shaman. A shaman was a mixture of wizard, prophet, history-keeper, doctor, and priest. Golinka looked a hundred years old and was said to know everything that went on in the *rancheria.* His filthy smock hung loosely on his skeleton frame. Dirty-snow-colored hair straggled to his ribs. There were, Choctaw guessed, ten million lines wrinkling his Chinese-yellow face. His name meant Skunk.

The old man studied the approaching soldiers. His eyes were as bright as new black paint.

Choctaw counted maybe two dozen cavalrymen, Hamilton and Second Lieutenant Riordan leading. The cavalrymen reined in and their horses milled in dust. Robertson walked over to them. "Lieutenant Hamilton."

Hamilton asked Robertson, "Where are all the men from this camp?"

"Sergeant Tyson went off with a bunch gathering mescal. Na-Han-Te moved his band up the creek. After better water and graze."

Hamilton turned in the saddle. He shouted (he had to shout over the rising wind), "Lieutenant Riordan, send two men out to find Sergeant Tyson's party. I want them brought in here. Take a dozen men and Primitavo and bring all of Na-Han-Te's people back here too. Use your discretion, Lieutenant. Don't panic them."

Riordan counted off his men; they rode off into dust.

Hamilton dismounted the remaining eleven cavalrymen. Most of the soldiers sat or squatted leeward of their horses, using the animals as windbreaks. Robertson asked, "What's up, Lieutenant?"

Because of the wind Choctaw couldn't catch all of Hamilton's reply. Apaches had faded into their wickiups to sit out the blower, or went about their business wrapped in blankets. A string of children ran about, shrieking. Kids went a little crazy in a high wind, Choctaw knew; also, the ponies and mules, snorting, pawing, and milling in the rope corrals.

Choctaw's own horse, the sorrel, was ground-hitched nearby, in an out-of-the-wind spot back of a lean-to. Choctaw wandered over to the red horse and fed it some of his corn cake.

He thought about Alope. He would tell Robertson, Choctaw decided. What would be the harm? Robertson once had a squaw himself. Anyway, what was there to be ashamed of? So why was he frightened of telling anyone? Why was part of him ashamed? Alope was a woman to him, not a squaw. *Damn John Shadler!*

He watched Skunk. The old man didn't seem to notice the wind; he was gingerly snatching at a corn cake on the hot stone. He seized one cake, gasped with pain, and tossed the cake between his hands, crying, "Ah! Ah! Ah!" He dropped the cake underfoot and crumpled down after it, knees and elbows scrabbling.

Choctaw started to grin at the old man. It was a small, silly, childish thing to laugh at he knew, but mirth took hold of him. He buried his mouth in one shoulder and laughed until his stomach hurt. He hoped no one was looking; Apaches never made fun of a shaman. Especially one who was old and maybe a little crazy. That would make him doubly holy, and his medicine twice as powerful.

Hamilton strode over and talked to Robertson, close enough for Choctaw to hear. "Did you get anything out of him?" The officer spoke to Robertson but he was looking at Skunk, down on his hands and knees searching for the lost corn cake.

Robertson shrugged. "You know how it is. An Indian wants to clam up . . ."

"That's not what I asked you."

"I got most of 'em accounted for. I know where most of 'em was when that massacre happened. When them five men was killed."

"Most of them? Who isn't accounted for?"

"Klosen. Seems a bunch of the young *broncos* foller him. He says they was off hunting wild pigs when the massacre happened."

"Wild pigs?"

Robertson scratched his throat. "Chased 'em so far into the hills, it got dark 'fore they knew it. So they slept out there and didn't come back to the camp 'til the next day."

"So they went off without permission. And no escort."

"No escort. No witnesses. No *white* witnesses, that is."

"Klosen, huh? Do you believe him?"

"I don't know."

259

"You think they joined that raiding party?"

"I told you, Lieutenant. I can't read their minds."

"Neither can I. I can't read what's in any of their minds. In Klosen's mind. Or in Coyote's mind. Where the hell is Coyote, anyway?"

Choctaw saw movement. West of the *rancheria,* there was a scatter of timber, on a rise overlooking the creek. Horses and riders bristled onto this rise, moving between the trees.

The boy pointed. "Look."

Hamilton lifted his field glasses and inspected the horsemen. He shouted orders that the boy didn't hear. Cavalrymen mounted up and moved forward in a skirmish line. Choctaw asked, "What's going on, Lieutenant?"

The horsemen broke from the timber and rode down towards the creek. There were many of them, perhaps fifty riders. About half of them were men in white cotton pants and shirts, riding mules and ponies.

Choctaw shaded his eyes with one hand. "Those Mexicans, Lieutenant, can you see?"

Hamilton leveled his field glasses. "I'd say Papago Indians."

"If they're Papagos, then those is Arizona Volunteers."

"That's right, son."

Choctaw reached for his Spencer, leaning against the windbreak. Fifty men, well enough armed, determined enough, could ride right over this camp. The soldiers wouldn't be able to stop them. Would they even try? For Apache women and kids? Some of the troopers here might have been the same men who'd crept up in the darkness, ready to fire into the Apache sing. At least Alope was safe, she was up in the Pinal *rancheria*.

Apache women had seen the riders. They began to swarm around the wickiups. "Tell them to get back in their huts," Hamilton barked. "Tell 'em they'll be safe there." Robertson began to shout at them, in Apache and in Spanish. Some halted and listened; they snatched up protesting children or herded them into wickiups. Others careered around the huts like mindless things. A woman began to scream hysterically. She was crying, "My children! Where are my children? My children!" But all her children were dead, Choctaw knew, massacred by Arizona Volunteers.

Hamilton had his field glasses trained on the north, looking for Riordan and the other soldiers Choctaw supposed. Choctaw strode over to Robertson. The scout eyed the nearing riders grimly. This was an old story for him too.

The cloud of riders had fanned wide. Now horses slowed. They halted in a line, shoulder to shoulder, perhaps three hundred yards distant. Dust smoked over them, thinned, pooling around the horses' hooves like white water, and was sucked behind them in long vapors by the wind. At the western end of the line riders held still. The eastern line was full of movement, as Papagos milled about on their ponies and ribshot mules.

Now the wind fell altogether. Quiet dropped on everything. It rubbed against the boy's ears. Quiet made a soreness he wanted to scratch.

Hamilton scanned the north with his field glasses. Choctaw knew there was no chance of his missing soldiers yet. In the hot, still quiet Choctaw heard a shod hoof knock against a stone and a cavalryman spit.

Half a dozen riders moved from the line of Arizona Volunteers and trotted forward. They rode to within fifty yards of the soldiers, then halted. Hamilton walked out to them, with Robertson a pace or two behind. Choctaw stepped into the saddle of his red horse and walked the horse after them, although no one had invited him.

Choctaw saw two of the six horsemen were Indians, though one wore the white cotton shirt and straw sombrero of a Mexican *peon.* He was a young man with a fox-like, narrow, very dark face. A horizontal bar of vermilion crossed his thin cheeks. He was as nervous as a cat and his wiry yellow mustang moved nervously under him. The other Papago sat a scrawny mule calmly, his broad face peaceful, a heavy man with a lot of gray in his clubbed, chest-length hair. To his surprise, Choctaw saw Alfredo Ruiz was there, and Oliver Wentworth. The Englishman wore a canvas jacket, duck pants, and a needle-crowned sombrero. Flanking him was an Anglo Choctaw didn't know: a man with a fringe of red beard and mustache, in faded, nondescript clothes and battered slouch hat. He might have been a miner. Or anything.

The sixth man was Jack Adams.

Hamilton stopped close enough to Wentworth to reach out and touch the bridle of his horse. Robertson halted a few yards behind Hamilton. Choctaw reined in his horse at the scout's side.

Hamilton said, "Mister Wentworth."

Wentworth declared, "Lieutenant, five men were murdered here last week!"

"I know."

"Did you also know that the St. David settlement has been abandoned?"

"I didn't know that."

"All thirty families have pulled stakes and moved back to Tucson. Isn't the army supposed to be advancing the frontier? Not watching it retreat? Five men have been foully murdered and what have you done about it?"

"I've sent two patrols into the mountains . . ."

Adams leaned forward in the saddle of his chestnut horse. "Why look there? We know where those killers is. Right here in this camp."

"No."

"Tracks lead this way, don't they?"

"The raiders went on through. On to the Apache war trail. Down to Mexico, or to join Cochise."

"I'll tell you what they did. They got off their horses in this very camp, and they're still here. And the first thing they did was have a good hard laugh at the damn fool army. Feeding 'em and keeping 'em safe, so they can keep on raiding and murdering."

The red-bearded man was making strange noises. He was breathing hard through his nose and made sounds with his closed mouth like words muffled by a gag.

Hamilton said, "Mister Wentworth, this is a military establishment. As of now, it's off-limits to you and your . . . Arizona Volunteers."

"You can try and protect them, Hamilton, and make excuses for them. But their hands are bloody and there'll be a reckoning."

Adams put in, "You better sleep with one eye wide open, soldier boy."

Ruiz added, "We know how to take care of your pets."

Hamilton sneered. "Like you took care of that boy, this morning? How old was he — five or six?"

Adams grinned. "Old enough. Any Apache around me gets to five or six, they'll be damned lucky." He laughed.

Wentworth said, "Two weeks ago Apaches ran off some mules from the Papago Reservation and killed an old woman and a boy. Cut their throats. What did the army do about it? Nothing as usual. The Apaches have made the rules in this war. Let them reap the whirlwind."

Hamilton nodded towards the two Indians. "Ask those Papagos which band of Apaches stole their mules."

Ruiz replied, "We have already. They say these Indians . . . the Aravaipas. Tracks lead here."

"Yes, and on to the Apache war trail, and down to Mexico."

Adams said, "No. I say let's settle these red niggers right now."

It was just talk, Choctaw thought. Hamilton had stood these men off. They weren't going to try a contest of arms with a dozen soldiers. But he wasn't sure what the Anglo with the red beard was going to do. He began to walk his horse up and down, as if to work off a rage within him. His grip was so tight on the rein his hand trembled.

Hamilton argued, "If the Aravaipas are doing all the raiding, where's the stock they've stolen? Can you see it around here?"

Ruiz declared, "It's hid out. Or maybe they sell it off. To buy bullets and guns."

Adams told Hamilton, "Could be they sell it to you."

"Damn you, mister!"

Redbeard spoke for the first time. "Hold up, Adams. I ain't saying that. But . . . all I know is . . . there's a hell of a lot of Indians here, and you haven't got the men to watch 'em all. Or *have* you?"

Hamilton asked, "Do I know you?"

"I'm Billy Parker. My brother was . . . one of those men the Apaches . . ."

"I'm sorry, Mister Parker —"

"Sorry ain't enough! My brother never

hurt any Indians. But he was murdered, and you don't seem to be doing nothing about it —" The man's voice choked off, and he turned his horse and rode off a dozen yards.

Choctaw felt embarrassment; he felt pity for Billy Parker, yet he felt a grin pulling at his mouth. It must be an instinct with him, he guessed. When he saw someone else in pain the first thing he wanted to do was grin, because it wasn't happening to him. He'd never be made to look so ridiculous, like Robertson or Billy Parker; he'd never let himself be hurt like they'd been, no matter how long he lived.

Oliver Wentworth addressed Choctaw. "Young Calvin Taylor. I'm surprised to see you here, boy."

"Mister Wentworth."

"What are you doing here?"

Adams said, "Easy to figure what's he doing. He's after the same as Robertson. You're squawing it. Another squaw lover. Ain't that it? I heard about it."

It was true, of course, but Choctaw cried furiously, "You lying bastard!" He kneed his red horse forward.

"If it's dark meat you're after —" Adams said, and twisted sideways to grin knowingly at the other Arizona Volunteers, "— there's plenty in Tucson for —"

Choctaw spurred his horse. The animal jumped forward. Adams tried to spin his horse away and the chestnut reared, whinnying fiercely. Choctaw dove from the saddle, striking against Adams. He clamped both arms around the other's chest and the two men fell between their pitching horses. Adams hit the ground hardest, because he was underneath. Dust boiled over them. A hoof grazed the boy's shoulder and he scrambled to his feet. His red horse backed away from him, walleyed, tossing its head in terror.

Adams was slower rising. Choctaw punched him right-handed and saw blood fly from Adams's nose. Adams hit Choctaw in the ribs and on the jaw. The boy found he could take these punches. There was nothing to this man, he decided, but threat and sneering. A little triumphant song began to sing in his head. Choctaw hooked a left into the man's ribs. Adams doubled over and grunted and went to one knee. The boy charged him, knocking him over, falling on top of him.

Adams grabbed at Choctaw's face, twisted his nose, fingers clawing for his eyes. Choctaw grabbed the other's testicles and squeezed. Adams gasped. He kicked out, his knee numbing Choctaw's arm and broke the boy's hold.

Both men rose, slowly. Adams swung a fist at Choctaw's throat but caught him high on the chest. Choctaw struck the man on the mouth with a right punch. Adams rocked backwards and fell, sprawling.

He took a long time sitting up. His mouth overflowed with blood. It ran over his shoulder and down the side of his shirt and into his pants.

Choctaw paused, breathing hard. For a moment, looking at Adams, weakness twisted in him, he felt revulsion and self-disgust. Then, in his head, the boy heard Adams say, "squaw lover." He heard the triumphant song again and lifted his fists and took a step forward, to finish this, to pound down on Adams until the words *squaw lover* were smashed from him.

A hand grabbed Choctaw's collar from behind. It was the lieutenant yanking him backwards. Choctaw struck at the soldier's hand and Hamilton shouted, "That's enough! What's the matter with you? He's finished."

Adams pushed himself to his feet. He stood, eyes unfocused. His mouth hung open, leaking blood.

Adams took three stiff-legged paces towards his horse. Choctaw saw the butt of the rifle in the saddle scabbard there and moved forward, but was too late. Adams slid the gun from the scabbard. It was a Henry carbine. He aimed the gun at the boy's stomach and began to work the lever.

# Chapter Twenty-Five

Choctaw froze.

It was about a dozen paces to where Adams stood, backed against his horse, the carbine leveled in his hands. In the time it would take Choctaw to throw himself across that distance Adams could shoot him, maybe twice. The boy decided if he was still alive in one minute, he'd take to wearing his holster gun regularly in the future. But even if he was wearing it now, Adams would still have the time to shoot him at least once before he could reach it. So again, Choctaw had jumped into something without thinking about it. Like he had running after Finn to rescue him, and what seemed a lot of times since. How many times could he rush into these fool things and get away with it?

He watched Adams brace the Henry's stock against his side and poke out his tongue and lick his bloody lips. The barrel of the carbine lifted slightly. Choctaw felt fear again, his belly filling with icy water. His feet were like iron weights and his head whirled with dizziness, like it wanted to corkscrew off his shoulders; and he knew he'd used up his ration of plunging into things unthinking, of pushing his crazy luck, because luck ran out, and his had run out, finally, here and now . . .

Wentworth called, "Adams!" He touched his horse's flanks lightly with his spurs and rode between the boy and his opponent.

Again he called, "Adams!"

Slowly, Adams lowered the gun. His eyes lost their craziness. The man swiped at his bloody mouth. He booted the carbine, stepped into the saddle, turned his horse, and rode back towards the Arizona Volunteers.

Choctaw swallowed a fair-sized mouthful of relief. He started to tremble. In a voice that was also shaky he said, "I'm beholden, Mister Wentworth."

Wentworth looked at Choctaw over his right shoulder. A faint smile curled his lips. For an instant his eyes looked into the boy's. Choctaw blinked at the contempt in them. They said, *"squaw lover."* The boy felt his cheeks warm, and his ears burn, and he balled his hands into fists.

Something changed in Wentworth's face.

He lifted his eyes and looked past Choctaw, towards the *rancheria.* Wentworth reached down unhurriedly and lifted his rifle from the saddle scabbard. It was a Yellow Boy Winchester.

Choctaw turned. To the east he saw riders coming on in a broken line. Through the dust that trailed behind them he saw other men running. Apaches.

Apache women began to emerge from their huts. Some of them shouted to their men.

Around Wentworth, weapons appeared. The line of Arizona Volunteers, three hundred yards distant, quivered with movement. Stars of brilliance leapt from metal all along the line as guns came up.

Robertson lifted his arms, palms forward, signifying halt. He began shouting at the oncoming riders in Apache. Hamilton went to join him. Some of the cavalrymen milled their horses in confusion.

Apache horsemen, nearing the village, fanned wide. Some of them were whipping their mounts into a dead run with their bows.

The riders forked into two bunches, drumming around the outermost wickiups. At a rifle shot from the nearest of the Arizona Volunteers they began to rein in their animals. Dust rolled and fell. Coyote pushed forward into view, riding his silver mule, Klosen and Zele flanking him. For a minute the Indians let their mounts shake their heads and blow.

Zele's face was black, covered in black ash and dirt. This wasn't war paint, Choctaw knew, but a sign of mourning. Klosen was in war paint. Spokes of yellow ocher radiated from a center at the bridge of his nose. Other Apaches had split their faces with a horizontal stripe of white, running from ear to ear. Some only had daubs of dirt and clay on their faces, token markings added hurriedly. Most of the Aravaipas had turned in their guns when they surrendered, but they bristled lances, some eight or nine feet long, knives, stone-headed clubs and hatchets, and many had arrows knocked to their bows.

Hamilton called, "Robertson! Talk for me." Through Robertson, Hamilton told Coyote, "*Jefe*, this must not happen."

Zele was shouting at the Arizona Volunteers in English. "You dirty bastards! You fucking bastards!" In a choked voice he told Hamilton, "They killed my son! May a snake eat them!"

Klosen cried, "They killed our children!"

"Are we men?" Coyote asked. "Do we

stand by and let them kill our families? Would white men let that happen to their families? They look just like the ones who butchered our women and children once before."

Hamilton said, "You mustn't fight, *jefe*. Tell your young men to wait. The Arizona Volunteers will go. I'll tell them and they'll go."

Coyote said, "You don't understand us. I'm not like a soldier chief. I can't tell them what to do. Each man does as he wishes."

"But they'll listen to you. Hold them back and I'll make the Volunteers leave."

Behind his war paint, Klosen grinned his broken grin savagely. He said, "Let's kill them now, so they can't come back and kill more of our helpless ones later."

Hamilton took the bridle of Coyote's mule. Coyote jerked the rein, the mule tossed its head, and the officer staggered forward, falling to his knees.

Hamilton rose slowly. Carefully, he brushed pink dust from his trousers.

"All right," he told Coyote. "Go ahead then, *jefe*. Fight! Look after your band by getting all your men killed."

Coyote scowled. Choctaw could see that struck home. Maybe the chief was wild with rage and grief, but he wasn't stupid. The

Arizona Volunteers outnumbered the Apache men; they were better armed, they had the choice of ground. On the other hand, the Aravaipas were encumbered with their families and their ponies were blown. Choctaw didn't doubt that the Volunteers would have a time of it, winkling the Apaches out of their *rancheria,* should a fight develop, but there could only be one outcome.

He could see Coyote and Klosen were thinking about that. But Zele was too far gone in his grief to see anything that clearly. He was another man crazy with loss, like Robertson before or Billy Parker now. He shouted, "What are we waiting for? They killed my son!"

Hamilton said, "The boy's still alive, Zele."

Coyote stared ahead grimly, studying the ground between the *rancheria* and the Arizona Volunteers. He said nothing.

Zele jerked on his mount's rein brutally, whirling the paint horse in a tight circle. "Well then. It's just me."

Hamilton told him, "But the boy isn't dead."

Tears mixed with the black ash and mud on Zele's face. They ran charcoal trails down his throat and stained the top of his polka dot shirt. Zele wore a bandolier in which three cartridges glinted. He carried a single-shot Springfield, the stock of which was broken and tied with rawhide. He had a bow and a lion-skin quiver rattling with cane arrows. "I'll take some of those snakes with me. Those cowards! Hey, Klosen, you know my black horse? The one with the three white feet? It's yours."

Hamilton cried, "Robertson, tell him the boy isn't dead!"

Coyote and Klosen both looked at Zele but said nothing. It was as if a glaze had scummed over their eyes, and a new dark skin lay over their copper faces.

*They're going to let him do it,* Choctaw thought. Zele was going to take on all fifty Arizona Volunteers single-handedly, and they were going to let him.

"Good luck, Zele," Coyote said.

Zele started to walk his pony up and down. He began to sing a monotonous low singing from deep in his throat that seemed to be just sounds, with no formed words.

Robertson said, "Listen to me. Your boy isn't dead, Zele. *No muerto!*"

Zele reined in his pony.

"Listen! He's with the soldier *médico.* Your woman took him there. He's still alive."

Zele stared. "Still alive?"

"Yes! It's true!"

"Can the *médico* make him live?"

"He'll do what he can."

Coyote gave a long sigh. Klosen reached over and gripped Zele's shoulder. "See, Zele. No need to die just yet." He grinned. Zele laughed shakily and put his fingers to his eyes and wept more black tears.

Coyote spoke to Hamilton. "You're the soldier chief. Make these dogs go now."

The lieutenant walked over to Wentworth and his party. "Get your people out of here, Mister Wentworth."

Wentworth said, "Lieutenant, I don't hold with what Adams said either. But you're wrong. These savages are playing you for a fool."

"Are they?"

"You're going to find out they are — too late."

Choctaw expected Wentworth to launch into a farewell speech. He was surprised and relieved to see the Englishman turn his horse and ride away. Billy Parker, Ruiz, and the two Papagos trailed after him. After a few moments the Arizona Volunteers moved off in a body and faded off to the west.

Hamilton stared after them. "I just hope that kid *is* still alive. Zele's boy."

Robertson said, "Hell, he better be. You said he was."

"He was two hours ago."

Choctaw said, "Christ, Lieutenant. You take some chances." He rubbed at his left-side ribs fiercely, where one of Adams's punches had hurt him after all.

Robertson advised, "I think you better send for some more soldiers, Lieutenant."

"From where? No more soldiers to be sent."

"When does Alford and his escort get back?"

"Two weeks, maybe three."

Robertson frowned. "What are you going to do until then?"

"I'll take Mister Adams's excellent advice."

"What's that?"

Hamilton smiled. "I'll sleep with one eye open."

# PART FOUR

PART FOUR

# CHAPTER TWENTY-SIX

Alope woke him as she slipped from under the blanket.

Choctaw opened his eyes reluctantly. It was false dawn, only a little color showing in the sky.

In Spanish he asked, "What is it?"

"A ghost bothers me."

That meant she'd had a bad dream, Choctaw knew. It didn't take much to arouse Apache superstitions — dreams, an owl hooting at the wrong time, animal tracks in a particular place, noises the wind made in a canyon. Although he couldn't see her, he knew what Alope would be doing. She carried some *hoddentin* — green tule seeds ground to a powder — in a little drawstring fetish bag. She'd be scattering this powder on the earth. He heard the girl mutter some words in Apache. Tossing *hoddentin* onto the ground, chanting a brief prayer, that was how Apaches placated a bothersome ghost.

Choctaw listened to the stillness and the early quiet. No one had a life as sweet and rich as his, he guessed. He turned the ring on his little finger where it was gripping tightly. The ring was a band of dull silver. Choctaw had bought it for a dollar from a street peddler in Tucson. Choctaw wondered what Finn was doing right now. Was he back in Tucson, or sweating over some haul to Yuma, or elsewhere? Probably he was waking now with early morning horniness, thinking about Little Gold Dollar. Choctaw smiled. Finn thought Little Gold Dollar was something. Finn had his one-dollar Mexican whore and Choctaw had Alope.

Coyotes started yelping, snarling, and howling in the chaparral. The racket they made brought a phrase into Choctaw's mind: "The wailing and gnashing of teeth." It must have been something his father had said. The old man fancied himself as a Bible shouter, especially when he was the worse for drink, or was working himself up to anger. The closer he got to God, it seemed, the meaner his temper became.

What would Pa think of his son now? A man, now, accepted as such by both whites and Apaches. Choctaw had killed a hostile Indian (or at least helped to); he'd fought for his life several times; and not only had he lost his virginity, he had a woman. He could make his way in the wildest country on the frontier.

There was a water bag, made from deer gut, hanging from a mesquite branch nearby. Alope drank, then passed the water bag to him. The girl said a few words in Apache under her breath. Another prayer, Choctaw guessed. He said, "It's only a dream."

Alope slid back under the blanket. "But dreams can tell you things. Don't you believe that?"

He kissed Alope on her shoulder and on her neck.

She said, "You don't believe in anything."

"Not much."

"What do you believe in? Do Anglos believe in *U-sen*?"

"Sure. God."

"Do you believe in God?"

"For Christ's sake!" Choctaw said in English. Returning to Spanish he admitted, "I don't know. Sometimes."

"The People believe *U-sen* is always there watching over us."

"Anglos think the same about their God."

"So, if God is always there, watching, how come you only believe in him sometimes?"

"Maybe . . . sometimes I want to forget he's there, watching."

"Why? I don't understand."

Choctaw rubbed the back of his head. "Anglos think . . . God's always trying to catch us out . . . catch us doing something bad. You know what God was watching closest, a while back? You and me . . . while we was making love."

He'd been trying to steer the conversation away from God into something funny, but it wasn't working. There was enough light now to see how earnestly Alope was watching him. Apaches laughed easily at most things, but not at their religion. It was a damn serious, almost life and death, business to them. They had no sense of humor about God.

Alope frowned. She asked, "Why? Were we doing something bad?"

He could see she'd taken it all the wrong way. "No."

"You think what we were doing was wrong. Why? Because you're white and I'm an Indian?"

"No." He hugged her to him. "No, it wasn't anything bad. It was good."

The girl squirmed away from him. She pushed up out of the blanket. "You think what we were doing was bad."

"No. There was nothing bad about what

we were doing, Alope."

She went and stood a distance from him. In English Choctaw said, "Shit!" He pulled on his drawers and his jeans, shook out his boots, and squirmed his feet into them. He went over to her. Choctaw put his hand on her arm and she shook it off.

After a long moment the girl half-turned towards him. Not looking at him fully Alope said, "At the White River there was a black-robe who talked to us about God."

"A priest?"

"He said God loved the white man and the Indian both. Coyote said, 'I guess he must love the white man more, because the Indian has always been cold and hungry since the white man came.'"

Choctaw smiled.

She said, "We'd better get back to camp."

Choctaw knew what was eating at her. It was rubbing away at him, too. It was all this skulking about, sneaking out of camp, covering with small lies, finding hidden places to meet . . . Choctaw remembered Adams. Was the man just talking, flinging out the worst insults he could think of, or were they really discovered? Did Coyote know what Alope was up to? Did he even have time to care? His younger wife was near her time; he had all sorts of other problems . . .

Choctaw could come out in the open. Give Coyote two horses, maybe a bottle of whiskey, and a few odds and ends, and he and Alope would be married — Apache style — providing Coyote accepted his gifts. But how would Coyote feel about it? And how would Klosen react?

There was no possibility of marrying Alope white man fashion. By Arizona law, whites weren't permitted to marry Indians. Even if he could marry her, there'd be no living amongst the settlers out here, not with an Apache wife.

If he was going to live with an Apache girl, anywhere in white society, it would have to be far away. Back east, perhaps. But that was a fantasy. He could never take Alope out of her world. Everyone knew wild Indians sickened and died in exile, as if the wilderness itself was life to them. All they could do was carry on, in secret, as they had been doing. But Choctaw decided to tell Robertson. He'd have to tell someone soon, or go crazy.

Alope left on foot, for the *rancheria*. Choctaw was supposed to be out hunting, so he rode up into the hills, following a deer trail. The boy found a sheltered place to roost, overlooking a water hole. Around midmorning a band of black-tailed deer

288

came to water. Choctaw shot a buck and gutted and bled his kill. He slung the carcass over the withers of his horse and rode back to the Aravaipa camp.

Robertson was there, talking to the Skunk. Robertson said, "Well, hell, you shot something. I was just about to give up on you shooting for the pot."

"I figure I'm just getting my eye in." Choctaw tried not to smirk when he said that.

Robertson gave him a sharp look. "I suppose you was hunting overnight again."

I'm going to tell him, Choctaw decided.

Instead he said, "Soldiers coming."

Two cavalrymen rode up, Lieutenant Hamilton and his orderly. They dismounted and strode over to the two civilians. Choctaw was surprised when Hamilton addressed him first. "I want a word with you, boy."

"What about?"

"Want to earn some army money?"

"Doing what, Lieutenant?"

"You've got a good horse, haven't you? I'm sending some dispatches to Tucson. I can only spare one man for the job. Would you pair up with him?"

"Why can't he go alone?"

"Not safe. Especially right now." Hamilton frowned and Choctaw knew he was thinking about the massacre on the St. David road. "There's one lot of dispatches for Fort Lowell." That was the Tucson cantonment, just outside town. "I want those to go right away. There's another set for Camp Crittenden. They're not so urgent. You can have a day or two off in Tucson before you deliver them. Hear the owl hoot."

"Where's Camp Crittenden?"

"About fifty miles south of Tucson. Chiricahua country, so you'll have to watch out. You still want to go?"

"Yeah. If the money's any good."

Robertson asked, "Sure your dispatches'll be safe with this here crazy kid, Lieutenant?"

Hamilton smiled. "Seems to me he can take care of himself. I've got to talk to Coyote. Come to my quarters afterwards and I'll give you the dispatches. We can talk about money then."

"Okay."

"Robertson, will you come interpret for me?"

The scout nodded. The officer turned and walked towards Coyote's wickiup, Robertson following.

# CHAPTER TWENTY-SEVEN

Coyote said, "Sit down. Have you eaten?"

Hamilton smiled. "Thank you, *jefe.*"

Robertson and Hamilton settled themselves on pallets on the floor of the wickiup, easing their backs against the breaking boards. Coyote also sat. A small yellow dog nosed around his legs. He fondled the pup's ears and pushed it gently towards the entrance of the wickiup. The dog left the hut, tail wagging.

Coyote handed out *macuche* cigarettes and they lit up.

Coyote looked tired, Hamilton thought, and there was strain in the smile he was trying to keep. He looked restless and defensive. He asked, "How's the child?"

Through Robertson, Hamilton told him, "He'll live, the doctor says."

"Good." Coyote studied his cigarette. He might sit in silent contemplation for thirty seconds or thirty minutes, Hamilton knew.

Indians didn't worry about time like a white man. They thought they had an eternity in which to do things.

Normally Hamilton would sit and let time drift and work his way 'round to what concerned him by degrees, but now he said abruptly, "*Jefe,* Klosen isn't in camp."

Coyote looked faintly surprised at Hamilton's rudeness. He replied, "Two days ago was the counting day. He was here then."

"But he isn't here today. And he wasn't here yesterday."

"Maybe he's gone hunting."

"I must know where everyone is, every day."

"Then you'll know more than I do."

"*Jefe,* that's no good and you know it. If some of your young men go off raiding . . . if they've gone on a revenge raid, because of Zele's son . . ."

"Klosen hasn't gone raiding."

"The last time you said he'd gone off hunting wild pigs."

"That's true, he had."

"And where is he now?"

The smile was altogether gone from Coyote's face. Irritation built in his voice. "I don't know . . . maybe he's left the band. I'm not like a soldier chief. I can't tell Klosen to stay here, or go there. All I can

292

do is kill him." He scowled and flashed Hamilton a hard, accusing look. "Do you want me to do that?"

In his mind Hamilton saw the two men tied to the wagon, heads pointing down into the torture fires. *That might be the best idea,* Hamilton thought, and was instantly a little ashamed of the thought. There was no proof Klosen was on that raid, or any other.

Coyote explained patiently, "The young men know what I've said to you, that the fighting's finished. If they still want to fight, they have to leave this camp."

"Is that why Klosen left?"

The Apache's face grew stony. That was something an Indian could do easily, make his face unreadable.

Hamilton said, "You know how hard it's going to be to make this work. There are those who'd like to see the fighting start again. White men *and* Indians. And others think your band should be moved to the White Mountain Agency." Hamilton paused and added, "Your people *would* be safer there."

"We've talked about that."

"*Jefe,* understand me. I'm only a soldier. I have to do as my chief tells me, and what his chief tells him."

"Will they tell you to move us to the White

Mountains?"

"They might," Hamilton admitted. "They could give me that order."

"Will you obey them?"

"I'll have to, if I want to stay a soldier. Otherwise all I can do is take off this blue coat and leave the army. Like Klosen . . . like you said . . . if he can't live at peace, he has to leave the band. Is that what he did, *jefe*?"

"Will you take off your blue coat, if you receive that order?"

"I can help you better as a soldier."

Coyote's mouth twisted. For the first time Hamilton saw open hostility in the man's broad, tired face. "Help to herd the People around like cattle? Your chief tells you, and his chief tells him. No one asks the Apache."

Hamilton leaned forward. "*Jefe,* once the Apaches were the power in this country. Your power was terrible. Everyone was afraid of you. Things have changed. Now the white man decides what will happen. He may say the Aravaipas have to go to the White Mountains for their own protection."

"Sure." Coyote sneered. "And after the People have left their own country, the white man will protect it. He'll take good care of it."

Hamilton had to smile at the other's

sarcasm. "All right, that's true. Long ago, the Aravaipas did the same. They took this country —"

"This is Aravaipa country and always has been."

"No, *jefe.* You came down from the north and took this country from other Indians. You did that because you were strong. Now it's being taken from you."

"What other Indians? As long as anyone in this camp can remember this has been Aravaipa country."

Which was probably true, as far as it went, Hamilton thought. He asked, "Where's Klosen, *jefe?*"

"I don't know." Coyote began to build another cigarette carefully. "I think maybe he went up north to visit some relatives."

"Relatives?"

Friendly relatives on the White Mountain Agency, Hamilton thought, or hostile relatives in war paint, among the Pinal bands? He could see from Coyote's face that he wasn't going to find out. Coyote smiled and it was a friendly smile, but it was a shield also. Behind the shield his face was inscrutable, a bronze mask. The interview was over. Hamilton could sit here the rest of the day and would learn nothing more.

*"Buenas tardes, jefe."*

Outside the wickiup Hamilton blinked against the sunlight. Coyote's dog came to sniff around his boots. The lieutenant asked Robertson, "Well, what do you think?"

Robertson lifted an arm to shade his face from the sun. "Something seems to have got Coyote pretty down in the mouth. Maybe he's been listening to the shaman. Looked at a lot of signs and portents and such. Said the future for the band looked pretty bad."

"He wouldn't need a shaman to tell him that." Hamilton crouched and rubbed the ribshot flanks of the yellow dog. The animal sat on its haunches and scratched its side furiously with a hind paw. "I think it's something else. Maybe he knows Klosen's gone on a raid. Goddammit!"

"Maybe Coyote was telling the truth about Klosen."

"Sniff around camp, would you? See what you can find out. See how many others might be missing besides Klosen."

"Why not have an extra counting day? Get them together and count them?"

"I'd rather not do that."

"You figure if you do that, the Aravaipas might panic, might break out?"

"I don't know. I think Coyote's expecting his band'll be moved up to the White Moun-

296

tain Agency."

Robertson frowned. "So he probably thinks he's betrayed his people."

"Find out what you can, Robertson. But ask quietly. If anything else spooks them, this camp might blow up right in our faces."

Choctaw smoked a cigarette, waiting for Robertson and Hamilton. He was watching some Aravaipa men and women down by the creek. They had dug straight furrows and had planted corn and beans in them. Now Skunk was blessing the crops. He threw *hoddentin* on the newly turned earth and shook a rattle, a tortoiseshell full of stones, tied to the end of a stick. He began to croon a monotonous song and danced a slow, stamping dance on the planting ground. Some of the onlookers, leaning on their wooden hoes, added their voices to his. This would be the harvest song. Alope had told Choctaw the words and he was glad the others joined in, as they hid Skunk's awful, out-of-tune singing.

*When you plant in the spring,*
*You hope in the summer it will bring*
*A good harvest in the fall.*
*A good life, if there's enough for all.*

A party of women had come in from cutting hay. They left their hay bundles in piles and went over to join in the singing. When the song was over, they stood about, laughing and talking, whilst Skunk continued chanting and scattering *hoddentin*. They looked a pretty happy bunch, with the prospect of something in their bellies this fall. Alope was amongst them.

Robertson and Hamilton emerged from Coyote's wickiup. The two men stood talking, then the soldier moved off. Robertson walked over to Choctaw.

*What would be the harm,* thought Choctaw, *if I told Robertson?* But he knew what the harm would be. John Shadler had said it. "If there's anything worse than an Indian it's a white man who squaws with 'em." Jack Adams had said it. *"Squaw lover."* Oliver Wentworth had said the same thing with the look in his eyes. Choctaw thought of Alope and knew they were wrong, all of them. But as Robertson came and stood alongside him, the words Choctaw needed to say died in his throat. He stared at the earth and said nothing.

Robertson began to make a cigarette.

"Funny," he observed. "Things are happening faster than I'd ever have believed."

He paused, maybe inviting the boy to comment. Choctaw remained silent.

Robertson said, "I thought this country would be wild forever. But I've seen how it's changed. In ten years, it'll be a different world. Ranches, towns all over. Won't be any free Indians then. They'll all be rotting on some miserable reservation. Or dead, maybe."

"Why you telling me this?"

Robertson looked at him, glanced over at the Aravaipas by the creek, then back at Choctaw. "Just something to think on."

Choctaw stared at the earth a minute longer. He walked over to Alope.

She looked up in surprise at his approach. Alope glanced over his shoulder at the other women, at Robertson, and there was fright in her eyes.

Choctaw twisted the ring from his little finger. "This is for you."

All at once it didn't seem enough, a dollar trinket, even if it was all he had to give. "It was my mother's," he lied. "Her name was —"

Alope lifted a hand. "You mustn't say the names of dead people. Ghosts are listening for you doing that, and they'll bring you bad luck."

Most of the fear left her eyes. She looked at the ring and a nervous smile trembled on her lips.

Choctaw felt Apache eyes on him. He could see Robertson watching him. The boy's ears grew stinging hot, and he felt his cheeks and his neck warm with color. He slid the ring on her next-littlest finger, the third finger of her right hand. He said, "I don't believe in anything, Alope, you know that." He touched the tips of her fingers. Choctaw turned and walked back to his horse and stepped into the saddle. Riding out of camp, he saw Robertson was still watching him.

# CHAPTER TWENTY-EIGHT

Private Kenney turned his horse and rode out of camp. Choctaw followed a short distance behind, on his sorrel horse. Hamilton watched the riders until they shrank to almost nothing amidst the saguaro and chaparral.

The officer walked back to his quarters. Hamilton sat at his desk, then poured a drink. He noticed that his hand holding the tooth glass trembled slightly.

Scanlon entered.

"Drink, Pat?"

Hamilton poured for both of them.

Scanlon sat carefully on a chair made of mesquite wood. "The kid'll be all right. Looked a lot worse than it was."

"Good."

"Did you find your missing Indians?"

"Coyote said they might be off hunting. Or they might have left the band."

"Does he know? Or care?"

"They could've left the camp. Gone back north."

"You look tired, Austin."

"Aren't we all? I could sleep for a thousand years. I will, soon as Alford gets back."

"Not on army time you won't." Scanlon turned the glass in his hand. "You sent for more men?"

"Vain hope. But with fifty troopers I can't do a damn thing. I can't do the job I was sent here to do in the first place. I can't stop the Apaches from breaking out, or Arizona Volunteers from raiding in."

"Oliver Wentworth wrote to General Stoneman, do you know that?"

"How do you know?"

"I heard."

"There's no accommodating these people, Pat. They don't even want the agencies. They won't be happy whilst there's one live Apache in Arizona. All they know is hatred."

"Do you blame them?" Scanlon poured himself another two fingers of mescal. "The likes of that feller, whatshisname, Adams . . . for him it's just an excuse to let out his sickness. But Wentworth, Ruiz, men who've built up this country . . . you're not a saying it's the same with them?"

"On that issue, maybe it is."

"You're wrong, Austin."

"Everybody seems to think so."

"These are sane men. They see things the way they are."

Hamilton lit a cigar. "And I don't, is that what you're saying? I look at an Apache and see a human being. They see a murderer, a bloodthirsty, treacherous savage . . ."

"Well, aren't they? Savages? Isn't it your job to look after your own?"

Hamilton smiled. "Good question. That's it . . . in a nutshell."

"I see you sent Private Kenney with the dispatches."

"Not my first choice. He was the only man I could spare."

"Do you really expect to see him again?"

"Good riddance."

Scanlon emptied his glass. "But you should see that boy, Choctaw, again. He'll come back. I hear he's got a squaw up in the Indian camp."

"Huh?"

"Just repeating tittle-tattle."

"What squaw?"

"That one . . . whatshername . . . Alope."

Hamilton studied his glass. "I never took you for the village gossip, Pat."

Scanlon eased himself to his feet. Quick pain crossed his face; perhaps his leg was hurting. "My new role in life. Pathetic, isn't it?"

"Come over after taps. Maybe we can get this bottle finished, finally."

"If I can."

Scanlon limped across the yard towards the post hospital. Hamilton stared into the distance. Down the Tucson road he couldn't even see the riders' dust now. Looking at the desert, the mountains edged like knives, the sky a metallic shield, he remembered gentle country, with fences, green fields, plentiful houses and people. About Arizona they said, "Everything that grows pricks; everything that breathes bites." This hard, alien land didn't belong to the white man, Hamilton decided. It belonged to the coyotes. And the Apaches.

He returned to his desk. Hamilton stared at the bottle on the table. So the boy was sparking Alope? In his mind Hamilton saw the boy and Alope together, and then the picture changed, and Hamilton was Alope's partner. He pushed the thought away. No woman for him, just Camp Walsh, loneliness inside him and an unfeeling vastness outside. He couldn't ever remember feeling so tired. Hamilton lifted the bottle and splashed mescal into the tooth glass, up to the brim.

Choctaw and Private Kenney reached the outskirts of Tucson at dusk the following day. Both men dismounted on a hillside overlooking the town and sat in a patch of bear grass. They rubbed cramps from their legs while their horses blew.

Kenney said, "Hey, kid. I got an idea."

"Oh?"

The two riders hadn't talked much in the fifty-odd miles from Camp Walsh. Choctaw hadn't taken to Kenney. He didn't care for the evasiveness in the man's narrow-set eyes and Kenney smiled too much for a man with his splayed, rodent teeth. You couldn't help the way you looked, of course, but Choctaw didn't trust the soldier.

"Instead of laying over in Tucson," Kenney said, "why don't we go straight on to Crittenden? Say around dusk tomorrow, when these animals have rested up. Safer traveling at night. And we can make up some time, so we've got more time to spend in Tucson on the way back."

"What if these horses ain't up to it?"

"They should be."

Choctaw thought about Tucson. Something about the town made him uneasy.

305

Perhaps he'd been out in the wilds too long. The boy said, "Okay by me."

They delivered the dispatches to Fort Lowell, then Choctaw rode into town. He cut the trail dust with a drink at the Elephant, then wandered over to the Lucky Strike. The same large, red-bearded man was there, tending bar. Choctaw bought a St. Louis beer. A hand struck him firmly on the back. He spilled a little of his beer and Finn laughed. He said, "I figured you was going to drink it, not take a bath in it. Horse-screwer."

"Finn, you one-dollar whoring bastard."

"Choctaw, you piece of clap-ridden mule shit."

"Son of the Great Whore."

"Fornicating piss ant."

Pleasantries exchanged, the boys bought each other drinks. Halfway down his second beer Choctaw asked, "How was the run to Yuma?"

"Just awful."

"You get to California?"

"No. Why? You fancy joining up again?"

"No thanks. Town's quiet, ain't it? Where is everybody?"

"Ain't you heard?"

The bar dog, running a drying towel over dirty glasses, told Choctaw, "Apaches hit a place nine miles outside town. Folks are out chasing 'em."

Finn said, "Them devils run off some horses and mules. Carried off a Mexican woman."

The bar dog frowned. "Atanacia Rodriguez. Terrible thing."

Apaches sometimes kidnapped women and children to make up their war losses, Choctaw knew, though this practice seemed to be fast dying out.

Finn said, "John Shadler went after 'em with one bunch and Oliver Wentworth another. We'll catch 'em this time."

Choctaw sipped his beer. "Nine miles."

The bar dog declared, "They've never swung so close to town before. I expect any day now them Camp Walsh Indians'll come howling right down main street there."

"Who says the Camp Walsh Indians done it?"

"Everybody knows it's them soldiers' pets." The bar dog gave Choctaw a knowing look with his one good eye. "Ever since they got settled at Walsh, the raiding's been worse than ever. Never been so bad. I say kill the lot of 'em. I wouldn't leave a live Indian up at Walsh. And that damn soldier, Hamilton, I'd shoot him first. If he came in here, right now, I'd kill him myself."

The barman moved over to other customers.

Choctaw asked Finn, "How come you ain't out with the posse?"

"My mule got a stone bruise. Anyway," Finn added hastily, "the outfit's set to be moving out again."

He was sounding defensive, Choctaw thought. *Maybe he doesn't want me to think he's played the coward again.*

Quickly Finn went on. "Talk is . . . there's going to be a raid."

"A raid?"

"Oliver Wentworth's been talking to folks in town. To the friendly Indians — the Papagos. And around the Mexican quarter."

"A raid?"

"On Camp Walsh. What's your plans for this evening?"

"What's yours? Little Gold Dollar?"

"Why not? Don't you get lonely for women?"

Choctaw smirked. "I got a woman." It was said, out of his mouth before he'd even thought what he was going to say.

"Like hell you have."

"Oh no?"

"Ain't no women up at Walsh. Only soldiers' women come payday. Only soldier'll go with them."

"Let's drink someplace else."

"It's all right here. You got yourself a soldier's woman, Choc?"

"It ain't a soldier's woman."

"You got a soldier's woman? You got a soldier's woman, Choc?"

"Fuck yourself, Finn."

"Fuck yourself, yourself."

There was a racket of hooves in the street outside, a clamor of voices. Some men entered noisily, Anglos and Mexicans. Straightaway Choctaw identified Billy Parker amongst them. There was another man he knew there, a scarecrow-thin Mexican. Yesquez, Vasquez? The man was part of a Tucson outfit that freighted to Camp Walsh. He and Choctaw had spoken a few times.

The newcomers were talking all at once, grinning and laughing, slapping each other on the back. Vasquez started waving a pair of saddlebags around his head and yelling. Other men, entering, shouted questions and the din thickened. It was a time before Choctaw could make out words, or sort out what was happening. Parker, Vasquez, and the others were possemen, hot from the Apache chase. Men were asking them, "Did you get them? Did you get the Indians?"

Vasquez cried, "We got this!" He lifted something from his saddlebags; it hung from his fist, a couple of feet long. In the glimmer of coal-oil lamps the hair still had its sheeny blackness. The room erupted in whoops and cheers. Vasquez declared, "She is prettiest shot I ever make."

It seemed the Apaches had zigzagged for fifty miles through bad country, trying to shake pursuit, but in Tanque Verde Wash the posse came in sight of the raiders at last. The Apache rearguard, a young man on a staggering pony, had been trying to herd the mules up a canyon, but got within range of Vasquez's Sharps rifle. The Mexican had made his pretty shot and got his scalp. The posse had recaptured the mules but the other raiders had escaped, and there was no sign of Atanacia Rodriguez.

Vasquez had his back pounded until it was probably sore. Drinks were thrust into his hand. "That was me, a month ago," Choctaw told Finn. Someone asked Vasquez, "Who do you figure it was? Cherry-Cows?"

Vasquez, enjoying his glory, grinned triumphantly and announced, "Camp Walsh Indian sure."

"How do you know?"

"I know him. That one I kill." Vasquez stabbed a finger into his mouth, pressing his fingertip against his front upper teeth. "I remember him from tooth out here. I seen

310

him up at Camp Walsh plenty times. I think I even talk to him once. He's called Klosen."

"Sure," agreed Billy Parker. "Klosen. I seen him too. Just after the St. David massacre. After the Apaches murdered my brother — and other good men. Fat, with his front teeth missing. I seen him up at Camp Walsh."

Choctaw heard Parker yell, "Now we know the truth about them soldiers' pets!" Then the din closed over Parker's voice, and all other individual voices. The possemen, and most of the onlookers, crashed out of the Lucky Strike and into the street. Vasquez would be taking his scalp around the bars, Choctaw guessed, milking it for all the free drinks it was worth. Around him Choctaw heard men talking in excited and angry voices. The posse had dosed the savages in their own medicine. It was about time too; the words *Camp Walsh* and *Hamilton's pets* came again and again.

"Well, now we know," Finn said. "It's got to be them at Walsh, whatever that Indian-loving soldier says."

Choctaw stared hard at the glass in his hand. "If it was a Camp Walsh Apache they killed."

"You heard, Choc. That Indian had his tooth out at the front. How many Apaches

311

are there gonna be like that?"

"Not so many, I guess."

"Only one, I figure. This Klosen. Damn treacherous savages." Finn wiped foam from his lips. "Hey, Choc, you were up there. Maybe you knew that Indian they killed?"

"Huh?"

"Maybe you knew that Indian they killed?"

Choctaw finished his beer. He was suddenly afraid. His mind was shouting: Alope, Alope, Alope. He said, "I knew him."

# CHAPTER TWENTY-NINE

A meeting was called, to discuss the "Indian menace." It was to be held in the court-house, at eight o'clock the next evening.

Finn didn't plan to attend. He spent the next morning and afternoon working in the Schmitt and Gottlieb freight yard, repairing wagons and mule gear. After work Finn poked around the mescal shops and stores in the Mexican quarter, looking for Choctaw. From some soldiers he learned his friend had ridden out of town on army business. Finn went back to the saloons and found himself drinking with Danny McClure. Just before eight he followed the Ulsterman — and a crowd of other men — out of the Elephant and into the courthouse.

The meeting wasn't held in the courtroom but in a large office to the side. The office was reasonably full, perhaps sixty men attending. Almost all of them had to stand. Mesquite fires glowed in several stoves and kerosene lamps scattered smoky, dark-yellow light across the room.

Finn saw Alfredo Ruiz and a handful of Mexicans in the crowd. The rest of the congregation were Anglos. Sitting behind a pine-top desk, on a raised platform at one end of the room, was Oliver Wentworth and, next to him, John Shadler.

Wentworth rose to speak first.

He told the assembly that, following the massacre on the St. David's trail, he'd written to General Stoneman himself. "I told him we were slowly being murdered off by the protected Indians at Camp Walsh. If nothing was done about it, up to five hundred stockmen in the immediate vicinity of Tucson would remain in danger of their lives, or be driven from the territory. Alas," Wentworth stared gloomily at the desk top a moment, "the reply was all that I had cause to expect. And fear. Paltry excuses about the lack of men, the shortage of good horses and remounts, the confusion over Indian policy directed by Washington. Excuses why the army could not be more effective in subduing the Apaches. The essence of Stoneman's reply was this: *five hundred stockmen should be able to look after themselves.* In short, gentlemen, we pay our taxes for the army but we can expect no help from them."

Angry voices were raised in the room. Somebody called, "No, they're too damn busy protecting the savages," and other men shouted in agreement.

Wentworth continued, "I then thought of writing directly to President Grant himself. But what would be the point? We know where Grant stands . . . on the side of those lily-livered apologists for Poor Lo — for the noble red man — for fiends, thieves, and murderers. Even if Grant did reply to my letter it would only be to send his Quaker friends out here, to cure the Apaches with kindness.

"Kindness? Kindness for these killers? These cowardly, treacherous assassins? I say no! I'd show them the same kindness they show to their victims. I say strike them and strike them hard."

Listeners shouted "Yes!" and "That's right!" and formless words of agreement, and a few punched the air. It was turning into a regular camp meeting, Finn thought. He prepared to enjoy himself. Wentworth began to recount the details of one Apache atrocity after another. He even spoke of the attack on the Schmitt and Gottlieb wagons. That was nearly three months ago but mention of it made the boy's skin feel tight and hot, and he noticed he'd made his hands into fists. Finn's throat was dry with the same fear he'd felt during the attack. He glanced over at John Shadler. Shadler was still ash-pale from his wound and his eyes remained feverish, his mouth set in a hard, unforgiving line. As Wentworth described, "Teamsters going about their honest business brutally slain . . ." Shadler's mouth tightened.

Finn found his thoughts drifting, back to the saloon last night. So Choctaw had a woman, had he? Or was he just lying? There weren't any women up at Camp Walsh except those soldiers bought with their pay. Those women only went up to the camp on payday, made their money, and came back to town the next day.

Just for a second another thought struck Finn. What if Choctaw had an Apache squaw up at Camp Walsh? The idea frightened him; he didn't know where it had come from. Finn hated and feared this country and all that went with it. But Choctaw was a strange one, he felt differently. He'd moved back into the wilderness, leaving the safety of town for Camp Walsh, out on the edge of nowhere. Perhaps there was a strain of wildness in Choctaw that answered to the desert and the Indians.

Maybe that's why the idea of him having a squaw had come.

Finn didn't want to think of Choctaw squawing it; he didn't like where those thoughts took him. He pulled his attention back to the here and now.

Wentworth was saying, ". . . Now we know the Camp Walsh truce to be nothing more than a cruel farce, as many of us feared. We have the evidence of the kidnappers of poor Señora Rodriguez — the one raider killed in the performance of this dastardly act has been positively identified as a Camp Walsh Indian. Perhaps General Stoneman gave us the answer we need after all. Five hundred men *can* look after themselves . . . *if we have to.* We know what we have to do, and have been given free rein to do it.

"Not only has the white race suffered. The Mexican community has its own grievous losses to mourn. The Papago Indians have always been our friends. Their people have been killed, their stock stolen. Despite their loyalty and hospitality, the army does nothing to ease the suffering of the Papagos. I say the situation is intolerable for all concerned — Anglos, Mexicans, and friendly Indians — and that joining together, our three races can prevail. I have spoken with the Papagos. They can send us a hundred

317

men. Señor Ruiz has found recruits among the Mexican populace. I have the promise of a shipment of arms. We have the men. The time to act is now!"

There were cheers. Wentworth asked, "Mister Shadler, would you care to speak?"

John Shadler took his time standing up, getting ready to speak. Maybe he was still slow from the old wound, or maybe it was for effect. No one was talking when he began. Instead there was a thick, expectant silence. Some of the Mexicans, who'd only been half-listening to Wentworth, now stared sharply.

Shadler told his audience, "I'll keep this short as I ain't one for speeches. Mister Wentworth can do that better than me. But he doesn't just talk, he does, and the time for doing's here. Like Mister Wentworth said, ever since that miserable, Apache-loving son of a bitch Hamilton has been using United States soldiers to protect those that murder its citizens, this country's been going all to hell. There was a cowboy who came into town from the back country only last week. He came to get himself measured up for his coffin. He figured the way things are going, the corpse should be available any day."

Finn was surprised to hear men laugh at

this, but it was bitter laughter, full of anger. "Men, what with Grant, Stoneman, and that damn specimen Hamilton, what are we to do? Lie down in our coffins and wait until it's our turn to get our throats cut?" He paused, and the room listened. "I say the hell with that!"

Men took up his words; the room was filled with shouts of agreement. Finn hadn't taken Shadler for a natural stump orator, but, with a few sentences, he held this crowd. They shouted with him, and for him. When he leaned forward to speak again, the room quieted.

"Men, you've heard Mister Wentworth — we've got Mexicans to help us, and Papago Indians. And we've got guns. But we need Americans in this, too." Shadler looked gravely at his audience. "Now there's plenty mouth fighters in this town. Fellers talk a good fight. If hot air killed Indians, way they talk it up, there wouldn't be an Apache left in Arizona now. But I don't want any of those with me — damn cowardly blowers. I want men who'll be there when it counts. When the bullets fly. Men with the guts to side me in a real fight."

He had them, if the shouting from the floor was anything to go by. Shadler lifted one hand for quiet. "If you're with me, there's one thing you need first. A damn close mouth. I want men who can shut up and keep shut up. There's leaky mouths all over Tucson. There's even some Indian lovers in this town. It wouldn't do for them to hear about this, or the army.

"Second, you need a good horse or mule, supplies for a week, and a gun that'll kill Indians. So get it cleaned. And be ready to move in five or six days. If everybody keeps shut, and holds fast, we'll have something to celebrate — and soon. We'll give the Apaches a lesson they'll never forget. They'll think twice, or a hundred times, before they dare murder a white man again. Or a woman. Or a child." Shadler had to lift his voice over the cheers of the crowd. "We've all got scores to settle, and now's the time. We know who, now, and where. I go with Oliver Wentworth. I say like him — strike them hard! Strike them hard!"

Shadler sat down. Men were clapping and shouting and cheering. Finn found himself shouting with the rest. It was fun, like listening to the fiery speeches of camp meetings. Even as he cheered, however, Finn knew responding to hot talk about dead Apaches, in the safety of a crowd, was one thing; fighting live ones, up in the mountains, was entirely another. How many of these men would still be there when the rifles snarled and the bullets flew?

Finn came to a decision. He wasn't going to be one of them, one of the mouth fighters and blowers Shadler scorned. Finn had played the coward once, shaming himself when the Apaches jumped the freight wagons. It wouldn't happen again. He'd side John Shadler this time. He'd do all he was required to do, and more, in whatever came next.

Choctaw and Kenney left Tucson late in the afternoon, traveling partly through the night. They laid up during the worst of the next day's heat and rode into Camp Crittenden in the early dusk. Their horses needed to rest the next day, so Choctaw spent the time loafing around the camp, a scatter of adobes and tents, sitting in the middle of a lot of emptiness, not unlike Camp Walsh. He played cards with some soldiers, drank green Mexican beer at the sutler's, and was thoroughly bored. Next morning, he looked for Private Kenney and couldn't find him.

A corporal told him, "Looks like your friend's skipped."

"Huh?"

"Deserted. Horse's gone, and all his gear.

He probably made a run for the border. First Mex town he gets to, he could sell his horse, or his gun, or his saddle, and end up the richest man in town."

Choctaw remembered Kenney's anxiousness about not dawdling in Tucson, wanting to push on south. "Maybe."

"Still . . ." The corporal fingered one handlebar of his mustache. "He might be unlucky. Border's only thirty miles, but the nearest town that way's about a hundred. Bad country 'tween here and there. Bad water, bad Indians. Horse only needs to go lame . . ."

"I suspicion Kenney'll make out. He's the type."

"Who knows?"

"You seem to know all about it. Maybe you thought about going over the hill yourself?"

"Sure. What the hell else is there to think about, in a hole like this?"

"I got to get back to Tucson."

The soldier started fingering the other wing of his mustache. "By yourself?"

"I can lay up part of the day and get some travel done at night."

"Pretty risky. You got to sleep. Who's gonna watch out for wild Indians then? You're better waiting 'til someone can be spared to go with you."

"I've got to get back to Camp Walsh."

"Why? I hear it's even worse than this place."

"I got reasons."

"I think you're crazy, kid."

"I got reasons."

Choctaw rode back to Tucson alone. He saw no Indians the first day. On the second day he saw moving dust about ten miles south of Tucson and went into cover until it passed. Where the dust had been, he found tracks of shod and unshod horses and mules, and moccasin prints. He also found a club, made of hard mesquite, ball-like at one end, tapering to a point at the other, where there was a looped leather thong.

There was too much dust and sign for it to have been hostiles so Choctaw guessed they had been Papagos. Perhaps they were hunting off their agency, or going to trade somewhere.

Choctaw tucked the club in his saddle-bags. He forgot about the Papagos and rode into Tucson, reaching the old pueblo shortly after dark.

He made for the Schmitt and Gottlieb freight yard, hoping Finn was about. He thought he recognized a man crossing the street by the teamsters' yard. Choctaw rode towards him, calling, "Robertson!" But when the man turned and stepped from the shadows into the early moonlight, Choctaw saw it was John Shadler.

# CHAPTER THIRTY

Choctaw didn't want to look at Shadler. He thought: *he'll see the guilt in my face.* But he looked and was surprised to see a guilty expression on Shadler's face also.

The wagon boss took Choctaw's horse by the bridle. "Choctaw. How're you, boy?"

The boy smiled but he could tell his smile was a weak, frightened, defensive thing. "Mister Shadler."

"How's the leg? All healed up?"

Something was wrong with Shadler. His voice was muddy, he moved sluggishly. For an instant he swayed on his heels.

"Yes, sir."

"Now, don't start a-sirrin'. That's for the British and such. Not us."

"No," Choctaw replied and, before he could stop his tongue, put "sir" after it.

Shadler smiled and Choctaw felt some of the fear ease out of him. What was there to be afraid of? "Can't cure you of that, can I, Choc?"

"No."

"You hear about the English earl, or lord, or some such? Come out here and went straight up to a cowboy. 'My man,' says the Britisher, 'Where's your master?' The cowboy said, 'The son of a bitch ain't been born yet.' "

Choctaw grinned.

Shadler told him, "Sirrin' ain't for us."

Choctaw understood Shadler's thick voice, his unsure movements. The wagon boss was drunk. Shadler stared foolishly at the earth for a long time. His mouth was slack and hung open, his eyes were wide and stupid and weren't quite focusing. It hurt Choctaw to see the wagon boss like that.

Shadler frowned. "You still up at Walsh with them Indians?"

"Yes, sir."

Anger worked in Shadler's voice. "You still up at Walsh with them Indians?"

*So now it comes,* Choctaw thought. *Squaw lover.* But he replied, again weakly, "Yes, sir."

There was a considerable pause, then Shadler asked, "How old are you, boy?"

"Seventeen. Nigh eighteen."

"Seventeen. That's a hell of a good age."

"Yes, sir."

"That's a hell of a good age. Any old bastard like me starts to tell you: 'don't do that, do this,' you don't listen, understand?"

"Yes, sir."

"You're only seventeen once, and you're a long time dead. Like Dutchy. Lying there dead, and no reason to it. No sense in it at all."

Shadler stared off into the darkness. Choctaw couldn't think of anything to say. Finally, the wagon boss released his hold on the bridle, and half-turned into the shadows. He said, "I got nothing against an Indian that's peaceable."

"No."

"I got nothing against an Indian that's peaceable."

Shadler moved off into the darkness. His path back into town was not quite straight.

The boy told his horse, "Come on, Red," and rode on into the freight yard. The door of the office opened and Gravitt was there, the Remington shotgun over his arm.

Choctaw said, "Don't shoot me, Mister Gravitt. I ain't after your coffee and sugar."

"Holler out next time, you young idiot, or maybe I will. You looking for Finn?"

"Yes, sir."

"He ain't about. I don't know where he

is. Your friend, that feller Robertson" — there was disdain in Gravitt's voice — "he was over at the Lucky Strike."

"Thanks."

"You want to leave your horse here, Choc?"

Choctaw did so and walked over to the Lucky Strike. He met Robertson coming out of the cantina. The scout greeted him and the boy smelt his mescal breath from two strides away. Choctaw decided everybody in Tucson was drunk but him.

The boy suggested, "Let's have a drink."

"You go ahead, boy. I am too old to drink anymore. Get that way, you should be put against a wall and shot. You got a place to bunk tonight?"

"No."

"I got a roost. You're welcome to spread your blankets there."

"Okay."

"I got a jug, too, if you fancy pulling a cork before retiring."

Choctaw said, *"Ugashay,"* which was Apache for "Let's go."

"I thought you wanted one in the Lucky Strike."

"I don't like drinking by myself."

Walking back out of town Robertson said, "Jack Adams is in Tucson."

328

"Why tell me?"

"You want to watch out. He won't have forgotten what happened here, and up at Camp Walsh."

Choctaw remembered Adams, sitting like a butchered animal, with the blood spilling from his mouth. "I don't know. Maybe he's got a reason for the way he is."

"Adams? Meanness is all. I know a bad story about him. After the Arizona Volunteers . . . after they'd been through an Indian camp. There was a baby left, squalling, on the ground. Maybe its people had been killed. I don't know. Adams sat down, among the dead bodies, and the burning wickiups and everything, and starts dandling the kid on his knee. He starts talking to it, you know, cooing, like you do to babies. Then he puts his gun against its head and pulls the trigger. The other Volunteers chased him all around the huts for that, and you know what kind of men *they* are."

"Hard to believe a white man could do something like that."

"All men can do anything, white, red, any breed. Maybe it's not true, but it sounds like Adams to me."

"Well, you'd better watch out too."

"What for?"

"Adams."

"I ain't losing no sleep over that son of a bitch." Robertson stumbled over something. He swore and kicked out and an object went clattering and rattling along the ground, a tin can maybe. Robertson asked Choctaw, "How long you in town?"

"I'm going back to Walsh tomorrow. Early as I can."

"What's your hurry?"

"I've heard talk. About a raid on Camp Walsh."

"So've I."

Choctaw halted. "You've heard?"

"Sure."

"Then you know about Klosen . . . it was Klosen they killed."

"I dunno."

"Billy Parker said it was him, and that Mexican, whatshisname, Vasquez."

"So?"

"So it must've been him."

"Seems like."

"Did Coyote know about it? About the warriors going on raids, when they were supposed to be at peace?"

Robertson thought a minute. "Maybe he did. Maybe he was back of it, all the time. Making fools of us all."

"I don't believe it. You believe that?"

"I don't know which side to believe. But

don't worry about anyone attacking Camp Walsh. They've been talking about that for a month or more. This town's got plenty mouth fighters. But it's just talk."

"I don't know . . ."

"It's just talk. If anything was going on, I'd know about it."

"Maybe."

There was another pause, and then Robertson said, "The worst of the lot is your friend Mister Shadler. He's keeping things stirred up."

"John Shadler?"

"Mister High and Mighty himself. Or he was, until the Chiricahuas and the Bedonkohes shot the hell out of his wagons. He was cut down to size, and can't forget it."

"It's not that way with Shadler. You talk like it's just hurt pride with him."

"Well, isn't it?"

# Chapter Thirty-One

Robertson's jug was almost full; Choctaw
awoke late next morning, muzzy-headed,
with a harsh taste in his mouth. Robertson
wasn't about. After a lengthy search around
Tucson, Choctaw found enough water to
wash his hands and face in, then he went
over to the freight yard. He considered riding out to Camp Walsh straight after breakfast but decided his horse needed more rest.
The immediate prospect of traveling sixty
miles on horseback, over a rough mountain
trail, wasn't appealing, anyway, as a hangover had descended on him in earnest.

Choctaw drifted over to the Mexican
quarter, bought a breakfast of tortillas and
beans, and managed to eat half of it. The
boy found a shady place off the plaza, sat
with his back against an alamo tree, rolled a
cigarette, and watched the morning turn
into a fierce afternoon.

Life went on. Slowly. Traffic passed, horsemen, mules bearing loads of firewood, dwarf oxen dragging carts down the streets, the wheels huge discs cut from cottonwood trunks. Men and women lounged and smoked in the shade of adobes, women slapping tortillas between their hands. Young women crossed the plaza, water jugs balanced on their heads. A few of them glanced at the boy in the shade of the cottonwood and smiled but he didn't respond.

It was entirely pleasant, spending the day this way, but as Choctaw's head quieted, he began to think about Alope. He eased himself to his feet and went looking for Robertson.

Walking over towards Fort Lowell, he found him. The scout approached. He had his arm over the shoulders of a soldier, a cavalry private, and they were both weaving along stumble-footed like caricature drunks, trying to sing in harmony and not even getting close. Choctaw thought it might be "Lorena" they were mangling.

Seeing the boy, Robertson called, "Hey, Choc! This is Private —" But remembering the soldier's name appeared to stump him. After a minute he seemed to give up, telling the private, "This here's Choctaw."

The private glared at the boy owlishly.

"Why, he an Indian?"

Choctaw decided he was going to get rid of that damn nickname. "No, I ain't no Indian. My name's Calvin Taylor."

The private said, "That's all right then." It was hard working out exactly what he was saying. On top of appearing to be three-parts drunk, the man had an accent deeply southern. "I tell you what, Calvin. Seeing as I got paid today, I'm in the mood to celebrate. And *you're* invited along."

"Thanks, but I was figuring on heading back to Camp Walsh."

"You don't understand, boy. On top of being payday, it's also my birthday."

"Well, happy birthday."

"First I aim to buy myself a decent meal. And then treat myself to a few drinks. And I'm buying. You fellers care to join me?"

"Like I said —"

Robertson leaned forward and punched the boy in the chest. "You mean you ain't gonna help this generous fellow celebrate his birthday?"

Choctaw's original plan was to go some-place quiet and shady and finish sobering up. Yet somehow he found himself following Robertson and the private into an Anglo eating house. Then they had a few drinks over at the Fort Lowell sutler's.

Later, Choctaw wandered over to the Schmitt and Gottlieb freight yard. By then it was dusk and there was a three-quarter moon. After seeing to his horse, the boy sat on an empty crate at the edge of the freight yard and smoked a cigarette. As his hangover had all but gone, he'd got his plan back on track. After he finished this smoke he'd get on the trail to Walsh. He found himself thinking of Alope. More and more that happened. He'd be doing something, or be in conversation with someone else, and it was Alope he was seeing, her voice he was hearing.

Robertson came over, leading his gray horse.

The scout said, "Come on. Get Red. We're going back to Walsh."

"Why?"

Choctaw saw anger and pain in the old man's face. " 'Cus I am a stupid old bastard, that's why."

Robertson turned and walked towards the corral. Choctaw caught up with him. "What's up?"

"Looks like you might've been right all along."

"About what?"

"About a raid on Camp Walsh. The officer over at Lowell, he's heard talk as well. He thinks there's too many people missing from town. John Shadler, Oliver Wentworth . . . seems a party of Mexicans left this morning . . . whilst we've been fucking about here. Whilst we were celebrating somebody's fucking birthday!"

Robertson went on but Choctaw wasn't listening. His head began to whirl. Thoughts came tumbling and Alope was in all of them.

They reached the corral and something Robertson said pulled Choctaw back from his thoughts. "That ain't all. A cavalry patrol spotted a band of Papagos moving through Tanque Verde Wash. A trail through there leads to Camp Walsh. A fair-sized band, all warriors . . ."

Choctaw said, "I saw some Papagos yesterday."

"What?"

"About ten miles south of town. A big bunch. I even found this club one of 'em must have dropped . . ."

"Jesus Christ! Yesterday! Why didn't you tell me?"

Choctaw felt terror. He'd made another mistake . . . he could have mentioned this yesterday . . . he became dizzy with fear. "I didn't think . . ." he said tonelessly. "I thought they was off trading or something."

"Carrying war clubs? Christ, boy!"

"I didn't think . . ."

Robertson was checking his saddle. "There's a hard ride ahead of us. We should make Walsh dusk tomorrow. If we're lucky . . ." the scout's voice trailed off.

Choctaw began to saddle his horse. He felt cold sober. His hands did their work automatically, whilst his thoughts raced ahead, sixty miles, to Camp Walsh. "Robertson."

"What?"

After a time, Choctaw managed to say: "I've been . . . going with one of them. An Apache girl. Alope."

Robertson faced him. In the cold moonlight, Robertson's face was tired and old. Choctaw had never seen the scout look so old before.

Choctaw said, "It ain't just squawing to me. It's like you and your . . . Yavapai woman. Alope isn't just a squaw to me."

"Then you're the same as me, ain't you, boy?"

Choctaw turned back to his horse. He said, "You know, for a stupid old bastard, you ain't —" and something struck against his back and knocked him headlong. He plowed into the dirt of the corral, chin first. Thick, flat noise rocked about him, as if God himself had clapped great hands together, right over the boy's head. Then Choctaw recognized the sound for what it was: a gunshot, and very close.

For a moment Choctaw lay stunned, then he snapped onto his side. His red horse was snorting and backing around the corral.

Choctaw remembered his Spencer was booted on the saddle. From the ground the boy scanned the freight yard and the squat blackness of the freight office, and the moonlit dark beyond. He didn't know whether he'd been hit or not.

Dazedly, he got to his feet and ran to his horse and ducked behind the animal. Keeping the horse before him as a shield, the boy pulled the Spencer from the scabbard. As he did so, he saw a glimmer of metal and sprang away from the horse as the second shot came. And missed. The boy ran to the corral fence and wedged himself against a thick corner post and rested his carbine over a fence bar.

Choctaw was surprised at his own calmness. He might have been an onlooker, calmly viewing these proceedings from a safe distance. His heart was thumping, but taking measured, regular jumps. He got his breathing steady, and waited until his fingers stopped trembling.

The boy studied the darkness and made

out a grayer object in the dark, a grayness that was slim and upright, like a snubbing post. He made out another shade of darkness against the upright, only it moved, and Choctaw knew he'd spotted his gunman. The boy tucked the butt plate of the carbine into his shoulder and lined up the sights.

The man rose and stepped away from the post. He turned and ran. Choctaw fired. The runner tripped and fell. He began to claw to his feet and Choctaw shot and saw the man knocked flat. The body stretched and half-rose and eased down against the earth and quivered and was still.

Choctaw tasted sickly-sweet black powder smoke. He blinked his eyes against the muzzle flash. The boy rammed another shell into the chamber, slid between the mesquite bars, and moved towards the fallen man. He looked around for the scout and called, "Robertson!" and in the tail of his eye caught a dim movement.

The man on the ground was rolling over, sitting up, the cold gleam of metal in his hand. Choctaw whipped the Spencer to his shoulder, caught the darkness where the man's chest should be in his front sight, and pulled the trigger.

As he fired, flame leapt from the earth.

The world exploded.

It was a blue explosion, a surf of blue fire that smashed against him. The explosion was silent also.

He couldn't hear anything, not for a long time. Gradually, he made out the murmur of distant voices. Sand was in his mouth and a flat hardness struck one side of his face, from temple to chin. He opened his eyes with difficulty (a warm, thick stuff was gluing down his right eyelid) and saw it was the earth grinding into his face. He was lying folded on his side. The boy coughed on the reek of vomit and the smell of blood. He squirmed an elbow under him and levered himself to a sitting position.

Shadows clustered around him, blotting out the moonlight.

Choctaw came to his knees, then his feet. The world reeled about him. He felt above his eyes, and his fingers came away thick with blood.

Shadows gathered in a circle nearby, pointing at something on the ground. Choctaw made his way over, squinting down at the something myopically. After a while he decided it might be a man lying there, twisted. It might have been Jack Adams lying there.

Choctaw asked, "Did I kill him?"

The shadows jabbered at him, but he

couldn't make out words. The shadows fell away and faded to fine gray smoke, then shaped into people, moonlight catching eyes and teeth and metal and shining leather. He caught snatches of words he could understand.

He remembered his horse and moved towards the corral, dragging his feet as if he were wading ankle-deep in mud.

Choctaw saw a man lying at the edge of the corral, facedown.

He looked closer and saw it was Robertson.

The bullet seemed to have taken the old man in the back of the head and exited through one cheek. Most of Robertson's face lay under him, in the dirt of the freight yard.

Voices became distinct. Choctaw heard a man say, "Poor old bastard."

Another commented, "I knew someone would shoot that Indian-loving son of a bitch."

Choctaw couldn't remember why, but he knew he had to get to Camp Walsh. It was important that he see Alope. He stepped towards the corral and the fence bars leapt up at him and knocked him, staggering. The boy grabbed a fence rail and kept himself from falling. He ducked through the bars and reached for his horse. The animal shied away from him.

Choctaw heard a man say, "Jesus, son! You're shot in the head!"

The boy thought about that. He was shot in the head; therefore, he was killed. But he couldn't be dead yet. Not until he saw Alope.

He grabbed the horse's reins. Hands reached at him from all sides. He struck them away. There was reaching Camp Walsh, and Alope, and nothing else was important.

A strange thing was happening to his horse. The animal began to whirl, like a coin spun on a tabletop, a blur of movement and the shadows thickened around him and Choctaw felt his legs sinking down into the darkness. He began to fall. He couldn't fall, he had to reach Camp Walsh and Alope, but he was falling, anyway . . . falling without landing. Now he was drifting down a long tunnel of shadows, a formless and weightless thing, like an echo in a canyon . . .

# CHAPTER THIRTY-TWO

Someone was speaking to him from far away and, slowly, the voice became more distinct. After a time, he decided it was Gravitt's voice. Gravitt was asking, "You want some water?"

Choctaw felt a canteen against his lips. There was tepid water in his mouth and a few drops ran down his throat.

The boy opened his eyes. He cried out at the room's brightness. Sunlight ripped into his eyes like sharp teeth.

Choctaw lifted a hand to his face and found a thick bandage across his temples. The rag was sticky with blood.

Gravitt said, "Lie still, boy. Medic thinks your skull might be fractured."

Choctaw opened his eyes again but only for a second, wincing with pain as he did so. He was lying on a pallet on the floor of the freight office. The office was windowless and inside was a hazy darkness, the only light entering in harsh brass strips above and below the steer-hide door. The trapped heat of the room was stifling. After working his jaw several times, Choctaw managed to say, "Medic?"

"From Fort Lowell. He's over in town. Looking after your friend Jack Adams. Adams ain't expected to live, what with three of your bullets in him. You better rest easy, boy."

That seemed a good idea. Choctaw had a pounding headache, his throat burned, and the dim light was hurting his eyes. He squirmed his head back into the improvised pillow. Gravitt said, "I'll tell the medic you're awake." The boy heard Gravitt step towards the office door, the door open and close.

The pain in Choctaw's head built mercilessly and under the bandage his wound began to itch. He started to think back, to piece together his memories. He remembered Robertson, and Camp Walsh, and Alope . . .

"Jesus Christ!"

The boy sat up and the world rushed at him, and the pain in his head was like a knife twisting, a knife with a long white-hot blade, skewering his brain. Somehow Choctaw found his feet, crossed to the door, and opened it. It was perhaps eleven o'clock by the sun. He'd lost more than half a day.

He found he was wearing only his red flannel drawers. He hunted 'round the room for the rest of his clothes and put them on. Several times he sat down while he was dressing, afraid he might faint, but finally he was dressed and he stepped outside the office.

The heat and the brightness of the day were terrible, but he managed to walk to the corral and to saddle his red horse. By the time he'd finished he was bathed in sweat, shaking uncontrollably, and at the end of his strength. It was all he could do to lift himself into the saddle.

He rode. The motion of the horse sent new waves of pain juddering through him but that would have to be put up with too. It didn't matter if his skull was fractured, nothing mattered except reaching Camp Walsh, and Alope . . .

A few miles later he found himself lying in the bear grass, whilst his horse grazed nearby.

Choctaw climbed to his feet and slowly remounted. He let out his belt a few notches and looped his belt over the saddle horn. Maybe that would keep him in the saddle if he passed out again. He spurred his horse into movement . . .

A lot of that journey was darkness, because part of the time Choctaw was traveling through the night, and some of the time he was barely conscious in the saddle. He remembered a few things — vomiting noisily, the sorrel stretching his long neck to drink from a rock pool, and the shine of moonlight on the cup of black water — but most of the journey was like a gray dream he passed through.

Then it was dawn and his eyes were blinking against the raw pink light of early day. Soon he heard voices. He glanced around him and saw the familiar shabbiness of Camp Walsh. Figures, then faces, swam into view ahead. A sentry challenged him, then someone grabbed the bridle of his staggering horse. Choctaw saw it was Sergeant Tyson. Lieutenant Hamilton came up on the offside of the sorrel. He exclaimed, "Good God, boy! What happened to you?"

Choctaw's head ached fearfully, and he wasn't seeing properly. Mirages and heat hazes had invaded his sight. Things he looked at whirled away, twisting out of focus, then loomed back sharp as arrow points. The faces before him melted into sunspots, dancing around in dizzy brightness, and then they became faces again.

Hamilton asked, "Where's Robertson?"

Choctaw said, "Get the Aravaipas back here, Lieutenant."

The officer replied, "Easier said than done. They've moved back up the canyon four, five miles, after the creek dried up. Most of the men have gone on a deer hunt. With an escort. There's only women and children in camp now." He smiled.

Choctaw said, "Tucson posse . . . John Shadler . . . Wentworth . . . big band of Papagos . . . left town day before yesterday."

Hamilton's smile vanished. He glared stupidly.

Choctaw shouted, "The day before yesterday, Goddammit!"

Hamilton said, "Lieutenant Riordan, form up your company. I want you ready to move in five minutes! See if you can find Primitavo."

Sergeant Tyson put in, "Nobody could find him yesterday."

Choctaw said, "I'll go with you. You don't need Primitavo."

Tyson advised, "You better get off that horse, son. 'Fore you fall off."

"No. I'll go with you."

"You'll kill that horse."

Choctaw swung the sorrel's head and broke Tyson's hold on the bridle. He spun

347

the animal about. Tyson said, "You dirty little bastard."

Choctaw couldn't wait for the soldiers; he kicked the horse's flanks and rode out of camp. The sorrel's breathing was now harsh and gasping; there was a brokenness in the animal's easy, mile-eating stride. When they reached the creek and the boy reined in, the sorrel hung his head and yellow saliva leaked from his mouth. The horse's coat was soapy and dark with lather.

Choctaw glanced up and down the creek, where the Aravaipas had planted corn and beans and sung the harvest song. But this old campsite was deserted.

He spurred the horse into the canyon.

Choctaw rode uphill over very rough ground, crested the ridge, and raised dust as he went downslope. Suddenly the horse fell to his knees and the boy jumped clear. Choctaw's legs buckled on the steep incline and he fell, sprawling, then twisted over onto his rump. He sat and watched the horse. The sorrel rose, staring at the boy with great liquid eyes full of pain and accusation. A trembling riffled over the horse's body.

Choctaw said, "I'm sorry, boy. I'm sorry, Red."

He coughed, an acrid smell biting at his throat.

After a moment he decided it was the smoke of mesquite fires. Choctaw turned and walked a few paces downslope, and a scatter of dim mounds humped out of the early haze below him, partially screened by a thick tangle of chaparral.

He saw these shapes were wickiups and brush shelters. Relief swept through him. It was the Aravaipa camp, about to awaken, and the smoke was made by breakfast fires. Everything was all right. He'd walk down there now and get the People together. He and Alope would have a quick breakfast of ashcakes and hot biscuits; she'd worry about the bandage around his head and he'd tell her not to; they'd listen to the women chattering, the shrill voices of the children, the snuffling of the ponies and old Skunk groaning his early morning prayer song . . .

Choctaw began to walk downslope and with each step he grew more uneasy. The *rancheria* was too still. By this time people should be bustling all over, and there was too much smoke. Apaches built small fires, burning the ends of mesquite branches and lifting only a thread of smoke, but these fires drove a gray screen across the *rancheria,* hazing vision. Perhaps most of the Aravai-pas had gone out after water and left their fires untended.

He almost stepped on something and Choctaw stared at it. It was a long time before he could make sense of what it was.

It was an Apache baby, a girl, lying on the earth.

Sometimes Apache mothers hung crying infants in their cradleboards on a low tree, or bush, until the baby learned not to cry. But the mother would be nearby, keeping an eye on the child. Perhaps this baby had fallen from her cradleboard. In which case, where was the mother?

Choctaw lifted the baby. The arms were flung wide, the tiny face shriveled in pain. There was blood all over the baby, and the left leg had been hacked away at the hip.

He lay the baby down.

It seemed he couldn't think, or act. But gradually he became aware that there was the broken-off shaft of an arrow in the child's back. It had two thick flights, not like an Apache arrow. He stared, fascinated, at the bloody thing at his feet.

Time passed. He lifted his eyes and saw the bodies of two young Apache women ly-ing nearby.

He saw there was a trail of bodies leading

down to the *rancheria.* There were people lying about the camp too, still figures scattered all around the huts. Most of them seemed to be naked. Some of the wickiups were still burning. He began to count bodies and gave up at thirty-three, but there must have been sixty, or seventy . . .

One of the two women who lay nearby was Klea, Coyote's younger wife. She'd been six or seven months pregnant, but knives had ripped open her stomach. Choctaw couldn't look at that, he glanced away. But in the tail of his eye he couldn't help but see her head had a caved-in, dented look. Choctaw remembered the Papago war club, with its large, ball-like, striking end.

The other girl lay arched on her back. Her deerskin shift was thrown over her head and there was blood on her splayed legs. He lifted the dress to see this woman's face. She'd been killed by a rifle butt. The weapon, a Spencer, lay nearby, broken at the stock. The butt plate had worked loose. The killer had used the rifle butt frenziedly, smashing the girl's face into blood and splintered bone.

As in a dream, Choctaw lifted the dead girl's right hand. He could tell by the ring on her next-littlest finger that it was Alope.

# CHAPTER THIRTY-THREE

Hamilton stood at the door of his office, a glass of mescal in his hand, an unlit cigar in the corner of his mouth. The lieutenant gazed at the sky over the mountains. He could look at the dusk, or the faces of his men, or the report on his desk, and for a time think this was a day like any other; and then there was a picture in his mind, something he'd seen today, or yesterday, in the Aravaipa camp.

He heard coyotes. Bands of them, and wolves too, would be drifting down from the mountains. Hamilton moved back to his desk. There was the report he had to finish. He lit his cigar. He took another drink, but that didn't help. He couldn't clear his head of today, and yesterday.

Hamilton wrote:

*In the aftermath of the massacre, all the survivors had fled to the hills. No amount of persuasion, or offers of money, could tempt my scouts to go after them, to make contact with the warriors. They feared the men would kill them, believing them party to the massacre.*

*I hoped all the trust I had built up over the months had not been completely destroyed, even after what had happened. So, today, I took out a burial party, to lay to rest as many of the Indian dead as we could find. So far eighty-six bodies have been discovered, of whom only six were men. Of those six, one was an old man, and another a boy, perhaps fourteen or fifteen years old. We tried to give all of them as decent a burial as possible.*

The soldiers were mostly silent as they worked, which told Hamilton what they felt about the job they were doing. They lowered several bodies into each long, narrow grave. The wind lifted, flinging dust into eyes and mouths, and then fell, and the sun struck through, bringing clouds of buzzing flies. The cavalrymen pulled bandannas over their faces against the rotten-sweet stench. Some of the bodies were bloating, turning purple and black. A few were already marked by the claws and teeth of predators. Some troopers didn't like to throw earth on naked bodies; they found old blankets or scraps of cloth to wrap the corpses in.

> . . . I thought an act of caring for their dead would be evidence to our Indians of our sympathy for them. This conjecture proved correct, for while the soldiers worked, many of the Apaches began to come in. They came from all directions, singly and in small parties, so changed in thirty-six hours as to be barely recognizable, during which time they'd neither eaten nor slept. Many of the men, whose families had all been killed, when I spoke to them and expressed my sorrow for them, were obliged to turn away, unable to speak, and too proud to show their grief. Children who, two days ago, had been full of fun and frolic, kept a distance, expressing wondering horror. Others, men, women, and children, indulged in expressions of grief too wild and terrible to be described . . .

Some of the Apaches fell facedown on the earth, beating at the ground with their hands. Hamilton saw one man spinning himself about, shouting a long "Aaaaahhh!" Others were keening, their voices lifted in a high, dog-pack snarling. It was, he supposed, the most human of sounds, and yet it was an animal sound, with nothing recognizably human in it. He heard Apaches scream and cry, howl and wail their anguish, cutting off fistfuls of their hair and tearing their clothes.

Some were still too dazed to mourn. They sat or stared, blank-faced. Others took spades from the hands of cavalrymen or got their own wooden hoes (those not burned with the wickiups) and began to scrape out graves themselves.

They toiled patiently through the day. Water was brought from the creek in clay ollas and watertight woven baskets, and the faces of the dead were washed, and painted. If possible, the dead were dressed in their best clothing. The few possessions salvaged from the ruins of the village were placed in their owner's graves. Hamilton noticed that bodies were laid out with their heads pointing to the west. The graves were filled in with layers of soil and leaves, then piled over with rocks and stones.

The Indians wept as they covered the faces of their people. Now and then lifted voices merged and Hamilton heard the keening. Some of the Indians sang quietly as they worked, or chanted prayers.

*The Apache chief, Coyote, was one of*

*the few men in camp when the attack oc-
curred. He was down at the creek, carrying his baby daughter, when the firing
broke out. At that point Coyote was armed
only with a knife. He attempted to reach
his hut, where his rifle was, but was driven
back by the rifle fire of Mexicans and
Americans.*

*He broke through the line of Papago
warriors and escaped with his daughter to
the hills; both were unharmed. But his two
wives, and his four other children, were all
killed in the massacre . . .*

Hamilton watched as the youngest of
Coyote's dead children was buried. This was
a boy, perhaps three years old. They had
washed the small, round face, and daubed
streaks of bright red and yellow paint on
the boy's forehead and cheeks. There was a
claw necklace on his chest, and he was
wrapped in a robe of bleached moleskin,
trimmed with beads and shells. They tied
belts of cloth tightly about the robe because
the boy had been slashed open, the wound
cleaving his chest and stomach. If the lips
of this wound weren't kept pressed together
the body would open like a split melon.

Coyote was kneeling by the grave, trying
to place objects into each of the child's

hands. One was a toy, a horse made of cloth and stuffed with grass. Into the other hand Coyote was trying to press a skin bag of maize, to feed the child on his journey after life. But Hamilton saw the little hands were claws, each finger a tiny, rigid hook, and Coyote couldn't unbend them.

Somehow Skunk had survived the massacre. He stood nearby. He shook his tortoiseshell rattle and scattered *hoddentin* on the earth by the grave. The old man rocked in an awkward, stiff-jointed, circling dance, making a wordless grumbling in his throat.

Coyote gave up trying to close the dead child's fingers. Tears were rubbing off the dirt he'd smeared on his cheeks, dripping from his chin and weaving dark gray rivulets down the front of his shirt. A man began a thin, high keening and other voices joined in.

Hamilton turned away. He felt dizzy. He drew several deep breaths, clenching his fists. His head ached and his arms trembled.

The lieutenant walked towards his horse. He saw Choctaw sitting on the earth nearby, staring at another of the day's new graves.

Tonelessly, Choctaw said, "I'm quitting, Lieutenant."

"I need you here, Choc."

"You've got Primitavo."

357

"You stand in well with Coyote."

"No. I'm going back to Tucson."

Hamilton noticed the boy's eyes were red and sore, tear tracks striping the dirt on his cheeks. The lieutenant remembered what Scanlon had told him about Choctaw and Alope. He knew, from the look on the boy's face, what had happened to her.

Hamilton asked, "You going after 'em all? As far as we can tell, there might be a hundred and fifty of them in on this. Where'd you start? Wentworth? Ruiz? John Shadler?"

When he said "John Shadler," Choctaw's mouth twisted and his lower lip trembled. For a second, he like looked an angry child, wronged, frightened, and dignified, all at the same time. Then Choctaw turned the hurt expression into a scowl and his face became a mask. It was something he might have learned from the Indians, making his face so still, rocklike, and unemotional.

"You'll get yourself killed, boy."

Choctaw stood up. "Will I, Lieutenant?" He spoke quickly, as if afraid his voice might betray him.

"They say Shadler's killed more men than the cholera."

"He didn't kill many men yesterday."

Choctaw strode off. Hamilton walked to

his horse. He mounted and rode back to Camp Walsh.

*I did what I could: I fed the Indians and talked to them and listened patiently to them. I sent horses into the mountains to bring in two badly wounded women, one shot through the left lung and one with a shattered arm.*

*One of the Apache men said to me "I no longer want to live; my women and children have been killed before my face and I was unable to defend them. Any Indian in my place would take a knife and cut his throat. But I will live, to show these people that all they have done, and all they can do, won't make me break faith with you, as long as you stand by us . . ."*

Scanlon entered. Hamilton offered the bottle and poured another drink for himself. They sat a long time without talking.

Scanlon seemed to have aged ten years. Hamilton guessed the last two days had worked the same trick on him.

Hamilton said, "We've found eighty-six."

"Eighty-six?"

"We'll find more. Wounded that crawled off to die. All but six of them were women and children."

Hamilton's voice caught when he said, "Women and children." He saw in his head women and children after bullets and knives and clubs had done their work. The Papagos had used their clubs on everything, even the camp dogs. He remembered Coyote's three-year-old son, his hinged, unbending fingers . . .

Hamilton said, "I betrayed these people."

"No."

"Didn't I?"

"You only did what you thought was right."

"What I thought was right. And everybody else thought was wrong. You too, Pat. You thought it was wrong too, didn't you? Only I wouldn't listen."

"You're tired, Austin. We all are . . . Jesus."

"It was my fault, Pat."

"No."

"I tried to stand in front of history. That's what I tried to do." Hamilton's tongue tripped him; he realized the mescal was reaching him, finally, but he didn't care. "But why did I do it, Pat? Why? Was it for the Apaches? Or was it for me?"

"I'll see you in the morning, Austin."

"I'm going to get drunk, Pat," Hamilton declared, and the words filled his mouth like sand. "I'm going to get drunk on duty.

Why not? Get this damn bottle finished at last."

Hamilton followed Scanlon to the door of his office and watched his friend limp back to the hospital.

The sky was mauve now, and would soon be an inky darkness. The mountains were indigo, turning deepest black. He smelled the early evening smells, the sage, the nopal, the curious fragrance of the earth giving up its warmth. He heard the lonely voices of the coyotes and then a low, dull, rumbling, far off under the mountains. He listened, and after a few minutes, identified the sound of hooves.

A body of horsemen poured from the darkness. As they came nearer, he glimpsed scraps of metal, and the shine of leather. The riders were challenged and formed up in front of quarters, perhaps twenty cavalrymen.

There was still enough light for Hamilton to make out the rider with the lieutenant's bars on his shoulders.

"Curtis!"

"Hamilton! We've just had a hot welcome back."

"What?"

"Just had a shooting match with your precious Indians."

"Where?"

"Four or five miles back." Curtis jabbed a thumb over his shoulder, towards the Aravaipa camp. "What's going on here?"

"What happened, Lieutenant?"

"Hot work for a while, back —"

"Just tell me what happened, Goddammit!"

Curtis's blue eyes hardened and his smile slipped and then became not quite a sneer. After a moment he said, "Alford sent us back, ahead of the rest. You requested assistance, I believe."

"Well?"

"Riding through the canyon back there, we were fired on. So much for your peace-loving Indians. One man wounded in the arm. Nothing serious."

"All right."

"It was a tight business, but we managed to drive 'em off up the canyon. Maybe killed a few . . ."

Hamilton said, "Lieutenant, give your men five minutes out of the saddle. Get your wounded man to the hospital. Then I want you and your detail to accompany me back there. I want you to show me exactly where the shooting happened. Orderly, bring up my horse."

Curtis talked at him but Hamilton wasn't

listening. His orderly brought up his horse. Hamilton mounted and led Curtis and his detail out of camp. They rode up the canyon and into the burned-out village. There was an eerie quiet; the village seemed deserted. Then shapes melted out of the darkness ahead of them. Cavalrymen, a burial detail Hamilton had left behind, under Sergeant Tyson.

Tyson said, "Glad to see you, sir. For a while there, I thought we was going to get massacred too."

Hamilton asked, "What happened, Sergeant?"

"Somebody fired a shot. Next thing there was hell to pay. Firing all over."

"So we fired on them," Curtis said. "They fired on us. We didn't see them until we were almost on top of them. One of them shot at us, so of course we fired back."

Tyson told Hamilton, "I figure the lieutenant must've run into a burial party, sir."

"Why did the Indians start shooting?" There was a long pause and Hamilton demanded, "Well, Sergeant?"

"I don't know, sir. All I know is somebody fired a shot. It might even . . . it might even have been one of my men fired that shot. Everybody was jumpy, the Indians were making their damn moaning noises, and it was already pretty dark in here . . . and then the lieutenant came up so sudden . . ."

Curtis said, "It was the Indians fired on us."

"Maybe it was." Hamilton looked around. "Question is, where are they now?"

Tyson said, "Looks like they've all run off."

Curtis declared, "They've no stomach for a close fight."

Hamilton twisted in the saddle. "You might've started this war again, you God-damned fool."

"Don't Goddamn me, Hamilton. I never knew this war was off. At least I know what my job is."

"Do you?"

"It's killing these savages, not nurse-maiding them."

Tyson said, "A few of 'em did fire on us, once the shooting started. I thought we were done for. But they didn't rush us. They scattered instead."

"Looks like your pets are long gone," Curtis observed.

Hamilton asked, "Any of your men hurt, Sergeant?"

"No, sir."

Curtis said, "I think we killed a few."

"I hope the hell not."

"Still the same Hamilton. Still the same bleeding heart."

"Shut your damn mouth!"

"You've been drinking, Hamilton. You're drunk on duty, by God."

Hamilton turned his horse and rode back to the village. He told a soldier, "Bring up that lantern." Hamilton lifted the lantern and saw the body of a man lying nearby. The figure sprawled, facedown, over a grave. Hamilton dismounted, rested his hand on his pistol, and walked over to the prostrate figure.

Carefully, he turned the man face up.

"Well, Curtis," Hamilton said. "You got one of 'em all right. Fierce fighting man you killed here."

Lying with his withered face tilted up to the cold moonlight was the Aravaipa shaman Golinka, the Skunk. He'd been shot twice through the back. The tortoiseshell rattle hung from one thin wrist by a loop, the rattle stones spilled. In his other hand the old man clutched a drawstring bag of *hoddentin,* the seeds Apaches scattered on the earth to bless the ground, raise the People's crops, and bring them good luck.

# CHAPTER THIRTY-FOUR

The killers made no attempt to cover their tracks. After they struck, they ran. Choctaw found their trail easily, within a mile of the *rancheria,* and followed it.

He didn't think about what he'd do when he caught up with these men. By now he guessed his skull wasn't fractured, even though the pain in his head was blinding. Adams's bullet had grooved a crease above his right ear and the wound throbbed angrily under the bandage. So he didn't push himself, or his red horse, still recovering from the hard run from Tucson to Camp Walsh.

By dusk, he felt dizzy and nauseous. He camped early and fell into a dreamless, exhausted sleep.

As soon as it was light, he was back in the saddle, following sign. His headache was worse. Soon he came upon a place where the killers had scattered in all directions.

Choctaw became interested in the tracks of one particular mule and followed them into the chaparral.

About midmorning he saw a turkey vulture, lazily quartering the same patch of sky. That meant a person, or people, on the desert immediately below. The vulture marked a spot and Choctaw rode towards it. After a time, he dismounted and ground-hitched Red. He took his carbine from the saddle scabbard and went on afoot.

He heard the murmur of voices.

Choctaw was deep in a tangle of mesquite and scrub oak. Sweat grayed his shirt and he fingered more sweat out of his eyes. Flies droned and bit. Nearby a rattlesnake clashed its tail. He listened, placing the voices. As quietly as he knew how he moved forward.

The boy crouched down and studied the screen of brush before him and what lay beyond it. A dun horse and two mules, ground-hitched near some palo verde trees. Three men. One man lay in the shade of the palo verdes. He seemed to be sick or injured; he was wrapped in a blanket and propped up against the base of a tree. Choctaw couldn't see his face. John Shadler squatted at this man's side. His Yellow Boy Winchester stood against a tree trunk four or five yards away. A third man was hunched on a rock nearby, his face buried in his hands. He looked up and Choctaw saw it was Finn.

Choctaw cocked the Spencer, making the smallest possible sound. He took the pistol from his jacket pocket and hooked it in his belt. He waited until his breathing became even and his arms ceased the trembling that had just come on them. Then he stepped out into the open.

The mules turned their blunt faces, and their long ears pointed towards him. Shadler saw that immediately, as Choctaw knew he would. Shadler crouched there like a trap about to spring and glanced over at the Winchester. Probably he judged it was too far away; he made no move towards the gun. He rose to his feet and turned slowly. Shadler's right hand reached across his body to the pistol holstered on his left hip. When he saw the Spencer trained on him, his hand slid away. The wagon boss stood very still, his arms at his sides. His face was expressionless, he didn't say anything.

Finn stared and his mouth hung open.

Choctaw kept his gun on Shadler and walked carefully over to the man in the shade. It was Danny McClure.

Choctaw lifted the blanket and flies buzzed greedily. The Ulsterman was in his

red flannel underwear. Strips of blanket —
which might have been an old shirt once —
were tied around his waist and abdomen.
The bandages were dark with old and newly
dried blood. McClure's eyes were closed,
and his breathing was low and irregular. His
face was gaunt with pain and might have
been gray under the yellowing of sweat.

Lying on top of some camp gear nearby
was an Apache belt, studded with turquoise,
something a woman, rather than a man,
might wear, on ceremonial occasions. A pair
of thigh-length Apache moccasins lay there
too. There was a long smear of dried blood
down the side of one moccasin.

Choctaw told Finn, "I figured it was you.
I figured those was old Daisy's tracks."

Finn stood up and smiled weakly. His eyes
were sore from recent tears. He said, "Why,
hello, Choc." He looked, moved, and spoke
like a man in a daze.

"I'm going to kill you."

"No, Choc. No, don't."

Choctaw nudged his toe under the Apache
belt and kicked and sent the object a yard
in Finn's direction. "Where'd you get this?"

"Please God, Choc, no, please, no, please."

"What happened to your Spencer rifle,
Finn? Where's your Spencer?"

Finn sank to his knees, bowing his face

almost to the earth. He began to cry.

"Please God, Choc. I didn't do nothing. I swear to God. Please, Choc."

Choctaw's mouth twisted. "You gutless yellow bastard. You always have been."

"That's right," Shadler agreed. "He always has been. Turned yellow out on the Ninety Mile, and up at Walsh too. Now he's showing yellow again."

Shadler's voice was unconcerned, conversational. He lifted a hand and scratched the red stubble on his chin. He gazed at Choctaw calmly. The Spencer pointing at him might not have existed. "That's why Irish is lying there. Indian playing possum, he jumped up and stuck a knife in McClure. Gutted the poor bastard like a fish. Finn was there. He could've saved McClure, he could've shot that Indian easy. But he couldn't do nothing. Just sat there shaking and crying like a damn frightened kid. Mc-Clure was the only man hurt serious out of the whole party, the whole hundred and forty of us." There might have been pride in Shadler's voice when he declared, "Otherwise it was sweet as molasses. A whole nest of the vermin cleaned out, and only one of us bad hurt. And that 'cus of Finn — 'cus Finn couldn't do nothing."

Choctaw said, "You could though."

"That's right. I could. And I did. And, by God, I'd do it again!"

Despite himself Choctaw grunted, a sound of admiration. This was the old John Shadler, the man he'd wanted to be. Death leveled on him from a few yards distance, the movement of a trigger finger away, and yet he sneered at it, arrogant, fearless, superb.

A voice in the boy's head told him, *Kill them now. Don't listen to any more talk. Don't ask questions. Get it done.* But, instead, he asked, "Why?"

" 'Cus there's white men and Indians. One ain't safe while the other's alive."

"Simple as that?"

"Couldn't rely on the army to protect us. They was too busy nurse-maiding those murderers, looking the other way while they was stealing and killing. Even after we killed one of 'em at it, and got the proof of it. So we had to protect ourselves."

"Against women? Kids?"

"Bitches drop pups, don't they? Nits make lice."

Choctaw's arms began to tremble and then to shake, so that the carbine barrel pointed at Shadler's face, then his chest, and then his stomach. The boy raised the Spencer to his shoulder.

After a long moment Shadler asked, "Well,

you gonna shoot or what? McClure's finished, he don't need a bullet. Just me and this yellow-bellied excuse here. All you need do is squeeze that trigger twice."

*That's all I need to do,* Choctaw thought. *Squeeze twice.* So why couldn't he?

Choctaw stared along the barrel of the Spencer to the front sight. He stared so hard what lay beyond became a blur, like heat haze on the desert. Shadler's voice came from somewhere in this haze. "Or maybe you're thinking about how I saved your life once. Me and McClure. I even got shot doing it, didn't I? Well, don't let that stop you. I wish I'd left you out there now. I wish to God I'd killed you when I tried."

"What the hell are you talking about?"

"John Shadler's famous shot. Shooting that Indian out from behind you. Except that was John Shadler's famous *miss*! It was *you* I aimed to hit, not that Indian. I figured you was better dead than left in the hands of those savages. I didn't realize you wanted it that way. I never figured you'd turn out like that old bastard Robertson — a squaw-fucking, red-nigger loving —"

Shadler took three paces forward so that the carbine barrel was only inches from his chest. "What've I got to do to get you to kill me? Why, you're just as yellow as Finn there!"

Finn cried, "Stop it!"

"You're just as gutless and yellow as Finn!"

It was true, Choctaw decided. He might as well try and drive his finger through a wall of steel as bend it into that trigger. Stinging tears spilled from his eyes.

Shadler took another pace forward so the muzzle of the carbine rested against his shirt front. "You and Finn are just the same. Two cowardly, spineless, sniveling —"

Finn pushed himself to his feet. He shouted, "Stop it!"

Choctaw turned his head towards Finn and Shadler grabbed the barrel of the carbine with his left hand. He jerked the weapon sideways, bunched his right hand into a fist, and struck Choctaw in the mouth. The boy reared backwards, retreating half a dozen crazy, bent-kneed steps. Shadler took the barrel in both hands and swung the weapon crosswise, the butt catching Choctaw in the stomach. The boy grunted, doubled over, and pitched headlong. He lay with his knees curling into his body, the wind driven out of him. He saw his pistol had slipped from his belt and lay on the sand. Shadler grabbed it, then flung it yards away. He reversed the Spencer, jamming the butt into his shoulder, taking quick, downward aim.

Finn yelled. He flung himself at Shadler, seizing the barrel of the carbine, wrenching it sideways and up. The two men wrestled for the weapon.

Shadler hooked a leg behind Finn's knees, tripping him backwards, but in falling Finn pulled the other on top of him. They rolled and white dust lifted.

Choctaw squirmed to his knees, trying to breathe.

Eventually he climbed to his feet. He half-walked, half-ran to the trees and snatched up Shadler's Winchester. He heard Finn cry, "You son of a bitch!" and turned and saw the fight end.

The combatants had struggled to their feet, still tugging the carbine between them. Shadler took one hand from the gun and grabbed a hank of the boy's yellow hair. He lifted Finn's head and struck him in the throat with his fist. Finn squawked and fell, clutching his throat. Shadler drove a kick into the boy's groin. Finn gave a choked cry and lay, writhing.

Shadler grabbed the carbine. He turned towards Choctaw.

There was a pause, three heartbeats,

whilst they stared at each other over the intervening distance. Then Shadler lifted the Spencer and Choctaw raised the Winchester and both men fired together.

Shadler was knocked onto his rump.

Then, slowly, he fell backwards. Shadler's feet lifted from the earth. For a second, he balanced upside down with his feet in the air, then he performed a slow, clumsy backwards roll and returned to a sitting position.

There was blood all over the front and back of his shirt. His face was gray with shock.

Finn sat up and began retching.

A little later the boy looked around and asked, "You hit, Choc?"

Choctaw said, "I don't think so." He was trying to staunch the blood leaking from his split lips.

Shadler lifted both hands and pressed them against his right shoulder. Pain twisted his face, his mouth quivered with it, then he got the hurt under control. He gazed at Choctaw and the Winchester still trained on him. He asked, "Well, ain't you gonna finish it? Or ain't you got the guts? Finn showed some guts at last, by God, but what about you?"

Choctaw found he was weary of John

Shadler's courage. He remembered Robertson saying, *"He was cut down to size and can't forget it."* The boy studied Shadler's face. It was a dull, red-dusted mask; there was no emotion in his face at all but for the hatred in his eyes. Choctaw guessed a thousand dead Apaches wouldn't exorcise Shadler's hatred. The boy felt his own mouth twist in disgust.

He said, "You ain't worth killing."

"You ain't got the guts for it."

Choctaw flung the Winchester from him. It hit the sand near Shadler's feet.

Cunning came into Shadler's eyes. He glanced at the Winchester, then back at Choctaw's face.

The boy turned and walked away unhurriedly. His back muscles tensed. His ears strained for the telltale small noises that would mean Shadler was reaching for the Winchester, aiming it. He listened for the sound of the lever being worked and waited for the smashing impact of the bullet.

Nothing happened.

Choctaw strode out of the clearing and made his way to his horse. He rode back on to the trail.

Looking at the sky behind him, he saw other vultures dropping down to join the first.

# CHAPTER THIRTY-FIVE

Hamilton and Scanlon sat at a table out front of the officers' quarters at Fort Lowell, partly in the shade of a ramada.

Scanlon reached forward and lifted a glass of lemonade from the table. A fly buzzed. He swiped at it with a folded copy of the local Tucson newspaper — *The Arizona Citizen.*

Hamilton inspected the toes of his boots. Then he leaned back in his chair and studied the ramada above him. If it wasn't for that awning of saplings and brush, the sun would have fried him like an egg. Tucson in late July was a breathless furnace. Anything that moved out of the shade would be simmered down to a grease spot in no time.

Scanlon studied the newspaper. "Know anything about this Crook fellow?"

"Huh?"

"This fellow who's replaced Stoneman."

"There was a Crook in the Second Cavalry. I wonder if it's the same one."

Hamilton sat facing Tucson. A few hundred yards away was the edge of town, the Mexican quarter. The adobes were colorless shells, bleached by the afternoon sun. Only a few women were about, going to and from water.

Scanlon combed through the newspaper, returning again to the main story on the front page. "They couldn't even get that right."

"Huh?"

"The number of Indians killed in the massacre. They couldn't even get that right. It says here one hundred and forty-four."

"No."

They had — finally — counted one hundred and eight dead Indians. Eight of them had been men aged fourteen or older.

The one hundred and eight dead Apaches had become news all over the country. The newspapers became full of a distant territory called Arizona and a remote station called Camp Walsh. In the western states and territories, the press applauded "the Battle of Aravaipa Creek." It was "justifiable revenge"; it was a lesson the savages needed to learn. The eastern newspapers talked of "the Camp Walsh massacre"; they used words like *outrage* and *atrocity*.

Things began to move. A commission had been dispatched to the Southwest to investigate "the Apache problem." Stoneman had been replaced by this new man, Crook, said to be mounting the first full-scale campaign against the Apaches since the war. But, most importantly, President Grant himself was stirred to anger. He called the raid "cold-blooded murder" and threatened to place Arizona under martial law unless the "perpetrators of the crime" were brought to trial — and soon.

Now it was Arizonans' turn to be outraged, especially the citizens of Tucson. The president's words stung them into speedy reaction. A court had been convened. The trial for murder of the forty-odd defendants — thirty-nine Mexicans under Alfredo Ruiz, five Anglos (Oliver Wentworth, John Shadler, and three others) — was held in the Tucson courthouse. (The Papagos, having no rights in the courts, couldn't be brought to trial for their part in the massacre.)

The proceedings had gone on for five wearing days, Lieutenant Hamilton giving evidence every day. Nervous days too. The mood of the town had been ugly. Now, with the jury in deliberation, Tucson was waiting.

Scanlon turned the page of the newspaper. "This one makes me laugh."

Hamilton poured himself a lemonade and turned his head at an approaching footfall. A soldier wandered by, a dozen yards away. Hamilton was nervous of his back these days. Only yesterday evening, as he'd walked out of Tucson, there had been a shot fired at him, not missing by much. For several days, men had shouted threats on the street, vanishing before they could be identified. He slept in his tent with a cocked pistol at his side, and would do so as long as he remained at Fort Lowell.

Hamilton drank. "What makes you laugh?"

"Huh?"

"Something makes you laugh, you said."

"Oh. This here." Scanlon lifted the newspaper. He read: " 'Señor Ruiz justified the massacre. He claimed a captured chief had admitted taking part in at least two atrocities: the raid on the stage station where Benjamin Price was murdered, and the kidnapping of Señora Rodriguez last April.' "

"The Price killing took place in December. Coyote's band didn't even surrender until February."

"I know. And how did Ruiz manage to interview a captured chief, when they didn't take a single adult prisoner?" Scanlon frowned. "They didn't take a single prisoner of any kind."

"Their whole case is that kind of moonshine," Hamilton said angrily. "I nearly laughed out loud when they brought out that breast pin. 'A breast pin found in the Aravaipa camp was positively identified as belonging to Señora Rodriguez.' I saw the damn thing. It was hammered out of a silver dollar and wasn't even marked. Half of the Mexican and Indian women out here wear them. It's all lies and nonsense."

"Not all of it, Austin."

"No?"

"What about that one they killed — Klosen? You can't argue with that."

"Can't I?"

"He was positively identified."

"So was that breast pin."

"A lot of reliable witnesses said it was him."

Hamilton stood up and walked a few paces, which was a mistake — it took him out of the shade of the ramada. The heat was like hot metal on his flesh and the glare was blinding. He stepped back into the shadows. He said, "Maybe. Maybe it was him. Goddammit!" He saw a lot of things: Klosen in his yellow war paint; Coyote

381

smoking a *macuche* cigarette; a man burned against a wagon wheel, head down to the fire; the stiff fingers of a murdered three-year-old child. He heard movement behind him, and began to turn, but knew he was too slow. If this was an assassin, if he was going to get it in the back, like Robertson, then he was a dead man.

But his ears, or his nerves, were playing tricks. The movement was a long pistol shot away. A file of riders.

Cavalrymen, and one civilian. Choctaw was the civilian, now on the payroll as a scout. It was strange how he'd stepped so naturally into Robertson's shoes.

The riders dismounted. Choctaw spent a minute in examination of his horse's legs and feet, then he strode over to Scanlon and Hamilton.

It was hard to think of Choctaw as a boy now. It wasn't just that he'd turned eighteen, that he was filling out his teenage lankiness, or that he'd let a young, dark beard start to grow. There was a look on his face that had nothing to do with boyhood. He'd aged, like the rest of them had, in the ashes of the Aravaipa camp. Already weather had put sun cracks at the corners of his eyes and mouth. His eyes were restless, not trusting things to be the way they might seem. There was a strain in the line of his mouth that didn't belong in the face of such a young man.

Choctaw was also dirty, powdered toe to crown in red trail dust. Not surprising, as the boy had just come off a ten-day scout through the mountains, in search of Coyote's Aravaipas.

For a few weeks after the massacre, the Aravaipas seemed to have vanished. Hamilton began to hope that Coyote might bring his people into the White Mountain Agency. But when Coyote reemerged, it was in war paint. He'd been positively identified in an attack on a ranch where several cowboys were killed. There had been reports of other raids. The cavalry had been looking for him for two months, culls that had rounded up a few tired stragglers — old people, women, and children — but had failed to contact the main band.

Choctaw halted by the table. "Lieutenant, Mister Scanlon."

Hamilton said, "Get in the shade, boy. Sit down and have a drink."

Choctaw did so. He made a wry face at the lemonade. "Christ! What the hell's that?"

Scanlon said, "That's what they call refreshment."

"It ain't what I call refreshment," Choctaw replied, but he poured another glassful, anyway, and drank it quickly.

Hamilton asked, "Any luck chasing Coyote?"

"No. Went right through that country and never saw one wild Indian. But we met a cavalry patrol, and they had news."

"Oh?"

"Coyote's whole band jumped an infantry detail on the Fort Bowie road. Ain't you heard?"

"We haven't heard anything."

"Five or six days ago. Anyway, Coyote had the detail pinned down. But his luck was out. This cavalry patrol came up on his rear during the fight. The Apaches was drove off."

"Casualties?"

"The soldiers had one man killed. They say they shot a passel of the Indians, but they always say that."

Hamilton smiled grimly. "What do you think?"

"Maybe they did, this time. They say they saw Coyote right out in the open. Wounded him, too."

"Badly? Fatally?"

"Who knows? Maybe. Could be the band scattered into Mexico."

Scanlon said, "If Coyote's been killed, or fatally wounded, then what happens here makes no difference, anyway."

Choctaw asked, "Ain't it over yet?"

Hamilton poured another drink. "We expect the verdict any time. Have some more refreshment."

"I intend to," Choctaw said, and got to his feet. "The kind with alcohol in it."

"In Tucson?"

Choctaw nodded and strode off towards the nearest cantina.

There were rumors about Choctaw, Hamilton knew, that he was a squaw lover. The boy was no safer in Tucson than Hamilton was. But the advice, the warning Hamilton might once have offered, he left unsaid. He couldn't talk to Choctaw like he was a boy anymore.

Scanlon observed, "Hell of a way for a young fellow like him to be spending his time, out chasing Apaches."

Hamilton watched as Choctaw entered the cantina. The adobe squatted at the soft edge of a white haze, the town beyond swelling and rippling and gently changing, like paintings on the skin of a bubble. There was some movement behind the haze. Hamilton heard shouting. There was an excitement in town. He saw a man striding towards them, the haze playing its usual games with the man's size and shape. It was Second Lieutenant Riordan.

Scanlon said, "Look at that damn fool Riordan. Rushing about in this heat. He must be crazy."

Hamilton sat up straight in his chair. "I guess we've got our verdict. I wonder how long Shadler and Wentworth and Ruiz'll get in prison?"

Scanlon gave him a bitter look.

Riordan drew up before them, breathless.

Hamilton said, "Sit down and have a drink, man."

Riordan said, "We've got the verdict."

Hamilton lifted a hand to the side of his neck and his flesh felt cold. Which was strange, on this day of blood-boiling heat. He asked, "Well, what was it?"

"Not guilty, of course. All the defendants acquitted. Wentworth, Ruiz, Shadler . . ."

"All of them?" Hamilton leaned forward. He saw Choctaw emerge from the cantina and stand, staring off into town.

"All of them." Riordan smiled, sleeved sweat from his forehead, and reached for the lemonade. He told them someone had timed the jury. They'd been out eighteen minutes, debating the evidence.

■ ■ ■ ■

Tucson celebrated.

The night was filled with celebration. The streets thronged with musicians: Anglos scraping fiddle-and-dance tunes, Mexican bands playing *ranchera* music, a brass ensemble blaring military airs. The saloons were choked with men laughing, cheering, slapping each other on the back. They were all brothers tonight; it was Christmas Day and New Year and Thanksgiving all in one. It wasn't just Wentworth, Ruiz, and the others who'd been acquitted. The whole town had been vindicated.

Choctaw moved out of the shadow of the cantina and sat on a discarded cartwheel lying in the street. The full moon spread chill, pale light. He tilted a bottle of mescal and filled a tooth glass. He drank the mescal off in one swallow. But he wasn't drunk enough yet. He could think back, remembering most of all the dead at Camp Walsh, the slashed throats and broken faces, the marks of bullets and clubs and knives. Remembering Alope. But it was no good, the killing anger wouldn't come.

Choctaw lifted his pistol from his jacket pocket, the gun John Shadler had given him.

He turned the weapon in his hands, admiring the brown cedar grip and the gray-blue luster of the metal.

Some men burst noisily from the cantina and Choctaw looked up. A half dozen Mexicans, who seemed to be fairly drunk. One of them flung his sombrero on the earth and began to dance the *jarabe,* the hat dance. Men ringed him, yelling and cheering. He crossed his wrists behind his back and lifted his knees and went off in a heel-driving circle around the hat, but then he lost balance and careered off into the audience, who shouted with laughter. Choctaw began to grin too. Then he remembered what these men were celebrating. Some of them, the dancer himself, might have been part of Ruiz's band of killers.

Choctaw took another drink while his thoughts and memories pushed at him with no outlet for them, no one he could talk to about them. Finn belonged to another life, and Robertson was dead, and Alope . . .

Choctaw looked up and saw a man approaching the cantina. His face was in shadow but Choctaw knew who it was. He'd recognize that silhouette, that walk, in the black gut of a midnight canyon.

There was the slightest weave in John Shadler's stride. He paused at the corner of the adobe. If he turned his head, he'd see Choctaw sitting there. Choctaw could draw his pistol and shoot him dead now, easy as shooting into a mark. But Shadler didn't look his way. He turned towards the cantina entrance, giving Choctaw one more chance of a shot as he stood framed in the lamplit doorway. A man came up to Shadler and slapped him on the back, then another did the same. From inside the cantina voices shouted a welcome. Shadler entered the building and the crowd inside swallowed him.

Choctaw drank another glass of mescal, but left the bottle unfinished. He went to the corral, mounted his red horse, and rode out of Tucson.

# CHAPTER THIRTY-SIX

Choctaw rode the thirty-six miles to O'Brian's Station, which he reached the following dusk. Ed O'Brian was there by himself. The two men ate, then O'Brian produced a stone jug of Mexican whiskey. O'Brian said his helper, Felipe, had finally quit yesterday, after an "excitement."

"What happened?" Choctaw asked.

O'Brian glowered. "Stage company bought some horses from Pete Kitchen's ranch. Some of Kitchen's cowboys drove 'em up here, put 'em in our new corral. Night before last."

Since the last raid on the station — the one Choctaw had witnessed — the stage company had fortified the corral. They'd built stone walls ten feet high, with a locked, iron-bound gate. One of Kitchen's riders had guarded this entrance, and the others bedded down all around the corral.

In the morning the horses were to be

taken out to pasture, so the gate was un-
locked. Suddenly there was yelling and firing; the horses stampeded out of the corral,
right past the onlooking cowboys.

O'Brian drank and wiped his mouth with
the back of his wrist. "Would you believe it?
Three or four Apaches had snuck in over
the wall during the night and laid in the
corral with the horses. Don't ask me how
they got in, or why the horses wasn't
spooked. When the gate was opened those
devils jumped on some horses and hur-
rahed the rest of them out of there. While
we all stood around like damn fools with
our mouths open."

"Shit," Choctaw murmured sympatheti-
cally, reaching for the jug.

"Kitchen's riders was game, I'll say that.
Went after 'em. The Apaches drove the
stock through a canyon. Halfway along" —
O'Brian pulled a bitter face — "there was
an ambush. Apaches up on top of the
canyon, both sides. They killed one cowboy
and drove off the rest. Got all the company
horses."

"What Indians was they?"

"Aravaipas."

Choctaw paused with the jug partway to
his lips. "You sure?"

"No doubt about it. One of them vaqueros, he'd been working up at Camp Walsh. He saw the chief — Coyote — plain."

"Coyote? But the army says they've killed him. Or wounded him, anyway."

"Well, he wasn't dead as of yesterday morning." O'Brian took a turn with the jug. "That vaquero swore blind it was him. He saw him up there on the canyon roof, directing the fire."

"Maybe."

"Anyway, that was enough for Felipe. He went off with Kitchen's riders."

"Why didn't you go with 'em?"

"Company promised to send me a relief. Only I've got the feeling they've suspended the stage runs, with all this trouble, and not bothered to get word to me about it, the bastards."

"You're crazy, staying out here by yourself."

O'Brian studied the jug he held, his face gloomy. "Maybe you're right."

Choctaw slept over at O'Brian's station, the two men taking turns to stand watch during the night. Next morning, Choctaw was grooming his horse in front of the corral when he saw a vehicle approaching. The army called these transports ambulances, but they were only mud wagons, with high canvas sides. Apart from the driver, three cavalrymen jounced about in the wagon: Lieutenant Hamilton, Second Lieutenant Riordan, and Hamilton's orderly. The vehicle was pulled by six black mules. Two escort riders flanked the ambulance.

The transport halted near the corral and the passengers climbed out, beating at the dust, rubbing cramped limbs. Lieutenant Hamilton came over to Choctaw and they exchanged greetings.

Choctaw asked, "You heading back to Walsh, Lieutenant?"

"Briefly."

"Oh?"

"I'm trying not to sound bitter. I've been relieved of command."

Choctaw stared. "What?"

"Lieutenant Curtis will be taking over as acting commander at Walsh. I'm going to California — to face a court-martial."

"What for?"

"For being consistently drunk on duty. There's also an inference I've been more than a little interested in . . ." Hamilton sneered. " 'Dusky savage maidens' I think they call them."

"Huh?"

"The local Indian girls."

"Jesus Christ, Lieutenant. That's bullshit!"

"I was drunk on duty once. I admit it. The

rest is . . ." Hamilton looked around. He might have been looking for something to kick, or spit on. ". . . what you said it was. I knew they'd try to get me for something."

"They'd get me for being a squaw lover."

A silence settled between them for perhaps a minute, then Hamilton asked, "Are you leaving Arizona too?"

"No. I thought I'd go over to Fort Bowie."

"Why?"

"The new general, Crook, he's supposed to be down there. Recruiting scouts."

"Scouts? You fancy being the next Kit Carson or somebody?"

Choctaw smiled. "Not exactly."

"You're not short of guts, anyway. Pretty dangerous way of earning a dollar."

"So's being a soldier, out here."

"Right now, I'm safer out here than in town."

"Me too."

"You know, Choc, Tucson's just like any other town. There's good people there, only we don't see, or hear them. They aren't all . . ." Hamilton seemed to be searching for words ". . . crushed under a burden of hatred."

Choctaw said, "Good luck, anyway."

"This court-martial nonsense?" Hamilton pursed his lips defiantly. "All I tried to do . . . all we both tried to do, Choc . . ." he let the words trail off. After another little silence Hamilton said, "Let them do their damn worst!"

The two men shook hands.

"So long, Lieutenant."

Hamilton climbed back into the ambulance and the vehicle moved off. Choctaw watched until the wagon was only the size of a crawling fly, dragging a white rag of dust. Then it disappeared into the haze.

Choctaw stayed at O'Brian's Station until dusk, then he saddled his horse.

O'Brian told him, "You're crazy, going down to Bowie, all alone."

"Crazy as you, staying here by yourself?"

"There's Indians all over that country. Cherry-Cows. Worst Goddamned savages on earth. There's the Aravaipas. And others."

"Full moon tonight. I'll get some travel done then."

"Luck, boy."

"Luck yourself."

O'Brian shook his head slowly. "I still think you're as crazy as a turpentine bat."

# CHAPTER THIRTY-SEVEN

Choctaw rode out of the station, taking the eastward trail. Dark fell. There was a full gray-blue moon. He rode across a desolate mesquite plain and after some hours came to a river, perhaps ten yards across, with enough water in the bottom to cover his horse's feet. Both Choctaw and his horse drank, then the boy rode on.

The trail began to climb and the ground became rougher. Saguaro and all kinds of viciously armed plants crowded on every side.

Choctaw found a place to bed down. He lay, fully dressed, in his blankets, with the horse's trailing lines laid under him. The boy was woken twice during the night by the sorrel pulling on the lines, and in between he tossed in a dream-filled sleep.

Once he dreamed he was making love to Alope. His mouth explored her breasts; her fingernails gouged and brought sweet pain;

his sweat ran with hers and made a phosphorescence over the darkness they lay in . . . he kissed her mouth fiercely and kissed a bloody pool, tatters of flesh on white splinters of bone; mouth and nose smashed into the skull by frenzied blows of a rifle butt . . .

He awoke shaking, wet with sweat, in full darkness. After a restless time, he slept again.

Choctaw awoke in the false dawn and watched the sun come up. Apaches liked to attack at dawn. The uncertain light gave cover and enemies were thick-eyed with sleep then, easy to kill. But nothing happened. Choctaw ate a quick, cold breakfast. He rode on until just before noon, when the heat became too fierce. He hunted a shaded place to rest, which was also a good place to fight from.

It was the sort of country he was used to — mesquite flats, treeless mountains, saguaro, brush-choked washes — only it seemed a bigger, and wilder, country. Choctaw might have been the only human being in this primitive world. He wasn't, though; he saw a fur of dust crawling along the southern rim of the plain, and later a thread of signal smoke climbed above the mountains to the north. But both the dust and the smoke were at least fifteen miles away. Late in the afternoon Choctaw started traveling again.

By dusk the boy was worried. He was afraid he might be lost. He needed to find water tomorrow, for himself and his horse. Choctaw was also concerned about Red's feet. If the animal went lame, if he was set afoot . . .

The terrain might have been designed for ambushes, and Choctaw was worn down by the brooding silences, and the heat. He only pushed on a little after dark, then searched out a place to camp. He found a patch of fairly level ground, over a slope of loose gravel. No Apache, however catfooted, could cross that slope without waking him. He rolled into his blankets, with the horse's lines laid under him. Choctaw planned to sleep until just before false dawn.

He was tired, and overslept. When Red woke him, jerking on the trailing lines, there was pink light already on the roof of the canyon, and the darkness on the canyon sides was turning gray. He saw crouching figures flitting through the grayness and heard running feet crash on the loose shale.

The horse snorted and reared, almost pulling the lines from his hands. Choctaw grabbed his rifle and lifted it but the blanket tangled him. He shook the blanket free and then it was too late. A shoulder rammed into his chest. He sprawled on his back. Hands clutched at him and wrestled the carbine away. An Apache hooked Choctaw's right arm behind him and knelt on his right shoulder. Another Apache laid the edge of a long-bladed knife across his throat.

A third Apache snatched up the lines of Choctaw's horse. The sorrel reared away. The Indian looked around and picked up a flat, round stone. He yanked on the lines and the animal settled all four hooves on the ground. The Apache struck the horse on the forehead with the stone. Red staggered, rocked his head, and gave up fighting the man's hold on the lines.

Choctaw tried to lift his head. The edge of the knife nicked his Adam's apple and he lay back. Other Apaches came up the slope, dim shapes against the yellowing light. They stood around him. They wore the usual war paint, a horizontal bar of white bottom-clay across the cheeks and the bridge of the nose.

One man found Choctaw's pistol and yelled in delight.

Another man crunched up the slope. He was chewing a strand of raw bacon, pilfered from Choctaw's saddlebags. He stared down at the prisoner. In Spanish he declared, "I thought it was you. I thought it was your horse."

The edge of the knife moved two inches from the boy's throat. He swallowed and said, *"Jefe."*

Coyote said, "Why shouldn't I kill you? Anyone can kill an enemy. You have to be stronger to kill a friend, maybe."

"Maybe."

Coyote smiled grimly. "You're a brave man, listener."

More light poured into the canyon. Choctaw recognized most of the Aravaipas standing around him, including a man wearing a white-spotted red calico shirt, the tail of the shirt falling halfway down his bare thighs. The red-shirt wearer spoke to Coyote and the two men talked in Apache, too fast for the boy to follow.

Coyote walked over to the prisoner and spoke to the men holding him. The chief limped, dragging his left foot. Choctaw remembered the talk about Coyote being wounded in the fight with the army. Maybe he had a stiff leg, now, to go with his stiff arm. The man kneeling on Choctaw's shoulder shouted something, and an argument broke out. The boy listened helplessly. The cruel edge of the knife rested against the underside of his chin, where his new beard was itching. This might be six months ago, during the attack on the mule outfit, another knife laid against his throat, another band of *broncos* arguing over his fate.

The man with his knee on Choctaw's shoulder got up, made what sounded like an angry comment, and stepped away. Then the second man rose. Choctaw sat up, his hand cupping his throat. He rubbed his right arm, which was hurting from being doubled behind him.

Coyote said, "We decided not to kill you. It's not because you saved my life, listener."

"No."

"You're the first and last we'll spare. You understand? If we meet again, it'll be different. I've no friends amongst your people now."

"I understand."

"You should have camped higher. Where are you going, anyway?"

"Fort Bowie."

"Watch yourself going that way. The Chiricahuas are gathering warriors. They want us to join them. They want a big war, to push out the Anglos."

*"Jefe,"* Choctaw asked, "do you think they can do that?"

Coyote smiled bitterly. "No, I don't think they can do that. The Chiricahuas will die, like my people died."

Choctaw got to his feet. "You don't have to die, *jefe,* you and your people. It's not too late. You can still make peace."

Coyote took two paces downslope. He gazed at Choctaw bleakly. There was no mask over his face now. He said, "We tried that once."

*"Adios, jefe."*

"Goodbye, listener."

The Apache in the red shirt squatted nearby, shaping a cigarette. All the other Indians moved downslope. One of them led off the sorrel. Choctaw felt a pang of sadness, watching Red go. Some of the Apaches mounted mules and horses — doubtless Pete Kitchen's animals. The Indians drifted down the canyon.

The man in the red shirt approached Choctaw. He said, "You're trying to hide your face."

"Huh?"

The Apache touched his chin.

Choctaw's hand went to his stubble. "Yes."

"Thanks for your gifts, listener, your guns and your horse. The pistol is very pretty. Thank you for bringing them to us." The Apache grinned. "I asked Coyote not to kill you. You know why?"

"I think so."

402

The Aravaipas moved up the canyon and out of sight. Coyote was the last to pass from view.

Choctaw told the red-shirt wearer, "I thought you were dead. The Anglos said they'd killed you, on a raid. That's why . . . that's why they attacked the camp. They said you'd been raiding."

"No. I went up north, by myself. I have another woman up there. But it wasn't the same."

"No."

Klosen threw the husk of his cigarette at the earth. "I don't think there's any Chiricahuas between here and Fort Bowie. If you travel through the night, you might be all right."

"Okay."

"*Adios,* listener."

Klosen made his way downslope.

Choctaw said, "Goodbye," but he used the Apache word, *"Yadalanh."*

# ABOUT THE AUTHOR

**Andrew McBride** lives in Brighton, England. His previously published westerns — *Canyon of the Dead, Death Wears a Star, Death Song, The Arizona Kid, Shadow Man, The Peacemaker* — have won acclaim. All feature Calvin Taylor, hero of *Coyote's People,* as the central character.

The employees of Thorndike Press hope you have enjoyed this Large Print book. All our Thorndike, Wheeler, and Kennebec Large Print titles are designed for easy reading, and all our books are made to last. Other Thorndike Press Large Print books are available at your library, through selected bookstores, or directly from us.

For information about titles, please call:
(800) 223-1244

or visit our Web site at:
http://gale.com/thorndike

To share your comments, please write:

Publisher
Thorndike Press
10 Water St., Suite 310
Waterville, ME 04901